Copyright © 2022 by **Emily Dodd**

All rights reserved. No part of this text may be reproduced, downloaded, decompiled, reverse-engineered, stored in or introduced into any information storage and retrieval system, in any form or by any means, whether electronic or mechanical, now known, hereinafter invented, without express written permission of the publisher. For permission requests, write to the publisher, addressed "Attention: Permissions Coordinator," at the address below.

Typewriter Pub, an imprint of Blvnp Incorporated
A Nevada Corporation
1887 Whitney Mesa DR #2002
Henderson, NV 89014
www.typewriterpub.com/info@typewriterpub.com

ISBN: 978-1-64434-203-9

DISCLAIMER
This book is a work of fiction. The characters, incidents, and dialogue are drawn from the author's imagination and are not to be construed as real. While references might be made to actual historical events or existing locations, the names, characters, places, and incidents are either products of the author's imagination or are used fictitiously, and any resemblance to actual persons living or dead, business establishments, events or locales is entirely coincidental.

THE FEMALE LYCAN

The Female Lycan Trilogy
BOOK ONE

EMILY DODD

type
writer
pub

*To my Wattpad fans,
for always being so patient with me over the years*

Trigger Warning:
The following story contain/mention scenes depicting rape, suicide, and gore.
Reader discretion is advised.

PROLOGUE

In the beginning, it is said that the moon goddess roamed the earth. She had descended from the moon to find the natures of earth. In a forest somewhere in Europe, the moon goddess came across a pack of wolves. She admired their hierarchy and how they looked out for one another. She thought they were just what the humans at the time needed.

She created an immortal creature of both man and beast; a man who had a beast within them that they can control at will. She created seven, who would go down in history as the original seven; and named them *lycans*.

One female, six males. Her goal was to create a world where both humans and the supernatural could live harmoniously. The lycans were to thrive for the protection of others. To be the pillars of the supernatural world. To protect humans and supernaturals alike, but also to be the guardians of our world.

But her plan failed. While six of the seven fought for peace and harmony, one did not. Franz Wolfe. He wanted power and authority. He didn't believe the world was capable of peace. He denied all rules and was set on destroying what little peace there was. This caused the lycans to drift, each getting their own area of the world to rule as they pleased. Creating tranquillity or destruction.

The moon goddess saw how much her plan had failed and how she had given them too much power. It is then she created werewolves in hopes to even out the playing field. A strong, but lesser species, one that wasn't immortal. This also bought mates. The other half of your soul that was made just for you, the only person that could truly make you happy.

So many people—especially Franz—wanted the one female lycan to be their mate; Alvery. When he found out that she wasn't his mate, he fought to have her. This caused wars amongst all the countries. All the wolf species.

There will always be people that will stop at nothing to get that power. No matter what. Even hundreds of years later, people hunt for the one last female, Alvery's lone daughter.

Della Rosai.

I am Della Rosai, and I am cursed to forever run, to forever be hunted, and to never have a fairy tale ending.

It's a life no one deserves.

CHAPTER ONE

DELLA

"Dee?"

I opened my arms to her. "Surprise," I said, but the brunette remained as stiff as a board. Slowly, I pulled my arms down. "What's wrong? You look like you've seen a ghost." My attempt to joke does nothing to her. It isn't until I hear a soft, old voice from behind her that Vanessa made any kind of movement.

"What's going on, Ness? Who's at the door—" Henry. He looks much older than the last time I saw him, not elderly just yet, but the wrinkles under his eyes and the slowness in his movements are not far off.

He, unlike his daughter, takes immediate action when he sees me. He pushes past his still motionless daughter and pulls me into a warm hug. "It's so good to see you," he whispers, pulling away with teary eyes.

"You too, Henry." I could feel my tears starting to fall down my own face. We quickly wipe them away, a small laugh escaping our lips.

"Are you well? Do you want some tea? Food? I made a quiche this morning if you want some," Henry rambled, pulling me into their room. My heart fills with the love I feel. I missed Henry so much. My parents died when I was very young. Without a proper parental figure for a long time, I had forgotten the feeling of a parent's love. But Henry feels like the father figure I have longed for.

"I would lov—"

The sounds of someone hyperventilating filled the room. Behind us, Vanessa goes into what I can tell to be an anxiety attack. It's something I can relate to entirely.

"Seven years! You waited seven years to see us, what the hell Dee!" Vanessa's face is red. Her tears started flowing in a fit of rage.

"Ness—"

"I get it, but we thought the worse you know. We thought you might have actually died." Her tears fell more quickly. "You send us a single cryptic email, then you show up out of the blue!" She started pacing the floor. "We could have prepared the place. Omg look at this place, it's a complete mess! I was not ready for a guest today, and you should have called us at least. I would have made up a room for you, or given the alpha a heads up that I won't be doing some of my duties . . ." Her rambling continued as she picked up a few items around the house.

I looked like a goldfish, not expecting such an outburst, but at the same time I should have seen it coming. Ness is the anxious type. I looked at Henry, who is also looking back at Vanessa but with a soft smile.

"Are you okay, Ness?" I approached her slowly. She shook her head furiously.

"No . . ." She dropped the objects in her hand. "I just miss you so much Dee. You know you're like a sister to me. I hate that I can't help you or have a normal relationship with you. I feel so overwhelmed and very caught off guard." Her breathing began to slow down. I could feel the smallest of pangs at the sight of her freshly marked neck.

I brushed strands of hair behind her ear and kiss her forehead, "Congrats on finding your mate Ness. Sorry I wasn't here," I said. She pulled me into a hug and let her tears fall. "I would love to meet him when we have a chance."

She started crying even more. "Thank you," she whispered. "I'm sorry, it's really good to see you."

I can't help but smile wistfully at Vanessa's red puffy face. I know this isn't easy, seeing me every few years. She's like a sister to me, and Henry a father.

I rescued Ness and Henry many years ago, when their old pack was run down by rogues. They were on death's row. Henry was barely awake, and Vanessa was trying her hardest to keep the rogues off them. I wasn't meant to interfere. It isn't my job to, nor was it worth my risk. If anyone found out my identity as a lycan, a female lycan at that, I would be putting them at risk. But for reasons I still don't understand, my lycan forced me to shift for the first time in hundreds of years and had us saving them and urging us to keep them safe for the years to come. They have known of our existence ever since. I don't regret saving them, but I hate the risk I am putting on their lives. I check in every few years to make sure they are doing okay, but under the guise of a human. No one suspects anything, as long as my lycan stays at the back of my mind, away from everyone.

'What are you doing here?" Vanessa asked, wiping her face before quickly adding, "Not that we don't enjoy your company of course. But this is so sudden and . . . dangerous." She looked between myself and her dad, who nods in agreement. "America is pretty risky for your situation," she said leading me towards the couches.

In all honesty, I am not yet sure as to why I picked America, of all countries. It probably wasn't the best decision, considering the cost and the risk, but here I am. Perhaps I long for a little bit of danger after all, or I'm getting adventurous in my old age.

"I missed you." I kept my answer as brief as possible, before pulling out a paper bag. "But I brought muffins," I said, putting them onto the coffee table between us. "I was at a cafe on the border and got some."

Vanessa's eyes narrowed. "You're avoiding the subject..."

I pushed a muffin towards her. "I recommend the apple and cinnamon, it's good." She's gotten older, much older. She would be pushing into her forties soon. I feel a small pang in my chest. I often wish I could age, grow old, die of natural causes but it's not that simple.

"Della"—Vanessa places a hand softly onto my knee—"what is going on?"

I could feel my lycan stirring within my mind. We are anxious to be here and because of why we are here. "I feel something stirring in the world, that's why I'm here." I sighed softly and looked at them. "Something bad is about to happen."

CHAPTER TWO

DELLA

"What do you mean? Is something happening that we don't know about yet?" Ness said quietly, as if afraid to say it out loud. She has every right to be a little bit afraid. I do not involve myself in supernatural business but if it's enough to warrant a warning from me it has to be bad. And it is.

"I'm not sure yet, but I can feel something. It's been bugging my lycan and I for weeks now. The moment I stepped foot into America, something didn't feel right." Henry pulls me towards the awfully bright yellow couches to sit down. Henry sits in front of me, while Ness sits to my right. My eyes teared up at the intense yellow blaring into my eyes.

"What's wrong Della?" he said softly.

"I don't know, not yet." I feel my lycan stir within my mind at the smell in the air. Something is not right. The air smells fowl, tainted, almost rotten. Very much like a rogue but stronger. It's causing my lycan to stir, something she hasn't done in years. I almost felt she had disappeared forever, then the moment I stepped onto American soil, she moved, and she wasn't happy about being here at all.

It's been pulling me towards the direction of Canada, meaning when I'm done making sure Henry and Vanessa are as safe as possible I should head in the opposite direction or out of the country. I shouldn't have come here, but I couldn't help but make sure they were okay, that they are prepared to run if needed. "I just needed to make sure you were okay and that you're prepared to escape country if needed. I have a few escape houses all over the world, I just need you two to be safe."

The feeling intensified ever so slightly. Vanessa sighed softly. "I'm sorry Dee, but I can't leave, not now, I can't." She shakily touches her marked neck. "I won't leave him, and I can't risk another person knowing who you really are." Her hand reaches out and softly squeezes mine. "I know how stressed you are over us knowing. I won't do that to you, I'm sorry." Ness's other hand finds my own, with a small squeeze she apologises. "I can't leave.

My eyes snap to hers. "But you must if things do end up bad. I can't bear the idea that you might get hurt, especially if I could have prevented it."

"I know Dee, but we aren't your responsibility, you are," Comes Henry's response from in front of me.

I looked at the duo in silence, unsure. They both bear the same dark brown hair and stunning green eyes, and the same knowing stare. I envy them. I always have and most likely always will. Her answer doesn't surprise me, being a mated wolf does that to you, but I grow frustrated anyway, signing more aggressively then needed. I nod, "Very well, but I cannot help you if it's not now."

With a pointed look they nod. "Thank you Della, but please consider your safety first and foremost, I'll think it over with Ness," was Henry's rather annoyingly professional reply.

Leaning back into the disgusting couch, I look to Ness. "Who is he then?"

Ness stares out into the darkening sky with a small smile on her lips. "His name is Rylan, and he is currently at his birth pack in Idaho." She looks back to me with a proud smile. "He's a pack doctor, one of the best in his pack and ours, but sadly his mother was attacked by a rival pack member. She didn't make it, a few of them didn't." As if reading my thoughts, she looks to Henry. "I couldn't go. I couldn't leave my pack in danger or Dad."

Spoken like a true head warrior, but her words stick out, "What do you mean in danger?"

"Rylan's birth pack is the Naught Pack, they are at war with their neighbouring pack. They have reason to believe that they are holding rogues in a camp on their grounds. Our neighbouring pack too has been suspiciously supportive." She looks to the window once more with a tired sigh on her lips. "They were right, quite a few packs around the states are holding rogue camps."

Could that perhaps be why we're uneasy in America? Then, I almost jump from my seat.

'Not enough reason to feel this uneasy.' It was almost unfamiliar. My lycan. I haven't felt or heard from her in many years, possibly a decade. With our current lifestyle, we saw it as too risky to communicate, and life has been rather uneventful as well to say the least. It hasn't warranted much talking from us.

'I missed you.' I thought into my mind where I knew she could hear me. She nuzzles our mind in reply.

"We don't think that's why we're here." I said to the duo. "It's something much bigger than rogue camps"

They went silent for a moment. Ness fiddled with her hair while Henry tapping his arm.

"Have you heard of anything else?"

They both shake their heads mumbling a no.

"It could be mate."

I hope for our sake and theirs it isn't.

*   *   *

"Do you know why we hide *Ma fille?*" said the soft angelic voice that's so painfully familiar. Her white hair glowed in the sun, with the ends touching her lower back. She had features of a beautiful goddess. She looks down to me and smiles.

Shaking my head, I looked over my mother's happy expression. "No, *Mere*," I said softly, hugging onto her leg.

She sighs and pulls me up onto her hip. "Because we are different Ma fille, we are one of a kind." She brings her middle finger to my nose softly, "We are guardians of a new and exciting world, Ma fille." She began walking. I'm not sure where but it seems nice and peaceful. Lavenders covered the fields around us, with a few trees in the distance. "And we must protect it, with our lives and heart." She brought her free hand to my own white hair, gently running her fingers through the tangles while taking her path amongst the flowers. "But we must not be seen, or . . ."

"Or what, Mere?" My attention was to the lovely lavenders at our feet, but she doesn't reply.

"Or I might find you." A nasally voice came next to my ear, a voice that brings my heart to a boil. Him. Shakily, I turned to see him. He gripped my throat as his eyes bulged from the sockets in a craze. He brought his face closer to my own. "I will find you Della." He kissed my cheek. "I will find you Della, and I will have you"—he turns to my other cheek and sloppily kisses that one—"even if it kills you," he whispered into my ear with a manic laughter. Before I could swat his hands away, he bites hard onto my shoulder.

Desperately, I grabbed his hands, screaming for him to stop. He does nothing to my protests but to bite harder. With a smile of a lunatic, he whispered, "You taste just as good as your mother."

CHAPTER THREE

Della

"Della. Della! WAKE UP!"
I bolted up and grabbed the person holding my shoulder. I tackled them under me, with my nails slightly longer. I glared at the person below me to see a shell-shocked Henry.
"Omg!" I quickly jumped back. "Henry I'm so sorry."
He slowly got up, concern evident on his face. "You okay?" Henry asked. "I didn't realise you still got nightmares. Sorry. You looked to be in pain."
I closed my eyes tightly and shook my head. "No I'm sorry. I shouldn't have attacked you like that. Even if it was a nightmare, I have no excuses." I opened my eyes and looked at him, hating the uneasiness I've caused him. "Let's have a look at those wounds," I said softly. I tilted his head slightly to look at where I got him on the shoulder. There were nail marks with drawn blood right on the mark from his late mate. Fuck.
"Henry, I'm so sorry." I frantically grabbed his shirt and moved it to get a better look at my stupidity. Why did I have to get his mark, the one thing left of his mate?
Henry grabs my hands and moves them from his neck. "Shhh, Della it's fine. It's okay, I promise." He pulled me into a hug, running his fingers through my hair. He whispers sweetly to

help with my nerves and racing heart, telling me how he's okay and how happy he is to see me.

Eventually, he leaves me to prepare. I put on some short blue jeans with a belt and an oversized black blouse that gets tucked into my shorts.

Before long, I'm being dragged to breakfast by Vanessa. I was then introduced to everyone, making me feel anxious.

Don't get me wrong, I can communicate perfectly well when it's one on one. But when it's with multiple people, my lack of social interaction becomes obvious. I'm so petty about it because wolves are social creatures, yet because of my situation I have grown to become very uncomfortable with large crowds. The more people I talk to, the more I fear for my safety. Understandable of course, but as a wolf I long for it deep down.

Vanessa being the social butterfly she is, introduced me to many of her warriors, friends and packmates. After thirty minutes, I began to feel my anxiety increasing. I need to get my own space. "I'm going to get some of the food before everyone eats it," I said to Vanessa and directed myself to the buffet set up. Despite Vanessa's protests, I left without listening.

Quickly grabbing a plate, I began to fill it with scrambled eggs. Not even a minute goes by before someone else approaches me.

"Tia Martin, I see you are still traveling the world." That was the snarky response of Alpha James Moore. He holds a lot of respect amongst his pack members like the kind alpha he is. Sighing in relief, I turned my attention to him.

"Of course, I've seen only a snippet of what this world has to offer." I pulled my hand out from under my plate, which he then gave a firm squeeze. "You're stepping down from the title soon I hear," I said, putting a few bacon strips onto my plate. He nods proudly.

"Yes, my son Arthur is of age next month, he will be alpha on the next full moon." He strokes his beard with a proud gleam in his eyes.

I smile up at the proud father. "Congratulations. Looks like you and that dear mate of yours will be the next to discover their wanderlust." I poured myself a nice cup of tea, he does the same, a small smirk on his face.

"Maybe" he nods, though I know he wouldn't leave Redstone, it's in an alpha's DNA to stay and protect what is his. Even if he is no longer the alpha, the need to be here for his son and pack will forever keep him rooted here. Something I have come to fear in packs. The unspoken rule of staying and never leaving. With my stature, I could never be a normal wolf within a pack. It's my birthright to be an alpha, nothing less.

"On a more serious note"—Moore sipped his own cup—"don't forget you have a spot here. If you do decide to settle, you are always welcomed here my dear. My son agrees that you have shown your trustworthiness many times over."

With a thin smile, I nodded. "Thank you Alpha Moore. I will think about it in the future. For now I'm quite . . . happy. I still haven't done everything I wish to do or seen everything I wish to see." I looked over to Vanessa and Henry who are idly chatting to the other wolves around them. "But thank you. I do appreciate it." I look back to the alpha and bow my head in respect.

He nods, his feet ready to take him over to his family when he stops mid step, "Oh yes, I must warn you Tia. I got word that the lycan king is arriving this afternoon. It'd be best for your own safety that you stay within your room during this time. He is rumoured to be rather . . . harsh. Please do tell Vanessa for me, she will need to be in attendance when he arrives."

My whole body froze at the new found information, a cold sweat glistening my skin, "Yes of course, I'll stay out of his way" Convinced he walks away.

The lycan king, rumored to be many things. But kind is not one of them. Discarding my food into the bin, I hurry towards Vanessa, a cold burning fire brewing under my skin.

"Vanessa, could you come with me for a sec, I think I forgot the way to your room" She looks up from her conversation, confusion written all over her face, "Um, yeah sure, okay" Getting up from her seat, she excuses herself, grabbing my hand she walks us towards her room. The walk is silent, just the way I wanted it and Vanessa could tell by the death grip I have on her hand, that speaking would be very unwise.

The moment that door closes, I start pacing the room.

"Della, what's wrong?" Ness asked, evidence of worry on her face.

"The lycan king is on his way here right now" I angrily growl, "the alpha just found out, he wants you to get ready" I spit.

The doors open with the hinges creaking loudly. Henrys face pops out from the doors opening. "Is everything okay?" Closing the door behind him, he takes in Vanessa's distressed face and my obvious fury.

Vanessa meets his eyes. "The lycan king is arriving this afternoon"

Henrys eyes widen, "Oh" In quick movements he goes to my room, rustling can be heard within. We follow to see him packing my bags in a messy forensic hurry. Worry evident within his eyes. Sighing softly, I grab his shaking hands, rubbing small circles on them.

"I can't leave Henry," I whisper not meeting his eyes, "The odds are too high to leave now."

"What if he is your mate?" she whispered. "Being a lycan, the odds are high."

I paced my room anxiously, my lycan following a similar movement within my mind. The closer he gets to the pack the stronger the aura becomes. The uneasiness to run is overwhelming. The trapped feeling is so close, it's about to be within its grasp. I am royally fucked. If I run now, it'll be too suspicious. My scent is everywhere. If there's the smallest chance I am the king's mate, I'll be followed. I hate it but I'm stuck here until he leaves. If I am his mate . . . he would reject me. My lycan whines softly. It's sad but true. No alpha male wants a weak human as a mate. No doubt he will reject me at first sight if we are fated. He has to. I can't reject him; the only way I can is by saying my real name. It won't work otherwise, but it won't work for him either. Fuck. I'll have to try convincing him to let me go or I'll run.

"Let's hope he isn't our soulmate."

Henry and Vanessa shared a forlorn look; one they share too often when it comes to me. I should have just stayed away.

CHAPTER FOUR

DELLA

I have done a lot of waiting in my lifetime. But this one, this one felt like the longest wait of my entire life.

"Is he actually a king?"

I look up to Ness, my spoon halfway to my mouth. Placing the spoon back into the bowl I shake my head, "No" Sighing I rub my eyes,

"A few hundred years ago, a band of lycans got together. The head of the Asian line at that time, wanted to put in the motion of there being a monarch. He had hoped that the motion would get appointed with him as the lycan king. But let's just say the tables weren't in his favor; Dxton Bosque, the youngest of the group, was appointed the position if he wished it." Looking down at my bowl, I swirl my soggy cereal around with the spoon. "Dxton was appointed, because his father was Ivan, the lycan of America. One of the first seven." Much like myself I think bitterly. "He turned the position down, ending the small period of lycan monarchy, but it still earned him the nickname Dxton Bosque, the king of lycans."

What a joke. As if being a lycan wasn't enough, having immortality and a natural higher standing in the world was nothing. It's disgusting of our kind, our ancestors would not be proud.

Dxton and I are the children of the original seven, while the rest of the lycans today are descendants. For a very long time, and still even now lycans were hunted for a chance of immortality. But of course it was all lies, consuming us does nothing. Immortality is something you're born with, not taken, not given.

My eyes focused on every entry into the room, but my heart raced faster than ever. Pushing my cereal away, I look back up to Ness. "Monchary is something that should have been left to the humans."

She shrugged. "Didn't stop the vampires." Scoffing, I roll my eyes. Or werewolves, those were dark times that got swept under the rug.

"Vampires have always been over the top." Huffing I get up to put my bowl on the sink. "They're the definition of extra."

Ness smiled. "Have you met the king and queen?"

I crossed my arms and gave her a pointed look. "Actually . . . once." They were in search of my mother at one point. I was but a pup then. That was a very long time ago.

Henry yawned from the cough catching my attention; his neck has a small scar where I had grabbed him this morning. Anxiety builds up in my stomach, from both hurting him and why I'm now hiding for dear life.

It's taking everything in me not to head towards Nevada, where I'll catch a plane or stay amongst humans. I have never met the "lycan king" and I definitely haven't met my mate yet. The chances are so fucking high, it's nauseating.

"I'm going to be sick," I breathed out, the anxiety increasing. Ness rubbed my back softly, but I could feel that she's tensed. She's trying so hard to keep herself steady.

I can sense his presence getting closer. My lycan became acutely aware of our surroundings. Her hackles were up and her teeth were in a viscous snarl. This male lycan is strong, that's for certain. You can feel his alpha dominance from here. The need to bow became harder for Ness and Henry to bear. Soon their heads are being lowered to a permanent angle to the floor, their wolves unable to resist the urge to show their necks to someone of a much higher status. Meanwhile I'm struggling to keep my eyes from turning their bright gold.

But it's the moment that I smell him that I know for sure, I am not leaving this pack unscathed. He smells so strongly of the forest, of a sure-of-himself male, but I can also smell a hint of caramel. The sweetness battled the salty scents. It's so addictive that I feel myself drawn to it. I want to smell more. I want to taste the caramel. I rose from my seat.

Ness and Henry gasped and begged me to calm down, no less seeing the shift within my eyes and the brightness radiating from them. It's then that you hear it. A roar so purely animalistic it has Ness and Henry whimpering. My lycan purred. My arms exploded in goose bumps, and my eyes watered.

"No." I'm going to be trapped. I need to run. I have to get out of here. "No." I backed up into the wall behind me. I desperately tried to maintain my restless lycan. Before I could blink, the door slammed open. A roar echoed through the room. Blinking profusely, I looked up to see the infamous man of the hour. His frame took up the whole door. His eyes were shining a bright gold, leaving me utterly frozen.

"Mate." One word, and I knew I was going to have a very difficult time leaving this man.

☐

CHAPTER FIVE

Della

"Mate."

It took everything in me not to let my lycan go. It took everything in me to not say the words back. My very core desperately wants to say those words at first sight. I want to mark him where he stands, to make him mine forever and mine alone.

He is nothing short of breath taking. His hair was dark with brown tones, cut short but enough to run my fingers through. His skin had a dark tan from centuries under the sun. I could feel my heart skipping beats.

Standing at the door was every pack member and two officials from the king's pack, plus a very starstruck Alpha Moore. Ness and Henry moved everyone out of the doorway. They closed the door behind them to give Dxton and I space. It's something I'm grateful for but also dreadful for. Last thing I want is to be alone with this alpha male.

And on cue, I was straight into his arms as his nose dug into my hair, I unintentionally smelt him too, allowing my lycan to get a good impression of his scent. I pushed him back gently to get a proper look at him. He really is handsome. I look tiny compared to him. I'm only 5'6 while he's 6'. I want to hug him again, but this time I want to stay there. *You have to try and play the human card, Della.* I repeated that in my head so many times in an effort to convince myself that I can't have this male. He might be mine, but he will never truly be mine. *You don't deserve a mate. Only your own company.*

"I'm—"

I put my hand up to silence him. No doubt he didn't like it. "I know who you are," I said softly, meeting his gaze. "Dxton Bosque, I heard you would be arriving today." I pick myself up from the floor and stood a few feet away from him. "And I believe it would be in your best interest to find someone else to be your mate, Mr. Bosque. I—"

"No."

"No?"

"No." He shook his head.

I straightened my posture. "Why not?" My heart tore at the very thought of him letting me go.

"I require a luna, my lycan would never accept anyone else."

I stepped back and looked into his eyes. "But I'm human."

"Your species doesn't matter to my lycan, he wants you regardless," he said. In other words, he himself doesn't want me. It's his animalistic nature that does. "What's your name?" he said, but I remained silent. "Very well, we will be spending the remainder of your life together. You have time to tell me your name." He straightened his tie and reached for the door.

"Wouldn't you prefer the female lycan?" I asked out curiously, halting him from leaving.

He doesn't look in my direction. "I can't desire someone that's dead." He sighed, aggravated. "I must sort out pack matters. Get ready to leave tomorrow." Not waiting for a reply, he exited the room.

I fell onto my legs. To make matters even worse, the haunting feeling I've had since coming here hasn't lessened. My mate wasn't the alarms going off in my head. Something is still happening and now that I have found my mate, I won't be able to escape. I'll forever want to go back to him if I were to run. He will no doubt look for me, hopefully after fifty odd years he will stop looking, when I'm "old" and unable to sire him children. Maybe then he would give up, assuming I'm dead. Our bond isn't nearly strong enough for him to feel anything from me. He would never know if I had died. All I would have to do is stay away from America. That's not so hard. If I go with him I will have to escape and be even more careful than I ever have been before.

Pulling my knees to my chest, I let out a soft cry. Not too long later, Ness and Henry came to my side to comfort me. But I know deep down that I wish it was him comforting me.

* * *

"Are you done hiding?"

I didn't bother to turn my attention to him. "I don't know yet." I sighed as I sipped my tea. I like coffee, but nothing beats a nice cup of tea with some scones.

I've made it my goal to be wherever the lycan isn't. I had food sent to Ness's room last night and today I had breakfast while I went on a run. At both times, the lycan came knocking on my door, and both times I turned him away. Him being close to me is sending shivers up my spine and is sending my lycan into a frenzy. She hates that we haven't claimed what is rightfully ours. She wants him, but we can't have him.

"You should pack your things, we leave for White Crescent Moon this afternoon."

"We? I don't recall saying I would leave with you." I turned my attention back to the forest around me. A small smirk was itching its way onto my face when I heard a small growl from the alpha male. He has probably never been told no before. It'll do him some good. "As far as I am concerned, you don't need me, not really. I'm sure you could find a nice werewolf girl, maybe even a female lycan." My arm that once lay peacefully on the small veranda was now held in his harsh grip. My tea got shattered on the wooden planks. I glared as I rip my arm away.

"You are coming back to White Crescent, whether by force or will. You will be in that car, we are going today!" His eyes went gold. I try not to scoff. Gold is our lycans coming through. It's our lycans fighting for, or are in control. Werewolves are similar, only their eyes glow a burning amber. It's a show of power, dominance, or in his case the fact that he has no control whatsoever. All I can see is a childish lycan playing alpha. If he can lose his temper this quickly, we are going to have some issues.

Turning to him, I roll my eyes to piss him off. It earned a growl from him. "I. Am. Not. Going."

"I won't tell you again—"

"And I won't tell you again either. I have no intention in going with you." I get closer to his face, glaring the entire time. "I am a human, not a supernatural creature. Your animalistic ways don't apply to me. Mate or not, if you want me to go with you, it would be to visit then leave." I stepped closer so that I could kiss him if I wanted to. "I am not going with you. Why would I? I would be trapped with you forever. Unlike you, I have a short life and I don't intend on using it to your advantage."

Dxton went quiet. Maybe he's speechless or maybe he's is trying to control his emotions. I hardly doubt he has been told no before.

"Who is he?" I nod towards the Asian man behind him. Sighing at the obvious change of subject, he straightens and gestures to the man to come forward.

"This is my beta, Dominic Singh."

A lycan. Interesting, lycans don't mingle, let alone serve under anyone. We're much to prideful for that. What would cause a lycan of the Asian bloodline to plant roots in America? Dominic is almost the same height as Dxton, just a little bit taller. Dom looks to be of a Chinese descent, which is also the only likely answer as not all seven lycans went on to have children. The Asian line has branched out to all of Asia. He has a nice tan though, I might add. I sniffed the air and caught a hint of someone else's arousal on him. A male's. A quick look to his neck and I note that he isn't however mated. Now that's a story. The Asian lines are all very strict to the old ways. Everything's coming together now as to why the lycan is here. But why would he be Dxton's beta? He very easily could have gone on to become an alpha elsewhere despite his obvious taste in men. Intriguing.

I put my hand out to shake Dominic's hand, but he instead bows and looks back to Dxton. "We are needed for a meeting, Alpha," he said. Awkwardly putting my hand down, I raised an eyebrow.

"I will be there soon," Dxton replied quickly, his eyes still on mine. Dominic bows and leaves. I wonder what his real name is. Dominic would be his western name. Maybe Dxton gave it to him.

"I will take you by force if needed."

"And I will make it my mission to make it hard for you for the rest of my life." Dxton grunted and moved to walk away. He looked at me from over his shoulder, but I glared. "I will never love you."

"I'm counting on it."

CHAPTER SIX

DELLA

"Dee?"
I hummed a yes, not looking at her.
"What are you doing?"
"Waiting."
Ness gets into my line of sight. "Okay, but do you have to stare at the door?" She brushes some of my hair behind her ear. "Maybe sit down, relax for a bit. You are about to leave when you just got here."
Feeling slightly guilty, I sigh and nod. "Okay, okay. I'll sit down."
Letting her drag me back to her disgusting couch, I roll my eyes. I'm acting so immature, meanwhile Ness is behaving like she's my mother. Looking to her stomach, I smile softly. She will make a great mother one day. Hopefully not now, now isn't safe for a baby.
Not even thirty minutes later, there's a knock on the door, sending my heart into a frenzy. Henry sticks his head out and looked at me. "I can hear your heart from here, girl."
I sighed and relaxed back into the chair. "Scared the shit out of me, Henry."
But before he could sit down, I could instantly smell him behind the door. Henry turns around and opens the door for the alpha.

Dxton instantly looks to me. "Time to go. Don't make this hard." Dxton grunted, his arms crossing.

Rolling my eyes, I turned to Ness and Henry. My eyes teared up slightly. I miss these two a lot when I'm away. It's always hard to say goodbye. I never know when I will see them again. But this time, it might actually be the last time. If I do run, I can't come back to America ever again.

"See you soon, okay?" Ness puts on a strong front but the moment I hug her, she absolutely loses it and starts crying into my shoulder. Dxton thankfully doesn't rush us. Pulling away, I kiss her forehead and give Henry a hug.

"Be safe," Henry whispered into my ear, but the lycan would have been able to hear it regardless. I pull away and nod, kissing his forehead. I go to grab my bag but see Dxton already carrying it.

I let out a sad sigh. "Bye, stay safe you two. I'll see you soon." I quickly left out the doors.

"They are free to visit anytime, or even transfer packs," Dxton softly replied as we descended the stairs.

"Thank you. I doubt they would move though." I wiped my eyes and looked forward.

Alpha Moore stops me at the car to bid his own farewells, before he and Dxton have their own chat. Dominic was already at the back with his phone. He looks up to nod before going back to his phone. I got in the front, stiffening slightly. The car smelt so strongly of Dxton that it was almost overwhelming, but it brought a calming feeling to my nerves that I stubbornly hate.

Dxton gets into the driver's seat not long later and begins the long drive to Washington. Stiff and anxious, I look solely out the window, not paying the alpha any mind. I ignore him when he looks my way. I need an escape plan. I've thought of many at this point, but I can't figure one out till I see his pack's layout and guard schedule. I considered jumping out of the car on one of the busy highways. If I scream bloody murder, someone is hopefully bound to stop and get the human authorities involved. I have a human record thanks to the black market network. Only issue is that Dxton must have thought of this because we haven't driven on any busy roads, and the lycan has clearly called in backup because we've had cars just like the one we are currently in following us the whole car ride. Besides that could go wrong in a few ways. I can't escape without it being obvious I'm not human. If I run too fast, they would catch on especially if they can't catch me. I would require using my lycan's help which would then leave a scent of a lycan behind me. There is also the fact that I will bleed jumping from the vehicle, instantly showing my lycan's scent.

    I got so caught up in my rabbit hole of outcomes that I didn't notice Dxton until he nudged my arm. I flinched. "What?" I look over to Dxton. Interestingly, his eyes are brown when he is in control.

    "What is your name?" *This again.*

    "Why does it matter? It's not like you'll see me often." The truth is I don't want him to know my fake name. Tia Martin feels wrong. I don't want to hear him say it or to refer me as that.

    "You are wearing my patience out for the last time, mate. What is your name?" Seeing his grip on the steering wheel tightening, I looked back out the window.

    "Tia Martin." I feel the smallest of pangs at lying to him.

    "Tia." The sound of the name sounds so wrong. I think of what my name would sound like coming from him as I closed my eyes.

    "Do you wish to see your family before we get to the pack?"

    I look over at him as he remains focused on the road. "Thank you, but that won't be needed. My parents are dead." As touching as this was, I have no one to visit. I looked back out the window.

    "Sorry," he said after a while. I looked at him and smiled, knowing he could see me from the corner of his eye. Calming silence passed after that, which I, for one, am very grateful for. I wasn't in the mood to talk to the two lycan males.

A few hours went by and still no chance to jump. The scenery was nice at least. It was a beautiful array of forest greenery. Animals darted away sensing the threat of the lycans, blurs of silver and tan. *Wait* . . . Looking into the forest more clearly, I noticed it again. Wolves, a dozen or so surrounding the car. They were protecting us, or more likely Dxton. I raised an eyebrow at this. *What could be so dangerous?* I'm sure the king hasn't told them he had found his mate yet, unless they know about this mysterious uprising with the rogues. Werewolves protecting their alpha wasn't an uncommon thing, of course. But something just seemed off, almost. Their attention was locked onto me.

"We are almost at my pack," Dxton said after I noticed the wolves. He sat a bit straighter with pride.

We drove off into a dirt path that takes us into a gated area. The gates opened instantly upon sight. We drove past a few people standing around the gate. The trees slowly started to fade away as houses came into view. Wooden cabins spread across the forest. A few people could be seen in a clearing, training in human and wolf forms.

Everyone looked up as the car drove past. Most of them bowed, feeling the strong aura of their alpha. Bigger houses started to surround the area as the forest ended. It was then I noticed a large building, a few stories high, maybe six. The pack house, I assumed. The car came to a stop outside the building. A few people stopped to look when I stepped out of the car while Dxton already have people swarming him.

"Welcome back, Alpha." The guard looks to me for a split second before turning to Dxton. He gazed over Dxton, indicating that the two are mind linking. The guard smiled at me proudly, his eyes focused on anywhere but my eyes as an accident old hierarchy trait. Looking into my eyes or anyone of a higher status would be disrespectful.

"Welcome Luna, to White Crescent Moon Pack," the guard said.

I nodded with a smile. "It's good to meet you."

Dxton looked towards the pack house. "Where is Alex?"

"On his way I belie— oh there he is." The guard points towards a couple in the distance.

Dxton placed his hand on my lower back which I shrugged off. He growled lowly but he led us towards the couple. I can sense strong wolves within them. The male isn't very tall, but he's very muscular. His face was plastered with the happiest smile I have ever seen.

"Alpha." The pair bowed their heads. The male straightened up, putting on a serious face that seemed rather unbecoming of him. "A group of five rogues came through the border while you were gone. We have apprehended two."

"The other three?" Dxton looked towards where the rogues are probably in right now.

The male smiled like a movie villain. "Dead."

Dxton nodded and turned towards me, catching the pair's eyes. They both started smirking. "This is Tia Martin, your luna." Dxton didn't get to say too much more before the male lurched forward.

"Alex McGavin"—he points towards his very pregnant mate—"and this is my mate, Jade." She bows politely with a hand on her stomach. Jade has golden blonde hair reaching towards her shoulders She has eyes the colour of the ocean. Alex's hair has a darker shade of blonde, almost a dirty blonde, and eyes the brightest green.

"It's a pleasure to meet you, Luna." Her smile is sweet, friendly, and very contagious. I looked at her stomach and smiled softly. The baby must be only three months along, but I can definitely smell her. She's small but she's there. I wonder who she'll look like more. Her parents are quite attractive.

Alex started to explain happily. "We're the gammas of White Crescent, the head of training and security if you will. We are the third in command after the be—"

"I know werewolf society Alex," I softly intercepted.

"Oh, well that makes this a lot easier then." He paused, taken aback. "Um, a tour then?"

Nodding, I look to the pack's forest. "I would love a tour."

Jade bows. "I apologise, Luna. Alex and I are very happy to meet you. We have been dreaming for the day that the Alpha would find his mate. We have watched many generations of gammas hoping to be the ones to meet you, and it's a huge honour to be your gamma." Her eyes started to mist over. Alex started rubbing her back.

"My mate is correct. I apologise for coming on a little strong. It's an honour," he said. They both bowed again.

I bowed back, earning a few surprised looks. "It's an honour to meet you. I will try to be the best luna I can for you."

I feel slightly bad for lying, but if I'm going to escape, I have to put up a happy, honoured front. Besides, being a luna for these kind people is extremely wrong of me. I don't want to watch them die and get replaced over and over again. It's easier for me and them if I didn't stick around to watch that.

"Alpha, we are needed in the cells, the rogues are conscious," the messenger said.

"Show Tia the grounds and introduce her to people she will need to know, mind link me when you are done and I'll meet you at my house." He doesn't let Alex or Jade, even myself respond before he leaves with Dominic towards where I guess the cells are.

"So Luna, where are you from? I can hear an accent, but I'm not sure from where. Jade begins walking away from the pack house.

"I just moved from Cardiff in England." Not a lie. I've been there for the last decade maybe.

"How did you find out about werewolves?" Alex butted in.

"I was on a study trip in America learning about the hormonal growth in plants when I came across a rogue attack on a pack. I was caught in the crossfire. I ended up saving a young she-wolf and was told everything." I shrugged. "Moved here about a month ago for a job offer . . . I guess I can't do that now." I looked to the ground, feigning hurt.

"Oh Luna, I'm sorry." Jade puts a hand to my shoulder which made me smile softly. She smiled back then turns to the building we're in front of.

"This is our pack house, home to over 200 pack members. We have about 300 members in our pack, but a few with families prefer their own space which is fair." Jade smiled, rubbing her stomach. "Alex and I live in the pack house so if you ever need anything, please let us know."

Alex nodded along with a smile still etched onto his face. The gammas showed me around the pack grounds and introduced me to the pack doctor. A few pack members welcomed me, meaning that the word has gone out that I am their new luna already. They showed me where the training grounds are and even scheduled me in for regular training by themselves and a few trusted warriors. I'll admit the training does sound rather exciting. I am surprised that Dxton would allow his human mate to train with werewolves.

"When are you due?" I asked Jade.

She smiles brightly, rubbing her stomach softly, "Three months" She looks to Alex with adoration, who was in the middle of eating a Snickers bar he had in his pocket. His attention was on a mind link. They are clearly in love and it's honestly adorable. "How long have you guys been together?"

"Seven years," she said as we descended a hill. I grabbed her arm for extra support, which she gave me a thankful smile for.

"This is the alpha's house. It's where you will be staying," Alex interrupted before I could say anything else. I looked to where he's gesturing and saw a house at the bottom of the hill. It's definitely nice.

The house is more like a fancy cabin. A wide veranda was all around the house with a swing on the railing. It made me smile. That's going to be my spot for sure while I'm here. The house is a two-story building with a lot of open windows and a bonfire just off to the side.

"He shouldn't be much longer. Hopefully a few more minutes, Luna."

"Please call me Tia," I said, stepping onto the front porch. "I haven't earned the title of luna yet, and I sure don't feel like one yet."

"We couldn't," Alex said, flabbergasted that I even thought to tell him to call me Tia. "Alpha would kill us anyway, he is big on titles and respect. You might be human, but you are still our alpha's mate. I'm sorry Luna, but we will have to use your title."

"How about when the lycan's away?"

Alex and Jade exchange a few glances, before shaking their heads. "Absolutely not," they said at the same time.

"Very well." I sighed, knowing I'm not going to get through to them. "Anyway how did you guys meet?" I may as well get to know them a little bit, just to pass time while Dxton gets here.

Jade blushed slightly, while Alex smiled sheepishly. "Jade and I met while attending the high school just in town. It's mandatory to attend the human high school so that authorities aren't on our asses. Jade and I completely hated each other because we were from rival packs, but when we both turned eighteen, we turned out to be mates and the rest is history." Alex sighed dramatically.

"Sounds like quite the story, one I've heard many times before if I'm being honest. Sadly, most packs are rivals these days."

Before I have to say anything else, Dxton walks down the hill, saving me from more small talk.

"It was nice meeting you, Luna. We will see you soon." Alex and Jade bowed, said a few words to Dxton, then left.

Dxton walks up to the porch, eyes locking onto mine. My heart beat quickly, especially when he looked like he wanted to say something and moved closer but he stepped back just as quickly and swung the door open.

We don't even get to step that far into the house before an elderly lady pops out from around the corner. "Luna." The elderly lady bowed softly. "I am Roxanna, the alpha's housekeeper. If there is anything you need, please let me know." Roxanna has a lovely blue dress on with an apron. Some pretty little flowers were embroidered on the hems. She had aged grey hair and soft brown eyes. I can already tell that I am going to have a harder time leaving this woman than Dxton. "Is there anything you would like for dinner tonight?" Roxanna looks between myself and Dxton.

"Whatever you wish to make us, Anna. You never disappoint." Dxton straightens out his coat and looks down to me. "On that note, please excuse us while I show Tia to her room."

"Of course, Alpha." She bows.

I smiled to Roxanna softly. "It's a pleasure to meet you."

Roxanna smiles back and bows once again to our retreating figures. The house's interior really is spectacular. The walls were painted soft grey instead of the typical white, with some stone walls here and there.

I peeked into the lounge room where I saw the biggest fireplace I have ever seen against the wall. Big brown leather couches surrounded the fire with a few plants here and there. I was pleasantly surprised to smell that they are indeed real. No doubt through Roxanna's care.

The lounge room opens out towards a fairly large backyard that stretches into the open forest line. Continuing on, we make our way up the stairs to find more plants and a few abstract paintings of wolves and forest scenery. We stop in front of a closed door.

Dxton's room is a few doors ahead in a more secluded part of the house.

"This is where you will be staying." Dxton opens the door, showing a very large bedroom. There was a king-sized bed located in the middle of the room, with a wooden splashback behind the poster bed and my own bathroom. The windows took up half of the room, showing off the most breathtaking view of the pack house and surrounding forest. I can see everyone and everything from here. Useful. I make my way towards the white covered bed. Plenty of pillows lined the bed. My bags and some new clothes were on the bed waiting for me. A small note with "Welcome" and flowers were also on the bed, causing me to smile. It's actually a nice gesture.

"I believe we should discuss our arrangement," Dxton said from the door. "You will birth me an heir and that is all. I do not wish to form any kind of relationship other than for you to be the mother of my son."

I don't know how I managed to keep my lycan in control, but she was not happy to be treated this way. To say we were angry was an understatement. I glared daggers at him. How dare he. How dare he think he can trap me here to be his incubator, to stay here forever just to birth him one son.

"If you only want a child then what is the point in keeping me here forever? Find someone else to be your mate!" I refuse. I won't do that, not again. I will not give him children. I won't do it. "I will not give you any children. I would rather die than give you a son." I spit, quickly slapping his cheek. "I refuse to be your bitch."

Dxton's demeanour stayed the same. He didn't flinch upon my contact, not even when the sparks flew. He looked at me for a few more minutes before he turned and left the room without saying a word. I rushed to the door. It's locked.

I'm high up, but if I get desperate, I am high enough to walk away from that kind of fall. I will not stay here.

CHAPTER SEVEN

DELLA

It's been one week since I got here. It's also been a week since I last saw Dxton. Good, he is the last person I want to see right now. Today I hoped to have a peaceful morning to get use to my new surroundings and to find escape routes. But the gammas had other ideas. They have also decided to keep me well out of the loop on these rogues.

"What's all the rush?"

"There was a rogue sighting on the border. Nothing the beta can't handle."

"And Dxton?"

Alex nodded towards a hallway just off the living room. "In his study at the moment. Did you want to see him?"

I look towards the hallway. I haven't been down that way yet. "No, no thank you." I'll be sure to avoid that part of the house. Taking note on which door, I turn to Alex. "Where's the rogue sighting? Maybe I can help?"

Alex shook his head and walks towards the front door. "You will remain here, safe."

These males. I shook my head at him, annoyed. "Oh but Jade will be around shortly. She wanted to go over some things with you and help get you used to pack life. Today is your first day of luna duties so she's going to help you get through it all."

I looked to the man standing at the side. "Who's that?"

"Oh right." Alex whistled him over. He's cute, I'll give him that. He has curly blonde hair cut in the typical fashion of today with the sides a little bit shaved, leaving the middle thicker but not quite a Mohawk. His eyes are an interesting shade of green, almost hypnotising with the raw colour.

"This is Terrance. He is the head warrior and will be your bodyguard for now on."

Terrance bows and gave me a warm smile. "It's an honour to serve you, Luna. I hope to be a good bodyguard for you. I promise to protect you with my life."

Alex mind links with Terrance for a few seconds, annoying me to no end. He then turned to me with a bright smile. "Jade is on her way. I will leave you here with Terrance. If you wish to have him not talk with you or anything of the kind, let him know. If you dislike him, I'll have someone take his place." He put on his coat and gave me a nod. "Okay?"

I nodded and waved him out of the house. "Okay, now go so I can read my book please." He laughed but did as I asked and left the room. I went straight to Dxton's library, the one good thing about this house. I grabbed the book *A Waltz for Matilda* by Jackie French then took a seat on the living room couch. I turned to my book happily, but I stopped when I feel the eyes of Terrance on me. "Yes?"

He straightens and quickly looks away. "Sorry Luna." *Bloody males.*

Hearing the door open, I look to the front door from my spot in the living room, annoyed. Jade bounced in. I eyed the alarm near the door, it's going to be hard to escape through the doors or windows. Maybe. I eye the chimney. It's a stretch, but maybe.

"Jade, would you like some coffee?" Roxanna said from the kitchen. She's been cooking all kinds of recipes with me here now. She made so many cookies, we ended up giving some to the children at the pack's day care centre. To say they were happy would be an understatement.

"Yes please Roxanna." She hang her coat on a hook then made her way over, bowing slightly. She takes a seat on the couch across from me. "How are you today Luna?"

Sighing, I put my book down. "I'm faring well. How about you?"

She nodded, bouncing her golden curls around her face. "I am also faring well" She giggles. "Excited to get started with your luna duties?"

I nod with a small shrug. "Ready as I'll ever be." I was absolutely shitting myself actually.

"I thought we could go over a few things and then maybe head out." She looks to Terrance and smiles. "And I see Alex has already assigned your bodyguard, good. Hi Terrance."

He nods with a kind smile back. "Hello Gamma."

Roxanna placed coffee in front of Jade on the table and tea for me, with a plate of blueberry muffins fresh out of the oven."

"Thank you Roxanna." Not missing a beat, Jade and I hurl into the muffins. I take a bite and hold back a moan. I love blueberries, they are quite an acquired taste, but they go with so many different dishes. I wonder if Roxanna would be up to making some blueberry jam.

"This is for you Luna. It's a phone so that we can talk to you when you need, or you us," Jade said with her hand over her face to cover up her mouth as she chews. Good, I hate bad eating manners. She hands me an iPhone. I don't know what version but it has a standard leather flip case. I pulled out an ID and a credit card from the case slots. I raised an eyebrow to Jade when I see the name is Tia Bosque.

"I don't recalling saying I do."

Jade blushed a bit and stuttered. "Sorry. I know that humans dream about their wedding day. I'm sure the alpha would have a wedding if it's something you really want to do. He set up the marriage certificate so that it was easier for you when you went out into the human towns."

He wants to be the first one to be notified if I were to leave more like it.

"Ah yes, the alpha has already arranged a joint bank account, so you have access to whatever you need. He has also ordered in a car for you as you had to leave your one behind. I believe he has a Honda on the way." She takes a sip of her coffee and does a little shrug. "He has also completed all of your paperwork so that it says you are married in case of any situation, and I believe he has also set up an escape house for you somewhere in Alaska."

She pulls out a phone of her own. "I have also added a few numbers to your phone. It's a little exciting. We've never really bothered with phones before. Only the alpha and beta have a phone, except for the offices of course since we all have one." Sure enough I find a few names in my contacts, hers, Alex, Dominic and of course two of Dxton. One labelled office, the other personal. He's pulled all the stops, hasn't he?

"How much is on the card?"

Jade thinks it over a little bit. "I believe $20,000. There is also a pack shared bank account that has roughly a few million in there. Just so we can get the resources we want."

I know that Dxton has a few companies under his name, but I didn't know if they were successful or not.

"Now." She claps her hands together. "Shall we go shopping?" She gets up grabbing her bags. "I'm sure you have clothes you would like to get or some items." She pauses expectantly.

"Um no." I looked perplexed so I shook my head. She rolls her hand expecting me to catch on then she looks downwards.

"What about toiletries?"

Shit, humans have periods. I didn't think of that. "Oh, do werewolves not get periods?" I stalled quickly.

"No, we get heats. When we've mated for the first time, a week later we go into heat. Which is one week of hell."

"Oh no I have an IUD, it's stopped my period."

Jade paused for a few minutes then shrugs. "Can I just say, I love your hair!" she adds.

"Thank you," I said, smiling at her while twirling a stray lock around my finger.

"Did you dye it yourself or get it done professionally?" she asked, looking over at me from the cart.

"Professionally," I said without hesitation. It's a question I've already been asked a lot. Jade gets up with ease.

"Well it looks amazing," she huffs out with a little laugh. I can't help but smile. She's cute. I dated a girl just like her once. She sadly died in a car accident thirty years ago, but I can't help but be reminded of her. My Angie.

I didn't realise I was blushing with a big grin on my face until Jade waved a hand in front of my face softly with a curious smile. "Everything all good, Luna? I was telling you about our schedule and I don't think that would bring on that kind of smile."

Blushing even more, I laughed. "You remind me a lot of someone I used to know."

Smiling, Jade looks out the living room window and grins. "She must have been amazing then." She turned to me and winked cheekily, making me grin back at her. She was.

"Let's go to the pack house today. I'm sure you would like to see your office. And since you don't want to go shopping, let me know if there is anything you wish to have and I'll order it in."

I muttered my thanks then made my way towards the door, making sure to lend Jade a hand up the rather steep hill just out the front. Of course, the moment we get to the top of the hill, Jade started feeling rather nauseous and began to almost fall straight down. Letting out a few French curses, I grabbed onto her shirt quickly, pulling her towards me. I let out a relieved sigh.

Ever the happy wolf, Jade didn't even acknowledge her misstep. "You know French?" she asked, her eyes glowing with excitement. I smile thinly and nodded. A small childlike excitement washed over me while talking about my home land. I wish I could go back. I miss it terribly. But for fuck's sake, this woman is going to be the death of me.

"I lived in France most of my childhood. French is my first language."

Jade continues the walk to the pack house, eyes wide and a grin that looks much like a Cheshire Cat takes over her face. "Oh wow, you speak English as if you grew up with it," she said, amazed.

"Well, I pretty much did. My mom was French. So I learnt from her but my dad spoke English. They both taught me their languages." I smile at the memories of my mum getting frustrated and rambling in French only to have my Dad sigh, waiting for her to finish so he could apologise. "I'm fluent in both, but I know other languages too."

"That's so cool, I've never met anyone who can speak more than one language." She gushed. "The Alpha can't and he's been alive forever." She laughs out. Taking the last steps, she takes a moment to let out a small exhausted huff. I wonder why Dxton never took up learning a different language other than his own? "What other languages can you speak?"

Humming, I start to list them on my fingers. "Arabic, Spanish, Korean, Swahili, a bit of Dutch, and only a little bit of Japanese." I have more but it might raise some eyebrows. I love learning new languages, it was a nice way to past by time and I can communicate with just about anyone.

Grabbing her arm to steady the pregnant woman, she gives me an appreciative look. Over my shoulder, Terrance is indeed still tailing us. "You'll get used to it," was Jade's response upon noticing me.

Not turning to her, my glance still on the male, I whisper, "You think? He looks quite bored." I imagine it wouldn't take much to leave his eye.

Jade too looks over her shoulder to find Terrance yawning, his gaze on the surrounding forest. "You're right." I took a quick glance in her direction and I see her eyes shining over, and sure enough Terrance is as straight as a tree, looking a lot less bored and a lot more awake. Jade rolled her eyes, continuing our walk and mutters something about males being useless under her breath.

Walking up to the pack house, Jade led the way up the stairs. I took a moment to appreciate the interior of the pack house. It's got a cabin feel to it with wooden walls and roof, but it has a more tech smart feel to it too, with touch screen systems and a TV that can disappear behind a wall. It's a nice set up.

Jade led the way towards a corridor. She pointed out which door leads to whose office, then proceeds to walk into one of the many doors. Dxton has two offices I have come to learn. One in the pack house, where we have a joint space, and one at his home. Based on the smell, I'd say he uses this space much more. The beta and gammas have an office space as well along the same corridor, both with a joint space for their respected partners.

The first thing that caught my eye is a portrait painting of Dxton with his father, Ivan Bosque and his mother, Josefina. She was one of the most beautiful people I have ever met growing up. Her eyes were always the amber of her wolf. Some called her the queen of the wolves. Royal titles must be a Bosque thing. But there was also a little girl beside a young Dxton. Her hair was unlike the rest of the family's, a dark auburn.

"Who's the girl? I thought only female lycans could have female children?" She would have been adopted. I didn't know Dxton had a sister. I have never heard of Ivan having a daughter.

"That is Lucia, Dxton's adopted sister. She was their beta's daughter but he sadly passed away along with his mate when she was only a few weeks old." Jade stared at the portrait with me and sighed. "She died from human hunters a long time ago. She's buried in the pack's cemetery. Dxton visits her often."

Understandable, and very sweet. She's gorgeous in her light blue evening dress. She has very calming features. She has soft eyes and lips posed in a sweet smile. I would love to have met her. I looked to Ivan and felt a small pang. He was a good man. He died also from human hunters. I didn't realise that he was protecting his daughter.

The space is quite big for an office. Dxton's desk is located in the middle with notes sprayed everywhere and crushed up paper littering around his desk, being anywhere except the bin. I expected him to be a neat freak, but this is a shit show. I guess even he gets stressed. Somehow that makes me a little happy. The walls are covered by bookshelves filled to the brim with books. Curious, I look through the spines and find many different books on management, money schemes, barefoot investors, and even a few on lifestyle balance. On the other side of the room lies a desk. My desk. It's an L-shaped table with a computer setup from the 90s, a filing cabinet and a few old looking pens that I doubt work. I can even spot a typewriter on the edge of my table. Everything old and worn. The desk definitely looks like it might break upon my touch.

Reading my thoughts, Jade speaks up. "Sorry, Alpha seems to like collecting antiques but he hasn't had them moved yet. I've order in a new desk, computer set up and a few storage units and new stationary. Hopefully it won't take too much longer." Jade pulls out an office chair that looks to be brand new, "Only the chairs came in so far." She laughs.

I'm about to respond when she gazed off into the distance in a mind link. "The Alpha wishes to speak with you, if that's okay?" she said while still in the link.

What could he want. "I suppose, if the alpha wishes it I can't really say no."

It doesn't take me very long to get back to the house. Upon arrival, Terrance takes a walk around the perimeter. Meanwhile, I barely stepped into the house before the no good alpha is in my face.

"Your Luna Ceremony will be taking place in a week."

Placing my coat onto the hook, I put a hand on my hip, eyebrows raised. The nerve of this male. I take a deep breath to keep my emotions in check. "Hello Dxton, it's good to see you too, how has your week been, hmm?"

Dxton, clad in a blue button up looks taken back slightly, before his eyes narrow. "You have been avoiding me just as much as I do, so don't give me that, mate." He goes and takes a seat on the couch, his eyes watching me as I continued to stand. "Very well, stand then."

Crossing his arms, I tried to keep my eyes focused on his. One blush and he might do whatever he wanted. "You should begin planning with Jade over how you would like to have your cerem—"

"No." I crossed my own arms. I give him my best stern expression. Luna Ceremonies require the luna to mix blood with the alpha as a means to connect me to the pack and the mind link. You can bind a lycan to the pack. But my blood with reveal my true form immediately.

I can't do the ceremony.

CHAPTER EIGHT

Della

"No."

Dxton looked at me with a questioning look. "What do you mean, no?" he said, raising an eyebrow. His voice was filled with such coldness it sent shivers down my spine. Roxanna noticeably stiffened at the sudden change in mood. She quickly rushes out, a plate of biscuits in hand.

I looked him dead in the eye and with the calmest expression I can muster. "No, I will not be having a Luna Ceremony"

He stiffened further. "And why the hell not?" he barked, his eyes getting darker, his wolf showing.

"Try and bring his lycan forward."

"What?"

"Bring his lycan out, you could get an answer from him. The human side is too stubborn," she said before disappearing once again. I looked up at him. It could work.

"Clearly I am not a fitting luna for your pack, as you keep clearly stating." His eyes got darker by the second. "I am only human. I can't lead a pack of wolves." His eyes flashed gold momentarily. He's trying to keep his lycan in check. "And I don't even get along with my 'mate,' if I should even call you that," I confidently continued.

A loud roar filled the air. The coffee table was thrown against the wall. I stay standing, calmly watching the raging animal before me. His pitch black eyes stare menacingly at me, shaking my very core. I ignored it and continue to look at him. He stalked towards me, rage rippling off him in slow waves. His eyes turned gold.

He stands in front of me and bends down so he is eye level with me. "You are my mate! Nothing can ever change that!" He gripped his fist together. I leaned forward and narrowed my eyes.

"Then act like it," I growled.

His eyes turn the brightest I've ever seen them, his lycan now in complete control. He smirks devilishly. "Oh I would." His voice darker. "Only"—his fingers brush hair away from my face, softly—"Dxton doesn't have a certain like for humans. I however, have been dying to mark you since I first laid eyes on you," he said right next to my ear, making me shiver. My calm expression was long gone, replaced with desire.

"Now, now, be like that and I might just mark you," he said through clenched teeth. He moves away from me, quickly. His fist clenched down by his sides, as he breathes heavily.

I blinked a few times before returning to my calm façade. "What is going on? Why are there rogue attacks?" I asked.

He calms down before looking at me with a small frown. "Most people would ask why their mate doesn't like humans, but the question you seek, I'm not allowed to answer. Dxton is trying his hardest to regain control. He doesn't want to let you in because he doesn't want to lose you. He is too stubborn to realise this."

Before I can ask anything else, he smiled softly at me. "You really are the most beautiful creature I have ever seen." He then closed his eyes. When they reopened, Dxton's brown eyes looked at mine. He frowned at me. A flash of sadness washed over him before he stormed out of the room.

I breathed out and put a hand to my forehead. I had not received even close to an answer. But I felt a tinge of guilt at his brief moment of vulnerability that I caused. Having had enough excitement for one day, I head to my room. Why couldn't Dxton be like his lycan?

Flopping onto the bed, I placed my arm over my eyes. I can't escape tonight. You would be counting on it, wouldn't you Dxton? For now, I'll continue being a good human. I grabbed my new phone and added Ness's and Henry's numbers that I memorised by heart.

"Why don't we tell him? He might—"

"No. I'm sorry." Sighing, I look through my few contacts. *"I really am. But I'm not risking a whole pack's life just for our selfish needs. If I reveal you, lots of people will try to get their hands on us. My mother killed herself because of what she went through. I don't want to go through the same."* Besides Dxton is onto something with these rogue attacks and he won't be in a hurry to tell us.

"Give him a chance, I'm sure he will come through and tell us."

I don't know, but let's hope so.

CHAPTER NINE

DELLA

"Imagine her," he said.
"But how will I know what she will look like?"
"It'll come to you," he said softly.
I closed my eyes and follow his orders. I could soon see a snow-white wolf. It was just like Mere's, with bright gold eyes.
A rush of pain spread across my body like wild fire. I screamed out and clutched my stomach. My bones snapped in multiple places which made me fall to the ground. My clothes ripped and fur soon sprouted. An eruption of pain followed suit. I laid on the ground in pain for an hour. My very first shift.
"Hello Della," a voice said in my head.
"Who are you?" I asked, panicky.
"I'm your lycan," she responded calmly.
"Do you have a name?"
"No, we do not possess a name."
"Oh."
"Della?" I looked up at my father who has a worried look. I tried to grin in my wolf form. He smiled and brought me in for a hug. "I'm so proud of you, little wolf."
I let out a happy bark and softly nipped at his skin, before sprinting off. Not long after, a huge black wolf came by my side.

He carefully but playfully pushed my side. I smiled and ran faster, but him being bigger than me, easily caught up.

We ran around for what feels like forever. My wolf's powerful legs took us at full speed for miles but somehow, she never got tired. I quickly stopped when I saw a woman ahead. Her arms were crossed, with a frown plastered on her face. Father bowed his head slightly with a guilty look on his face. When she looked at me, she smiled brightly.

"Della, look at you! I'm sorry I wasn't there to witness your first shift," she said, giving father a pointed look. "You look beautiful," she said, kneeling in front of me. I smile at my mother as she scratches my ear. I close my eyes, my tail wagging. When I open them, I was no longer in the woods of France, but in a dark murky room. A screaming girl caught my attention.

"Someone help me!!!" It was hoarser than before. There were rivers of tears running down her blurry face. However, no one answered. I stepped closer to her. It's a little girl with long snow-white hair and blue eyes filled with terror and tears. Blood covered her arms and her little body. She was strapped down on a table. It's then I got a clear look at her face.

"Della Rosai." I stiffened at the disgusting voice of Franz Wolfe.

"Come now, my princess. There's no need for tears," he cooed, giving a sickening, evil grin. He walked up to younger me and stroke her cheeks. She flinched at his touch, earning a growl from him. "Don't! You and your mother will bow before me. One way or another—"

She spat on his face, cutting off his overly practiced speech. Franz wipes it off with his hand. He glared towards her before growling menacingly. He grips onto her strapped arm tightly, lowering his face to hers with his fangs noticeable.

"No! Leave her alone!" I tried to roughly grab his arm but they refused to move. He didn't flinch or even notice, he only continued his activities beforehand. I thrashed my arms into his face. "Stop!!!" A smirk appeared on his disgusting face, before he snapped her arm. Her scream echoed throughout the room. "Leave her alone!!!" I could feel the pain in my arm. He started to inject two needles of wolfsbane and silver into her system. She cried out in pain as I fell to the ground. I can feel the wolfsbane and sliver taking effect as it ran through my blood and to every inch of my body. I can feel it all. I clutched onto my arm, desperately pleading for the pain to stop. My eyes began to feel drowsy, the drugs taking effect in me and her.

"Monster," I managed to say. My face makes contact with the cold floor, my eyes still on the younger me as she screams. Please stop. Please. PLEASE!

Then I shot forward, snarling at the person in front of me. I got ready to get up and pounce. The person staring back has her eyes flashing between gold and silver, defensive and ready to kill me. I realise it's just my reflection. "Oh my God." In a sweat, I got up quickly and frustratingly, gripping my hair. I scream into my dark room. I feel too worked up. It's been too long since I shifted. My skin is aching and itching badly at the long overdue shift. I feel restless. I can feel her moving around underneath my skin. She's been so patient for me, but she's growing restless too.

I took a minute to calm myself down. *Breathe in, breathe out.* If I stay here, I might forcefully shift from the stress and night terror. I grabbed my phone. "2:53 AM." Fuck's sake.

I put on an oversized hoodie, some sweats, and runners. I pull the hoodie up, covering my face. Luckily the house isn't creaky or loud with the fake wooden floor panels. Getting downstairs in front of the fireplace is the easy part. It's getting out of the house that's the hardest part, with the security system and my no way of knowing how it works.

I grab onto the bricks, on the side of the chimney. It's a big chimney but maybe too small for me. How else am I going to get out of here? I need to shift and I am not doing it here. Sliding into the chimney, I shuffle my way up. I just barely fit.

Barely making it out of the top, I quickly jump off the chimney's edge. Knowing Dxton's extreme lengths, I doubt he wouldn't put it past him to have security cameras everywhere. Jumping off a two-story building might not be very natural. Skiing down the second story, I made my way over towards the veranda's roof. I grab onto the roof's edge and swing myself around so that I'm hanging off the roof and drop down onto the railing, then jumped onto the ground.

The lake I saw just off the territory should help to mask my scent. I kept away from guard hotspots, having been tuning in to them the last few days. Sometimes I'll grab a book, when I'm actually listening to the guards patrolling outside the house.

It doesn't take very long to get to the lake from Dxton's house. I listened to the forest around me, sensing if anyone is close by. When I heard nothing, I quickly took my clothes off, tucking them next to a tree. The water is so calm, with the moon shining on the reflection. She's always watching.

I shivered when I dipped my toes, but quickly got used to the feeling. The water is freezing, but the need to shift and the heat steaming off makes me pay the water any mind, diving straight under. When I reached the middle of the lake, I slowly began the shifting process. My bones ached painfully, skin turned to fur, nails turned to claws, and eyes became even more enhanced. I can hear, smell, and see even better. I spotted a fox in the distance, and it takes everything in me not to let my lycan go chase after it.

A normal werewolf is about the same size as an ordinary wild wolf, except for lycans. We are about the same size as a shire horse, maybe a little bit bigger.

I tried hard not to howl, allowing my lycan small rein. She plays quietly in the water. She takes a moment to admire herself in the water's reflection. Our coat is pure white, but we have many scars littering our body. Some noticeable under the pelt some only we can see. She whines softly as our mind goes down our dark rabbit hole. Time heals wounds but some wounds stay with you forever.

We spent an hour playing in the water, soaking our limited time as a lycan. She sighs happily up at the moon. She will always remain loyal to the moon goddess, it's in her nature. My, just the thought about looking at the moon makes me angry to no end.

"We should head in," I softly said to her. She whines buts complies and started to head towards shore. Suddenly, a branch snapped just off to our left, right next to our clothes.

A light brown wolf emerged in the darkness, with bright amber eyes and its hackles flared. It's Alex and he is looking straight at us. In a split second to secure our secret, my lycan acts before I do. We darted out of the water quickly and snapped onto his torso. She threw him into the water with us. Quickly shifting back into a human, I grab his neck and lifted him high into the air.

Disorientated, Alex looked at me with a puzzled face. "My lycan and I prefer our secrets kept secret. If you even think about mind linking anyone right now, I will kill you," I said. He whined softly. "Shift." When he didn't comply, I pull into my alpha dominance. "Now!" Within seconds, he shifted against his will. Squeezing his neck tighter, I felt all of my emotions racing through me. I'm angry at myself and him, but my biggest emotion that I'm sure he can smell as clear as day right now is fear.

Glaring into his eyes, I see his wolf whimpering and submitting. "Do not tell anyone what you saw tonight! Got it?" He didn't react much, causing my hackles to become tighter and my anger to rage even more. "Do you get it?" He nods the tiniest of nods, with a barely audible yes.

"H—how?" He choked out.

"If you don't tell anyone, I'll tell you but"—I dropped him—"I have had a very shitty night, so now if you will excuse me I have a bed calling my name," I tightly said, walking over his body. He kept his distance on the way to the house, but I can feel him following me.

My heart beats a million times at the very thought of anyone knowing. I shouldn't have gone out for so long. I should have shifted, stretched and gone back inside. No one would have known I'd left. "Snitching bitch," I muttered. I'm going to kill him if Dxton knows.

At the back door of the house stands a very cross, a very livid Dxton. My heart starts beating frantically, not at being caught, but at being found out. If Alex told him, I'll kill him where he stands.

"Inside now."

CHAPTER TEN

DELLA

Pulling my hair out from its ponytail, I fell down onto the leather couch. Exhausted and angry, I sighed. I did not meet the eyes of the furious alpha. I avoided everyone's eyes except Alex's. I sent him the slightest of glares before focusing my attention onto my hands.

"Leave us."

"I um— Yes Alpha." Alex heads towards the door, took a quick glance in my direction then left.

Dxton gets right in my face, instantly annoying me to no end. This male does not understand boundaries.

"You are on house arrest till I can trust you."

You're joking. "House arrest, what the fuck!" I get up to get in his face. "You cannot house arrest me, do I look like your little bitch? I am not someone you can play around with!"

Dxton glares down at me. I note however that his lycan is nowhere to be seen. "Until you can act like an adult and not run away, you are staying here until I say otherwise." Seriously? I am almost two hundred years older than this male.

I jab a finger into his chest. "I have this thing called a heart. If this is how you are going to treat the other half of your soul, I will never love you." I jab him even harder, he even steps back a little bit. "I will make it my mission to hate you for the rest of my lonely existence."

I didn't wait for his response. I went straight to my room, where I proceeded to cry for my lack of soul.

* * *

"Why haven't you told the alpha?" Alex busted into my room just when I got out of the shower.

Removing the towel from my head, I rolled my eyes. "Morning to you too, Gamma." Flicking my hair over my shoulder, I turned towards Alex, "Can I help you?" I dropped the towel onto my bed then stood up. "Because last I heard, I was on house arrest, and I wasn't allowed visitors." I walk towards him and poked his chest. "And you are the last person I want to be seeing."

"Why haven't you told the alpha?"

I gave him my best glare. "Do you really think I trust that asshole? Do you really think I wanted you to know? This was a rookie mistake on my part, but you are thick if you think I'm going to tell that good-for-nothing king who I am." Getting in his face, I growl lowly, "If you tell him, I will kill you and make it look like a rogue attack. I don't care much for you. Call me a bitch. I just want to be as far away from anyone who would dare use my DNA."

Alex, growing furious, glares daggers in my direction. "Why are you still here then? Why waste your life away to hide? You could be helping us. We're on the verge of a war!"

Turning around I grab his neck and squeezed harshly. "You think I didn't try?" Slamming him against the wall, I growled. "Last time I played hero, it got a lot of innocent people killed!" Snarling, I snapped my fangs at his neck. "I am done playing my part as a lycan. As far as I am concerned, the female lycan is dead."

"You fail once, so you give up."

He did not. My lycan boils over from his clear disrespect. "I don't have to answer to you pup." I squeezed his neck even tighter, causing him to suffocate. "Last time I checked, I was still your luna and I command respect."

"You have the power of the moon goddess on your side, and you ignore it because you're scared."

Growing tired of his disrespect, I throw him across the room. "I refuse to communicate with that bitch!"

"But she could help us—"

I stomped my foot on his chest. "No, she won't. She's a goddess. They might have made us, but they don't care about us. If she did, then why have I been forced to hide forever? I tried playing my role as a lycan and it bites me in the ass every time. She loves playing with my feelings. I have pleaded and begged her to help me!" I point towards the glowing moon in the window. "She won't answer my calls! Every time I looked at the moon, she would just turn her back to me! I would die, only to wake up tomorrow healed like nothing had happened. I would beg and beg her to let me die but she wouldn't answer my calls. She left me alone! In a world against me!" I push away, feeling tears welling up in my eyes. I let out a small sob.

"Ti- I mean Della are y—"

"It's Tia to you," I quickly snap. Calming down, I mumbled an apology. "I'm sorry Alex, but this is a war I won't join, not as a lycan." Taking a moment to get my breathing together, I turn around to face him. "I do want to know what is happening. Something bad is happening and I want to make sure I am far away from it."

"But you're the luna, we need you."

Shaking my head I look outside. "You don't need me. Dxton has been fine this whole time without a mate."

Alex sits up and shakes his head. "No. No, he hasn't. He looked for you for so long, but he gave up after some time. He needs you, he just didn't want a human mate, personal reasons."

Personal reasons . . . his sister and father of course. That explains a lot, but that can't be the only reason why he dislikes me for being human. There has to be another reason. "I want to know what is happening around here, and you are going to tell me." I allowed my lycan just the smallest of a glance at him, enough so that he can feel her.

"Everything?" He gulped.

"Everything." Letting my lycan come back in, he breathes in, muttering a few curses. "What's with the rogue attacks? Something's going on and I want in on it."

He juggled his options and shrugged a little. "We honestly don't really know that much. It's eating Dxton not knowing what is happening under his nose." He pauses before looking at me. "Why do you want to know anyway? I thought you didn't care much for us." He sneers slightly.

The alpha in me hates that he's being disrespectful right now, but I can't blame him. "Ever since I came to America, something has been bothering me. I feel on edge always. Something is happening and I need to know what."

"We don't know a lot." He sighs but continues. "There is this leader, they control all of the rogues. They never reveal themselves properly. They leave notes, each note signed. But we don't have a lead yet. We do know one thing." He stops, letting me process this. I nodded, making him continue. "The only thing I know is that, they are after you." He stands up from the floor, keeping a safe distance between us. He runs his hand through his hair shakily. "It makes sense now. They believed that we had you, the female lycan, and were determined to take you away."

Of course, everyone does for certain reasons. The more popular option is a strong lycan army. With an immortal incubator, they could get a lot of full lycans from me. It's not the first time and it won't be the last.

"What's the note signed with?"

He hesitated to answer.

"Wolfe."

CHAPTER ELEVEN

DELLA

"Wolfe."

No, no it can't be. Please no.

Franz Wolfe.

"No, No, please no." I feel myself start to shake immensely. My heart was going out of control and mind going down the rabbit hole of memories.

He's taken me before, he could do it again.

He's taken me before he could do it again.

HE'S TAKEN ME BEFORE, HE COULD DO IT AGAIN!

I'm on the floor, eyes everywhere around me, looking for his eyes, his scent, him. I refuse to do that again. "Please no." I grip my hair tightly and feel myself becoming undone again. I need to shift. I need to run.

"I have to leave."

"Della!"

"I can't do that again."

Alex grabs my shoulders firmly. "Your lycan is showing, please calm down." When I didn't respond, he slapped me across the face, which worked very well because I'm on top of him, strangling him.

"I'm sorry," I whispered, horrified, and quickly got off him.

"It's okay," he whispered over and over again. "Della"—he sat up—"what is wrong?"

"Franz . . . did so much. All of it didn't make the history books." Only my family knows what he did. My parents died before they could even tell the story. Unless . . . no that couldn't be right. That can't be it.

After thirty minutes of breathing in quietly, the sun's out and awake. Alex soothingly rubbed my back for the whole time. His eyes blurred over some more. He's mind linking. "There was another attack, a pack member was killed. I gotta go." Giving my back a small pat, he gets up.

"If you tell that pompous alpha this, I will kill you." Alex stops in his tracks slightly. "You don't live as long as I have without some precautions. But also, thank you." He pauses and nods, a small gulp could be heard as he pulls the door open.

"And I want those notes!" I quickly add as he scurries off.

* * *

I can't do this. Sitting around, doing nothing, waiting. I have someone on my ass and they expect me to just do nothing. The rogue attacks are becoming more out of hand. In the small time I've been here they have had five rogue sightings, and three attacks.

Dxton. I need to talk to him about the notes or get them myself. I heard him talking to Alex earlier about him taking care of matters in the pack house. Maybe he has left the notes in his study here, or he took them with him.

The door is locked, of course. I know how to unlock it with a hair clip but last I checked, I didn't have any. Despite checking three times, I doubt they would magically conjure now.

With the door magically open, I waltzed out. *Heart, calm down . . . calm down.* I walk towards his study, hand on the door, I hesitated before slowly pushing the door open. Dxton's going to smell that I was in here, but I need to get answers.

His desk, much like the one at the pack house is messy and littered everywhere. There's paperwork everywhere, and there's not an ounce of neatness or professionalism. Makes me tick. He doesn't have much personality in here. There's one photo on his bookshelf of him with Dominic holding up fishes each. I didn't think they would take time for themselves. He has dark blue walls, with half being white wooden panels. Like the pack house office, he has a bookshelf covering one of the walls, and a big window behind his desk with white curtains. For someone quite moody, it's a surprise how much colour he has in here, or anywhere in the house really. I wonder what his bedroom looks like.

I heard the door to the house, but upon a small sniff, I can smell that it's just Alex. I continue snooping around.

"What are you doing?" he asked the moment he steps into the office. "You're meant to be in your room."

"Like a door is going to stop me." I roll my eyes at the gamma.

He stands in front of my line of sight and waves a hand. "Seriously, what are you doing?"

"I'm looking for the notes that 'Wolfe' is leaving behind. I want to know what is being said."

"You mean, these notes?" He pulls out a manila folder, a small smirk on his face. He is actually helping me, why? He is going against his alpha right now. I'm not officially his luna and besides, he has no reason to help me. I'm sure not helping him. I've been threatening him. "I was on my way to go give them to you, you might want to take a photo of them all."

"... Thank you." I grab the folder, not opening it quite yet. I look at him sceptically. "Why? Why are you helping me? You have no reason to."

"Because I want you to look back on this day, and know how wrong you were to even think about abandoning us. You'll stay because you want to." Cocky bitch. Leaning against the desk, he folds his arms, eyes focused on the wall in front of him. "Besides you will need all the help you can get with getting out of the Luna Ceremony. You aren't ready and to be fair, we aren't ready for the female lycan either. Last thing we want is to freak everyone out and draw attention to us during a potential war on the horizon." He plays with a pen on Dxton's desk, scribbling a note on his hand. "Most people will just see it as threat too, and I know that's not the direction the alpha wants with this war." Twirling the pen in between his fingers, Alex shrugs. "The alpha actually takes everything the peaceful route. He hates war and fighting."

It would be the age. After a certain point, you become numb to this world's stories and the actions you take and before you know it, you just stop interfering with the problems around you. It gets repetitive and insanely annoying.

"Any other reason you are here?"

Giving me a quick side eye, he rolls his eyes. "Alpha wanted me to take you to him to talk about the Luna Ceremony."

I didn't like this, not one bit. The blank disrespect and the Luna Ceremony talk. Sighing, I quickly took photos of all of the notes, not looking at them for too long. I placed them on his desk and left the office, with Alex following suit. We remained quiet for the length of the trip to the pack house. I know that I have lost all of Alex's respect and I can't blame him for that. But a small part of me feels a pang at the obvious dislike he has towards me. The happy-go-lucky persona he has is now long gone, which is refreshing but rather depressing also.

"You know where his office is right?" I nodded in response. Alex nods up the stairs, waving me up while he turns back around and buggers off. I can't believe the males in this pack.

Getting to the office doors, I stiffen up. I can smell someone. A female, werewolf and she reeks of males, and her horniness is so, so pungent. I try not to puke, waving a hand in front of my face. I took a deep breath and end up dry heaving. Angrily, I burst in through the door.

Dxton sat behind his desk with a frown on his face. His hands clenched tightly together in front of him in a business-like way. What I was most angry about was what stood in front of him. A tall slender woman, with great curves and soft features. You could see her breasts too much and her ass sticks out like a sore thumb. She screamed sex appeal. She clearly has no shame. She is not trying to hide the males she's concurred on and she is very much so eyeing up my mate. He is her next victim from what I could smell. I glared at her as I became physically and mentally sick by her presence.

Dxton got up and stood beside me, his hand resting on my shoulder. I want to shrug it off, but I keep it together for the sake of not causing a scene. I want to growl at him, but the way he is looking at me and his hand on my shoulder is putting me off. Sparks. Electrical currents ran up and down my arm, calming my nerves and muscles. I sigh into this touch.

"Tessa this is my mate, and future luna of White Crescent Moon, Tia." He smiles softly at me while he introduces me. Slowly I look into his eyes, he looks genuinely happy. Why? I tried to "escape."

Tessa puts me off instantly because the complete opposite of what I imagined happens. "It's a pleasure to meet you, Luna." She bows her head respectfully. "I hope you like the flowers I picked for you." She gestures towards the flowers on my desk . . . I hate that they are very nicely arranged wild flowers in a simple but nice pot. Fuck smell nice too.

"That was very kind of you." She gives me a big smile, and blushes slightly, a small thank you escaping her lips. *Don't judge a book by its cover, Della. You should know better.* Now I just feel like a jerk.

"If you aren't busy later I would love you to join Jade and I for coffee." Jade? Oh shit how did I not see it sooner? She's Jade's sister. They look exactly alike, except for her bright blue eyes, a shade darker hair, they may as well be twins otherwise. Then it dawned on me. He set me up. He wanted me to get jealous. *That asshole!*

I nod, with a small smile, "I would love to. I wasn't aware Jade had a sister."

"I live at our home pack. I haven't had the honour of finding my mate yet. I have brought news however. My alpha would like a formal dinner with you after your Luna Ceremony. If at all possible." Tessa smiles sweetly between the two of us.

"Do you know what it is about?" Dxton asked, rubbing circles on my shoulder.

Tessa gave Dxton a small smile. "I don't know why Alpha Bosque, sorry." Dxton nodded. They talked for a few minutes that I don't care to listen in too. I take my attention over to my desk, which I note is ironically the Ikea desk called Alex. Everything is new: desktop, stationary, and the flowers.

"I should get going," Tessa said, catching my attention. She gives us both a friendly smile. "Jade is waiting outside. Thank you for your time, Alpha, Luna. I will let Alpha Salomon know that you accept his offer." She bows her head and leaves out the door, not before giving me time for coffee later.

I get ready to leave myself when Dxton stops me by grabbing my hand. "I wish to speak with you." Turning around to face him, I sigh. He is dressed in a white button up and jeans today, and I note the first few buttons aren't done up. "Your Luna Ceremony, you need to start planning it with Jade right away. I have moved the date forward, as punishment for your escapade last night."

"Of course you did" I expected as much. "Was there something else you needed me for?" I asked, getting ready to leave.

Dxton remains silent, but I can feel his eyes burning holes into my back. "No." I look to Alex who appears by the door and allow him to take me back to the house.

Just before I close the door, I look at Alex. "Hey."

He turns around, one foot off the porch. "Yeah?"

"Thank you, and sorry for how I treated you last night. I . . . I'm not used to leaning on people for help."

He smiles for the first time since finding out my identity. "You're welcome, Luna."

CHAPTER TWELVE

Della

It's just a nightmare. They can't actually hurt you. It's just a nightmare!

"Allison!"

I looked over my shoulder to see people running after me but they are all covered in a shadow. They keep screaming.

"Morgan!"

"Estella!"

"Nicola!"

Those are names of my past lives, and they won't stop. I ran into a building, fighting to get up the stairs as quickly as I can.

"Wendy!"

"Chloé!"

"Tia!"

No please, stop yelling at me please. Please, I just want to live peacefully. "When will I just be Della!"

I closed the stairway door behind me, slamming it into the faces of the shadowy figures who at close inspection were all from my past lives. All of them.

"You should know better than to run away from me, sweet Della."

I stiffened upon hearing the voice, and slowly turned around to Franz, his hand around my mother's throat. He had a sick smile on his lips. "You will pay the price for running away." He ran his spare hand through my mother's hair. She flinched upon his touch. "You are going to watch me."

He grabbed onto her face and slowly made his way towards her neck where he snaps it, and he continues to keep snapping it every time it heals.

"Now, I want you to snap it." He grabbed both of my hands and forced me forward. I screamed out and desperately tried to get out of his grip.

"No! No please, I'm sorry! I-I won't run again." He forced me to stand above her healing form, her eyes a fraction open. She nodded, which sent me into tears. "Please," I whispered as Franz grabbed my hands and brought them to her neck.

"Snap it. SNAP IT NOW!"

I hear the loud snap of her neck. I could feel her bones shattering between my fingers. "Good. Now you are going to do it again, and you will keep going until I say stop." He reached behind him and grabbed gloves with silver laced in them. "And you will be using these."

"Tia! Tia! Wake up!"

I feel electricity shooting through my entire body, and hands tightly holding my arms. Screaming, I tried to throw them off me.

"LEAVE ME ALONE!"

"Tia. Shhh, it's okay." The person holding me softly whispered. "It's just me."

"Dxton?" I whispered. I looked at the figure holding me to see a very worried Dxton. He nods softly. Am I still dreaming? I look at the clock on the bedside table. 4:53 AM. I can read it. I'm not dreaming. I feel tears falling from my eyes, which he wipes away. I was too drained to stop him.

"How . . . how did—" I look to the door to see it completely shattered. How did that not wake me up?

"You were pretty out of it. Your screams were a lot louder than the door," he said, seeing my eyes on the mess. "I'll have it replaced. Do you want to talk about it?"

"Why are you trying to comfort me?" I said instead, completely avoiding his question. "Last time I checked, we hated each other," I said, rubbing my eyes wearily.

"No." He looks at me with a forlorn look. "Only you have said that." He takes a sip of his hot chocolate. I look out to the moon, shamelessly watching us.

"You still didn't answer my question."

"I heard you." He gestures to me. "Your nightmares, you have them almost every night." *Oh, I knew I had them often. I just didn't know it was that often.* "You do," Dxton voiced out. I had said that out loud. "Sometimes, I sit outside your room, seems to help sometimes. I can't come in when your door is locked, but sometimes it helps. Sometimes they don't, then I'll hear you waking up crying, screaming into your pillow."

I didn't think he could hear them, or even notice. I feel the bond tugging, which slightly startled me. It hasn't done that before. It's remained mostly dead. "It does that when you're in the heat of your nightmares, subconsciously you're asking me for help, seeking my comfort." He doesn't say it smugly, or even cockily, he states it softly. I never even sensed him by my door, or smelt him.

"You were a bit preoccupied," my lycan softly reminded as she nuzzles my mind. That is true I suppose, but part of me feels unnerved that he can sneak up on me.

". . . Thank you," I whispered. I look at his hands that are still on mine, small sparks fly up my arms, causing goosebumps to form. "You can let go now." He looks at me hesitantly but slowly let my arms go, causing me to take in a sharp breath from the lack of sparks.

I can't believe he has been hearing them. What if he could sense my lycan? What if I screamed out Franz's name? What if he already knows but is waiting for me to tell him, or if he is playing dumb to get a reaction? No, no you're just being silly Della. Dxton is the type that wouldn't play dumb in this kind of situation. He would bring it up if he knew.

"Are you sure that you are okay?"

No, "I'm okay, just childhood trauma." I don't bother putting on a big fake smile. I know he won't buy it and if anything it would probably just piss him off. "I'm fine."

Dxton pushes the door debris to the side, giving me one final look. He walks out the door, but I know that he doesn't leave the hallway. He stayed there until I fell back asleep. When I woke up again, I notice that Dxton is no longer in the hallway, but at closer inspection I can smell him. He was there for a while, and left not that long ago.

"What happened to your door?" Alex stepped over a few of the wooden shards, two coffee cups in hand. "Did you try to escape again or . . . ?" He handed me the coffee mug, which I mumbled a thank you for. When I took a sip, I concurred that it's a latte.

"No, I had a nightmare about Franz. It got vocal and Dxton got concerned," I explained, taking another sip. We both made our way towards the couches, which had become my favourite part of the house. It's in an open space. If something were to happen around me, I'd be able to hear it. Also, the couches are comfy.

"Have you looked through the letters yet?"

They weren't as useful as I had hoped. Nothing called out anything. It mostly said "you can't keep all of the lycans safe, especially the female." It really wasn't helpful. The ending was signed as "Wolfe," but it might not necessarily be the Wolfe. It could just be surviving members of Franz's pack, Dunkler Wolf. Or someone trying to send fear into our hearts.

"I have, but nothing really popped out. It's a dead end. Where's Roxanna?" I said, looking for her scent.

"She's stayed home today. Alpha's orders." Makes sense.

Alex looks off into the distance, eyes blurred. He taps the side of his coffee cup continuously. "Jade is on her way, the alpha really wants this ceremony planned."

Fuck. I breathed out, just what I needed right now.

"How are we going to cancel this ceremony?"

I ran my hands through my hair, learning back into the couch. "I don't know."

I don't know.

CHAPTER THIRTEEN

Della

Jade and I spent the whole day planning out the Luna Ceremony. She was determined to get it all done in one day. With only two days until D-day, she made sure everything was sorted from my dress, the food, the colour scheme, the location, and my speech.

I spent the majority of it nodding and yessing. My mind was too occupied with getting out of the ceremony. It annoyed Jade to no end that she ended up just planning the whole thing herself. I felt bad, but the ceremony is something that could wait. I even tried begging Dxton last night during dinner if we could postpone it but he wasn't budging. He was determined to have it over and done with. I even debated telling him why, but I kept backing out of it. I was too scared of the outcomes and the reaction. Alex and I conspired, but we couldn't come up with a concrete solution. He even suggested hiding the dress Jade brought, but that's easily replaceable. They wouldn't cancel a big event over a dress.

We were wasting time, and I only had one choice; reject the alpha in front of everyone before he could take my blood. It was the only solution I could think of. Hopefully before I could reject him, he will take me offstage and lock me in my room. My rejection wouldn't work, not unless I state my full real name.

But here I am, standing in a floor length Greek style chiffon dress. The dress has two slits up each leg, the material the softest I've ever worn. It's simple but works for what we are doing. Jade is currently putting my hair up into a neat bun. The roots in my hair are almost white now, something Jade of course picked up. Which ended in my terrible lie of "I redid the roots white."

I sigh softly as Jade pins down the last of my hair. Ceremony day was here, and I had no concrete way of getting out of it. I only had one choice. Rejection. But what if that doesn't work? What if he beats me to it? What if he sees it coming? What am I going to do? If he was nicer, more approachable, I could tell him the truth.

I feel myself starting to hyperventilate. I'm about to be revealed in front of hundreds of people. I have never been forced into this kind of situation before.

"Tia?" Jade quickly kneels down in front of me. "Hey, it's okay." She softly rubs my back. "It's going to be okay, it's not that scary, I promise." She wipes some of the tears from my eyes. "It'll be okay, you'll see."

"No, no, it's not." I walked away from her grasp. "You have been raised into this life, not me, I didn't want this for me," I whispered. "I didn't want to be in your world, to be a luna." I turned to her, my breathing still uneven. "I'm just a human! I can't lead a pack. I can barely look after myself." I look outside the windows of the pack house to see everyone seated in chairs. "I didn't even want to be here. Dxton forced it upon me." I just want to go home. I feel sick to my gut. I keep vomiting in my mouth. I'm so fucking nervous, I might faint.

Jade stood up. "Tia I ha—"

She stops short when she heard a scream. We both looked outside to see the pack hysterical. Some shifting, some running away.

"Rogues! Run!"

A few gunshots could be heard. Not to be that person, but *thank you*! This is the kind of distraction I needed. We live in a kill or be killed world. I'm going to take whatever I get to survive.

"We need to get out of here, the alpha has asked me to get you up to his office and to lock the doors." Jade grabbed my hand and starts pulling me into towards the stairs. We make it to the railing when I feel Jade's hand let go. A rogue that's managed to get inside has a gun to her belly and hand to her throat.

"You"—he gestures to me—"are coming with me, my alpha wishes to talk with you, Luna." He dragged the word *luna*. "Comply or I kill her and her pup."

I put my hands up. "Okay, okay. I'll do whatever you want, let her go," I said carefully, stepping just an inch closer. He pushed Jade away roughly then went to grab my arm. I quickly got out of the way, which causes him to clumsily pull the trigger, sending a bullet straight into my shoulder.

"Tia!"

Slapping the gun away, I quickly manoeuvred myself behind him and grabbed his head, snapping it. He drops to the floor. Because I had the audacity to think about the rogue attack, karma bit me in the ass, in the form of a bullet. Hissing in pain, I gripped my shoulder to stop the blood from flooding. The bullet stung and burnt my flesh. *Silver.* That's why they had guns. They wanted to kill Dxton, or possibly bring me out. I clenched my eyes shut, desperately trying to keep my eyes silver. Hopefully Jade doesn't smell my lycan. Please don't.

"Oh my god!" Jade starts fussing over me but I quickly push her away softly.

"Go find the shooter. Tell Dxton I'm fine." She doesn't budge from her spot. "Jade go! The rogues needs to be stopped!"

"Okay . . . okay I'll go get the alpha." Jade rushed out of the room, screaming for Alex, for Dxton, or anyone.

The bullet wound doesn't hurt. Even the small trace of silver isn't doing much in terms of hurting my lycan, but I am still bleeding. I got up from the floor and quickly ran up the stairs. I need to get away from everyone. The more people Jade brings in, the more I'll have to explain. Dxton is going to find out. I might be able to trick Jade, but I definitely can't fool him.

Kicking the door to our office open, I leant against his desk, quickly pulling the dress off. I elongated my nails and dug into my skin for the bullet, ripping it out. I threw it into the bin. The wound healed over instantly. I need to burn everything. The bullet needs cleaning. The dress, the dress needs to be burnt. I search for a lighter, or match or anything that could burn. I can feel Dxton approaching the door, his steps heavy and quick. I'm about to look through Dxton's drawers, when the door kicked open.

Dxton stood at the door, his eyes frantically zeroed in on the blood escaping my shoulder. "Tia ar—" His nostrils flared, taking in the overpowering scent of my lycan. His eyes went gold and furious. "Explain right now!"

"I-I—"

"Why do I smell lycan blood?" Dxton said stiffly. If the situation was different, I would have been drooling over him in the suit he is in.

"Um, uh, a werewolf who must have been a lycan came in with some other guys with guns and tried to shoot me. Some of his blood went on me," I blurted out pathetically.

"Bullshit." He wouldn't believe whatever story I brought up anyway. Sighing, I remove my hand from the wound showing the already healed over wound. "You're the female lycan," he said through gritted teeth. I nodded while he debated it over his head. "But how?" He sat down onto the couch with his hand going through his hair.

"My lycan hides her scent as well as herself. It's something I grew up with," I explained.

"Who taught you?" Dxton's eyes narrowed slightly.

"My mother. She picked it up herself and taught me. Which is how we moved around without people knowing," I said with a slight edge to my voice. He went silent for a while as he took this all in. It's not until I broke the silence that he looked up at me with a frown.

"Now do you see why I can't join your pack? I'll put everyone in danger and I don't want to bring unwanted attention here because of me. So please understand why I can't be your luna." I pleaded.

His dark eyes bore into mine as he calculates in his head, with his lycan. He nodded stiffly. He is silent for a while, before he mutters a few curses under his breath. He takes off his jacket and hands it to me, making me completely aware that I was standing naked. Mumbling a thank you, I put it on.

"I have things I must discuss with you then," he said, walking behind his desk where he sits down. I take a seat in the chair in front of his desk. His office is silent and full of tension. I can't help but notice his stiff shoulders and clenched fist.

"His lycan is on edge," my lycan said with a small whine.

"I know."

Because of this and the mate bond, I badly want to tell him it'll be fine and bring my hand to his. But that would probably bring more harm than good.

"The matter of the rogue attacks and strange happenings have been fresh on your mind for a while, yes?" He went straight to business.

"Yes," I said, straightening up with a serious face now plastered to my face.

"They are looking for you," he said swiftly.

"I'm aware of this."

"We don't have any suspects for who the leader of these rogue attacks are but he leaves notes. He searches for the female lycan and he thinks since my pack and the other lycan packs are allies, we might know where you're hiding. He threatened to kidnap and torture you. So we have been trying to keep this on a low profile in hopes you wouldn't find out and also because I didn't trust you," he said, looking me dead in the eye. This sent a numbing pain over me. I knew he didn't trust me but hearing him say it out loud just confirmed it. However, it's not like I trust him either.

"Because I was human."

He nodded.

"What else do you know?"

"In some of the letters it's in riddles or random words and the latest one says, 'when both moons align, darkness will fall.' We don't know yet what this means but we have a feeling it's something to do with the upcoming full moon, or lunar eclipse."

I nodded as I thought this through. I did see that part when I looked through the notes. This could be bigger than we thought and worst of all it could be anything. We always knew werewolves were involved of course, but this could get dirty with a full moon involved. A full moon doesn't make us powerful like it says in the legends. We just feel more in touch with the goddess and our loved ones. But this could still be a bad thing.

I look up at Dxton, who now has his jaw clenched and nails which morphed into claws digging into his desk. "You are lucky I was shot also." He lifts up his shirt to find a bullet wound in his hip. "It'll be an easy way to deny the smell." *That's true*, I thought to myself. "And you didn't think to tell me because?"

I stared at the male as if he grew a second head. "You're joking right?" I blinked at the male. "Oh you aren't joking."

"No."

This male, cannot be serious. "Why would I tell you?" I start listing the reasons with my fingers. "You are an absolute asshole, we can't communicate without arguing, and I don't trust you. Mate or not, I have no reason to trust you. You've given me the cold shoulder from the very beginning."

"You not being human changes everything."

"I know, that's why I didn't tell you" I sighed out.

"No that's not why." He looked at me, as if seeing me for the first time. "My issue wasn't you, it was that you being human meant I'd love you, blink, and you'd be gone . . . I wouldn't have had much time with you. I thought it best if I didn't have a relationship with you so when you did die, I wouldn't have my heart ripped apart." He looks everywhere but to me. "The moment I saw you, I wanted you. I knew I would never accept anyone else. It wasn't working. I thought you hated me. It would have helped, but it didn't." He looks into my eyes. "I already love you."

How? I choked on my own spit. How can you give me a bombshell like that? I know for a fact I don't love him. But what do you even say to that? "This changes nothing, I still don't trust you, and hate your guts," I quickly said in a flush.

He smiled the tiniest bit. "I know."

Luckily there is a shower on the office level, and also luckily they have bandages in there, and very oddly, Dxton also has human blood bags. "Why do you have bags of human blood?"

He doesn't even flinch handing it to me. "I looked in your file for your blood type and had it stocked in case you were to ever be hurt and needed an infusion." He handed me a towel also. "You can put some on the bandage, just to add to the human identity."

That is oddly sweet and terrifying at the same time. "Um . . . thanks."

Dxton helps wrap the bandage and put the gigantic bandage on it, even put some gauze on it just for safe measure. It was sweet. Too sweet. Please don't tell me he is going to start behaving like a real mate just because I'm not human now. That is very contradictive of him.

'He did also admit to being in love with us.' My lycan sighed out dramatically, causing me to instantly blush. Dxton looks at me strangely as I go red like a tomato.

"What's wrong?" he asked softly, though he started to smirk. The bastard.

"I'm fine," I said a little too quickly. Actually, he is really close right now.

Dxton hummed. "Are you sure?"

"Yes! Positive."

. . . What is happening.

CHAPTER FOURTEEN

Della

"I see that the alpha is aware." Alex called out.

I look up from my book, my mouth mid sip from my tea. "Pardon?" I put my tea down.

Alex crossed his arms. "I see that the alpha is aware."

"Oh yes. I didn't have many options." I put my book onto my lap, and gestured to him to sit down.

"True," he mumbled. "How did he take it?"

"Surprisingly well, a little annoyed that I didn't say anything sooner, and . . ." I blushed instantly. He also has rapidly shown new colours, rather sweet ones. This morning he brought me breakfast in bed. He claimed it was to look the part in front of Roxanna as a worried mate. But I didn't smell Roxanna's scent in the house.

"And?" Alex rolled his hand.

"And . . . he has started behaving differently."

Alex paused, about to grab a pastry from the platter on the coffee table. "Like?"

Crossing my arms, I raised an eyebrow. "I don't see how it is much of your business. Why are you here anyway?"

Alex rolled his eyes, biting into his choice of apple crumble muffin. "You are going on your first official luna business as the unofficial luna," he said with his mouth full. I slapped his head and growled out.

"Manners, rolling your eyes is one thing but do not eat with your mouth open." Disgusting. He choked on the muffin, causing a small smirk to form on my lips. "Anyway, what luna business?"

He quickly swallowed his bite. "Do you remember Jade's sister, Tessa? She came to ask for you and Dxton's presence at her pack. Her alpha has something that we need." He shrugs his shoulders. "She didn't know what, but Dxton thinks it's a letter from you know who."

"Right."

"Dxton had a bag packed for you, he is actually waiting for you outside," he said, taking the last bite of his muffin.

"Right now?" I was baffled. Talk about a late notice.

"Yep." Alex nodded, getting up. He stuffed another muffin in his mouth. "Right now."

I looked down at the PJs I have yet to get out of. Groaning, I put my book onto the coffee table. "I'll get dressed."

I tied my hair into a half-up bun. I don't bother with make-up, solely because of how late the notice was. Damn males. I might be hundreds of years old, but I still want to look good when I can. I put on a black crop top, some high waist jean shorts and an oversized white cardigan, with some white Converse.

I marched straight up to the male. "Thank you for the late notice of today's plans by the way." Dxton took a step back, putting his hands up in surrender. "I forgot all about it. Jade reminded me thirty minutes ago."

Speaking of the devil, Jade waved at me. "Luna, can I talk to you for a second?"

I gave Dxton a quick glare. "Still!" Turning away, I go over to Jade with a smile. "Course you can, what do you need?" I grabbed onto her arm. She's close, I can definitely smell her now. Little McGavin is gonna be a strong she-wolf. I feel a bit bad for whoever her mate is, they are gonna have a run for their money.

"So will our pup."

I choked at my lycan's response.

"*Let's not go down that road,*" I said. She rolled her eyes.

"How come I smelt lycan blood the day you were shot?" she asked with a serious look. Fuck, she did smell it. Her heart. It's beating out of time. She's nervous.

"*Is her wolf the same?*" I asked my lycan.

"*Yes, more so than the human. She fears for her pup.*"

"It was Dxton's probably. I tried to attack him, in hopes that he might have called off the ceremony." I shuffled around on my feet. "I drew blood, but he obviously didn't budge."

She shook her head. "I know what his blood smells like, Tia." Her eyes narrowed. "Is there something you want to tell me?"

Shit! Shit! Shit! I try desperately to keep my heart going at the same pace. I have learnt over the years how to avoid the rapid heart rate when lying, but I keep slipping up around this damn pack.

"Um . . ." I waved my hand frantically behind me in hopes Dxton or Alex can see my plea for help.

Sure enough. "Jade?" Alex called out. "I need help convincing the alpha that we are going to be okay for the weekend."

She looks over to the two behind me. "Okay!" She gave me a quick glare. "This conversation isn't over."

"*Chill, that was very chill.*"

"*Cold,*" my lycan said playfully. "*The term you are looking for is cold, not chill.*"

"*What do you know? You're an animal.*" Bloody bitch is right though. I can't believe I got one upped by a wolf.

"Let's go," Dxton called out. I nodded, getting into the SUV.

I sat in the back with my music playing loudly through my earphones as I drift in and out of consciousness. The beautiful French song of "*Non je ne regrette rien*" is playing. One of my all-time French favourites, also one of my mothers. We used to listen to

Edith Piat sing on the phonograph whenever we had the chance. Those were some of my favourite memories of her.

I feel myself start to fall asleep. I had yet another nightmare last night, and again Dxton sat at my door. A part of me wanted him to come into my room. Ever since he found out the truth about me, he's been sweeter and nicer. Mate material.

"Tia."

"W-what?"

"We're here," a gruff voice responded. I opened my eyes, seeing a blurry dark pair looking at mine.

"Okay." I sighed. Dominic went to give me a hand, but quickly decided against it. Wise move. Dxton wouldn't have taken lightly to that. "Where's Dxton?" I asked.

"Alpha Landon is greeting him on the porch. We've been instructed to wait for the alpha." I nodded and stretched out my muscles with a yawn.

"Ah, so it is true that the mighty lycan king has a human mate," a smug voice said behind me. I turned around to a lean, scruffy, and mind you, very unattractive man. A smug look was plastered to his face, with Dxton next to him. He smelt strongly of alcohol and sweat. He obviously didn't take his time to shower. I instantly wanted to get as far away from this male. As soon as possible too. He didn't have any good vibes. "You must be Tia, oh what an honour it is to finally see you. I've heard so much about you!" he said, grabbing my hand in his. Dxton instantly growls in warning. "Don't fret King, I'm simply welcoming the new luna." Landon lets my hand go, smugly looking at Dxton. There is something terribly wrong with this male, he's trying to get under Dxton's fur. A very dangerous move. He isn't a very worthy alpha. I can't believe this is Jade's former pack and alpha. How disgusting.

"I will not have you touching what isn't yours, especially since you killed your own mate," Dxton growled, moving in between me and Landon.

Landon didn't waver for a second. "She had it coming." He shrugs with a sigh. "Nothing but a lowly omega."

I clenched my fist tightly as I try my hardest not to kill this disgraceful alpha. Dxton, noticing my angered state, placed his hand on my arm, more of a warning than comfort.

"You are not worthy of your title," Dxton growls, glaring down at the smaller wolf.

"Maybe, but you can't change that, not if you want your answers," Landon states, moving to walk to the pack house.

Growling under his breath, Dxton looks to Dominic and gives him a sharp look. After a moment, Dominic nodded and walks to the forest. "What is he doing?" I was calming down, now that the disgusting alpha was gone.

"Checking perimeters, I don't want to take any risks." Fair enough. I doubt this idiotic alpha has a good guard system. I want to go back to White Crescent Moon, at least I knew I was safe there.

"Why is he still an alpha? You have the means to strip him of his title."

"I was about to. He knew too. I think he took one of the letters left by you know who. He's going to leverage it." Dxton growls lowly. "I'll kill him if he even thinks to try anything. Hell, I might anyway." He gritted his teeth. I suddenly had the urge to comfort him. "He isn't going to be alpha when we leave that's for sure."

I nodded and look towards the car. We should grab our stuff. I don't know if I can trust anyone in this pack to touch my things.

"I'll send some men to grab the bags later," Dxton said.

I looked up at him with a raised brow. "Reading my thoughts already?" He looked down at me with a twitch of his lip, before he started to walk into the house. I followed behind closely, my wolf silently alert.

81

"Ah finally decided to come inside I see." Landon said, walking out of a room.

Dxton gives a sharp nod. "If you don't mind, we would like to settle in. Before we get straight into business."

Landon smirks with a sly nod. "Of course." He turns to a tall man behind him and signals him over. "Aaron here, will help Tia get the bags, while us alphas have a nice chat in my office," Landon suggests.

"No—"

"Sounds great, have fun, Alphas," I said, stretching out alpha.

I turned around to start walking to the car when Landon yells, "She does talk!"

I rolled my eyes and walk out to the car. I look down to my hand in utter disgust. I'll have to wash it multiple times until his stench is gone. But at least now I can make sure no one touches my stuff.

The guy Landon sent to help me was very buff, with indigenous tattoos running up his arm, and earrings lining up both ears. Very badass and very dangerous. But he too smelt of alcohol.

I opened the trunk and started to grab some bags, when I felt the man pressed up close to my back and head too close to my neck. He breathes in my scent hungrily. "You are very captivating. I promised I wouldn't do anything rash but hell you smell too damn good," he said greedily, smelling my neck again.

I turn around and pushed him away hard. "Fuck off," I growled. He simply regains his stances and smirks sickly.

"Looks like I got myself a fighter," he purrs. I cringe at his words and move away from him. He continues to approach me with an evil glint in his eyes.

"You stay there or I'll scream for Dxton!" I demanded. I stop short when I felt the car against my back. This is what really sucks about hiding my lycan. I have to act weak, and well . . . like a human.

"Nowhere else to go," he said, putting his hands on both sides of my head.

Before he can even come closer, a thundering roar echoes through the sky. Aaron is thrown away from me, to a nearby tree. Dxton storms towards him, half shifted. Eyes bright gold and body livid with fur poking everywhere. "You'll pay for touching what's mine!" Dxton's claws slash at the man's chest. He pleads for Dxton to stop, but to no avail. Life slowly leaves his body but that doesn't stop Dxton from shredding his remaining body. Not even an hour and it's off to a very bad start, with one dead and one out of control.

Aaron's eyes stare into mine lifelessly. His brown eyes now faded over into a soulless pool. I let out a breath and sighed softly. Dxton's growl echoed through the forest as he stalked towards me. He was panting, his fists clenched.

Landon ran out of the pack house towards us, his expression one of anger and confusion. Some of his pack members trailed behind. "What's going on here? Why is Aaron in shreds?" he exclaimed, looking at Dxton pointedly.

Dxton ignored him and looks at me deeply. His eyes locked on mine. Worry and anger swam in the depths of his eyes, "Tell your men to stay away from Tia, or they will suffer the same fate," Dxton growls, glaring at Landon and the unmated males behind him who's started to cower away, baring their necks. Dxton rumbles in approval, before grabbing my arm firmly. Daring the males to make a move.

"Don't mean to be picky, but my men won't stay away too long. After all she is unmated and rather beautiful" Landon states while he lazily scratches at his scruffy, unkempt beard. This makes Dxton growl loudly as he stalks towards Landon murderously. His lycan on edge and ready to strike at the cocky alpha.

Even though I really wanted him to, I gently grab his arm and pull him back. Letting the sparks fly up his arm. He stops and turns his murderous eyes to me. "He isn't worth it" I whispered.

His eyes softened slightly as I gently rubbed his arm soothingly. He sighed. His eyes cast down to the bags at my feet. I went to grab them, but Dxton's faster, snatching them up. He throws them over his shoulder easily. He then guided me with his hand on my back through the small crowd. He was growling at every unmated male in sight. My lycan growled with approval.

"I'll see you for dinner," Dxton gruffly calls out before walking into the pack house, slamming the door shut.

I silently walk with him upstairs to a room. It's a small room with peeling wallpaper and ancient furniture. "Looks like termites are having quite a party," I muttered to myself before turning to Dxton, who looked to be having a battle with himself.

"Are yo—"

I was frozen, while his big arms wrapped protectively around me. I couldn't form any words or react towards his hug. I just stood there stiff as a board. Just as quickly, his arms were gone. "Your lycan is relaxing to mine," he said before leaving the room.

For a good five minutes I stood there relishing the feeling of warmth lingering on my skin. But even in my shocked mood, I don't get why he is now letting himself be more open to me. It's only been a day since he found out.

"We need to talk to him again," my wolf said softly.

"I know." I sighed, rubbing my temple.

"He clearly wants to try."

"I get it. I'm not going to die tomorrow from natural causes, but it's so heads on. I'm still in a headspace of trying to distance myself."

A few knocks on the door took my attention. "Come in." Dominic walks in and stands by the door.

"I've been asked to take you to the meeting room."

I nodded, mumbling a string of curses. "Lead the way."

After a few minutes of silence, I decide to break it and put on the innocent human facade. "So Dom, is it okay if I can call you that?" I asked. He nodded. "Okay, so have you found your mate?" Dom stiffened at my words and quickly shook his head. "Sorry if it's a sensitive subject, but with you being lycan, I can presume you've been around a while." I said softly.

Judging by Dom's scent, he reached maturity not that long ago. "I'm young for my kind, and finding a mate for a lycan is harder than the average wolf," Dom explained, looking in my direction. I pretended to let that sink in.

What he said is true. After all, I'm like in my 600s this year and I just found my mate. The oldest lycan was actually Dom's father. He died in 1294. But then again we can live for much longer. We just tend to be suicidal towards the end. Life isn't great, and immortality isn't everything. In fact, it's cracked up to be.

The double doors in front of us opened to Landon smiling wickedly. "Look who decided to come and attend, little human" he said slyly.

I roll my eyes and walk into the room. A short man, with tattoos lining his arms and scars looks to me. He must be Landon's beta. He gives me a short nod. My eyes catch onto Dxton who is motioning for me to sit down next to him. I sit on his right, while Dom sits on his left.

"Great so we're all here!" Landon claps. "Oh Tia, this is my beta Treva."

I nod in his direction, which he returns with a friendly smile. Which surprised me, to say the least. He must be the only white sheep of this pack.

Landon throws a folded piece of paper in front of Dxton. I look over his shoulder as he reads it.

I can see you
Can you see me?
Have you figured out who I am yet?
I am looking forward to the day you figure out who I am
You have the worst habit of biting your nails, Luna, I suggest you stop.

Dxton sighed and reread it. "Well they are taunting us," I mumbled, sitting back. I feel my heart elevate slightly. This isn't the first time they have started seeing me. He's watching us, but we already knew that. He's in the shadows, again already knew that. Doesn't take a genius to figure that out. But how are they getting away with it?

"Here, came the day before you guys. I haven't looked at it but it's got a name that might interest you," Landon said, throwing a letter in front of me.

Della Rosai . . .

CHAPTER FIFTEEN

DELLA

Della Rosai...

My heart started to beat loudly in my chest. The letter lay untouched in front of me. Were they onto me? Did they know I really was with Dxton? Worse, did they know I was his mate?

"What is this Landon?" Dxton growled.

Landon just shrugged. "Like I said, I haven't opened it. It was on the border. Figured since rumour has it that the female lycan is with you, you might want it."

Dxton nodded and grabbed the letter, putting it in his shirt pocket. "I'll look through it later. Anything else you have that I should know about?" He growled slightly.

Landon mockingly started to think. "Nope," he hummed. Dxton nodded and grabbed my arm.

"Very well then, we shall leave to our room," Dxton began saying as he rose from his seat with me.

We went to walk out of the room when Landon called out. "If it is true, that the female lycan is rising and a new world order is occurring. I'd watch your ass, King." He mocked towards the end.

"I'll keep that in mind," Dxton said over his shoulder, before dragging me out of the room. We walk past pack members that all quickly bowed or cowered away at the fuming alpha before them. Some even sent me worried glances. Dominic stood at the door, ready for action if needed. "Guard the door."

"Yes Alpha," Dom said. He proceeded to greet me with a firm nod. "Luna."

"Dom," I replied with a small nod.

The door closed behind us as Dxton ripped the letter out with a huff. He elongated his nail into a claw and went to rip it open. I quickly snatched it away and frowned at him with my arms crossed.

"Last I saw, it said 'Della,' and if I remember correctly your name isn't Della, Dxton."

He rolled his eyes and folded his arms also. "Whatever you say, Tia," he said, stretching out my name. I pulled the letter out of the envelope, my name printed in neat cursive, glistening smugly. A red seal with a coat of arms locked the opening of the letter together. It looked familiar. Too familiar.

"Look at the seal."

His eyes shine gold. "Franz." I nod. Ripping the seal, I unfold the paper and began reading.

Dearest Della,

Only Female Lycan to walk the planet.

What a lonely curse. Having to run from those that seek the power you hold. Must be daunting. Not even safe in your birth pack. After all your mother did die tragically, if only the story was true. Beaten and tortured by Franz Wolfe, but we both know how she really died.

I'm sure by now you have been made aware of our little hunting group. Our rogues sure have, after all we are getting reports of rogues being shredded in half, without a trace; I'm sure I have you to thank for that.

At the end of the day I will admit, you are one hard person to find. But that isn't a sign to start relaxing just yet. You may have been off the radar for years Little Wolf, but you made the grave mistake by helping those in need, with those certain wolves. How are the Burlings?

I'm sure the White Crescent Moon Pack is quite busy this time of the year, well at least that is what I've been told.

But that's enough about you. Who are we, you ask? Well that's a mystery all on its own. But I will tell you this, we will come face to face soon. I can assure you that. History is repeating itself and you Little Wolf are the main course.

Yours truly,

Wolfe.

"This is impossible," I breathed out, the letter dropping from my hand.

He shouldn't know the truth behind her death. I'm the only person that does. I've kept it from everyone for years. I spread a rumour saying Franz killed her. It's not because I'm ashamed, but because my mother didn't deserve it. She deserved to go out fighting in a blaze of glory, an honourable death. Not the title of suicide. She died fighting.

"Della!"

I snap my attention to Dxton. He's got his hands on my shoulders, shaking them. There was a worried look in his eyes.

"I'm going to kill him," I growled out, my fist clenching. My lycan was surfacing slightly.

"Della, you need to calm down," Dxton said softly. His eyes darkened. His lycan was also surfacing.

"I'm in control for now, much to Dxton's displeasure. Only until you start to calm down though," he said. His lycan's scent enveloped me, helping to calm my nerves. I took in a deep breath and slowly let it out.

"Smart move," I whispered.

His chest vibrates as he let out a laugh. "Yes, but we both know I just wanted an excuse to hold what's mine," he said with a smirk.

"Alpha, is everything okay?" a concerned Dominic asked from behind the door.

"See you soon, snowflake," Dxton's lycan said with a smile, before his golden eyes turned back to their usual dark brown. With clenched teeth, Dxton opens the door to Dominic.

"We're fine, he just wanted out to see his mate," Dxton coolly said.

Dominic nodded solemnly. "Of course, Alpha."

"Turn in for the night, you need the rest."

Dom's eyes widened slightly before nodding. "Thank you, Alpha." He then turned to a room next to us.

The door softly closes behind Dxton. "If you don't mind me asking, why did Dom guard the door, wouldn't a guard do that, instead of your beta?" I softly asked.

Dxton meets my eyes for a moment and nodded. "Yes, I would have a guard do it but Dominic always steps in. It's his way of showing his gratitude," he explains while he pours a glass of whisky. "I saved his ass once and gave him a place to stay when his family kicked him out."

Kicked him out? So my theory was correct then. "Because he's gay?

"Yes, his parents didn't approve so they kicked him out. Even now with his brothers in charge, he still isn't welcomed," Dxton said, looking at his now empty cup.

"Just because he doesn't like females? The Asian line is still quite old school," I said to myself. Dxton nodded in agreement. A thoughtful silence settles between us as we think of the letter and other small things.

"Snowflake, huh?"

"Damn lycan."

Everything was confusing. Once again I didn't know what to do. I usually had a clear understanding on what I was doing and how to deal with the problem. But now I have a dictator who has some power over me. Dangerous power that could get a lot of people killed. This is taking a turn for the worst. A turn back into history. It's repeating in ways that are getting out of control. These letters are somehow keys that must be figured out. He's leaving clues, clues that are right under our noses, making them even more dangerous in the wrong hands. It'll recreate an unfortunate war.

A war is brewing, a war that has happened before and is slowly returning. Only this time, we will be prepared. I will not let innocent lives perish or get involved in a war for power. This is something that can't happen again. The werewolf community has been through enough. The moon goddess made a mistake creating lycans, but we must use the power we were given for the better. We must make a change.

"Dxton, what are we going to do?" I said slowly. I was still shocked after the events of the letter that was opened no more than an hour ago. We've spent the past hour in thoughtful silence.

His eyes were calculating, and his muscles tense. He looked up at me. "I'm not sure." Sighing, I get up from sitting on the bed and walk over to the bar. Dxton raised a brow, but I ignore it.

Werewolves and lycans can have quite a bit of alcohol before they get drunk, which proves to have its advantages. I use to drink alcohol a lot when I was younger. When both of my parents died, I felt so lost. I had never been so alone before. I always had both or one of my parents looking out for me, in fear of something happening. I was young and naive. I took the easiest route to solve my problems. I drank. It wasn't until a few years later that I looked in the mirror. For the first time in a really long time, I really looked in the mirror. I saw how much I was destroying my life and how I was throwing it away. I was becoming careless. Everything my parents worked for, I was throwing out the window. I stopped drinking and started travelling. It took me a little over a hundred years for me to even think of picking up a glass again. But I refuse to go down that road again. I took a sip of the brown beverage; burning my throat along the way.

"Didn't think you drank," Dxton mused, handing him a glass of his own. I give him a pointed look.

"There's a lot you don't know about me Dxton," I responded, sitting back out on the bed. Dxton got up and sat down next to me.

"Alright then. Shoot, tell me something about yourself," he said while taking a swig of his drink.

I raise an eyebrow at him and look at his face in slight confusion. "Did my ears hear right? Did you just ask to get to know me? Your mate who you've been ignoring?" I mocked sharply. He huffed in reply. "Well what do you want to know?"

"Favourite colour?" Small talk, really?

"Of all the things you could have asked . . . soft blue. You?"

"Silver, much like your eyes," he said swiftly. Cheesy.

"Favourite place in the world?" I asked curiously.

"England. Not what most would think."

This piqued my interest, since my father was the lycan of England. "Why England?"

"It's peaceful and the scenery is beautiful," he said looking at me. I smiled slightly with a nod. "England is beautiful in the countryside." He smiled in return, which made me smile even more. But it dropped quickly.

"What's wrong?" My tone surprised Dxton.

"I lied."

I looked up at him, confused. "You do that a lot, Dxton."

"I lied about why I didn't want to be mates."

My heart picked up, placing my hand over it as I whispered, "What do you mean?"

"My mother. She was . . ." His hand distressingly ran through his hair. "She was amazing. Growing up, she was caring and kind. She was the best person other than father. But, when my father was murdered, it broke her," he said quietly.

"You don't have to tell me", I said softly, putting my hand on his arm, we weren't close, but I knew why he was telling me.

Taking a deep breath, he continued. "She turned into someone completely different. She was abusive and harsh. She treated me as her own boxing bag, but when that didn't justify to her, due to our fast regeneration, she started using silver. She would slash at my skin until it permanently scarred." He lifted up his shirt. On his torso, I found five long scars. They're so red and torn it almost looks like it was done not that long ago.

"Which is the real reason why I didn't want anything to do with you. I was scared. You being human brought memories and when you turned out to be a lycan, I was confused," he silently confessed.

I nodded softly as I let what he said sink in. Shakily I lift my hand and let it hover over the wound. When Dxton doesn't react, I gently place my hand over the scars. I traced the deep lines. I did something I didn't think I would ever do. I lift up my own shirt and turn my back to him.

"When I was ten, I was kidnapped by Franz. For about a year he tortured me, scarred up my back and poisoned me with silver. It took a few years before I was able to properly shift back, but the worst thing he did was take my virtue," I whispered, the memories flooding back. "I still have nightmares about it to this day."

I stiffened when I feel fingers gently touch my back. Dxton's fingers trailed up the jagged scars. I slowly relaxed into his touch. Small sparks flew with his fingers. But what surprised me most is when he turns me around looking straight at my lips. Before I could blink, his lips are on mine in a slow but gentle kiss.

For the rest of the night, we talked before I started to fall asleep. Dxton laid me down and pulled the blanket over me, his fingers softly trailing my cheek. "I'm happy you aren't human, I didn't want to watch you die." He said it so softly, I almost didn't hear him. But from the redness growing in his face, he knew I did. He pulled away but I grabbed his hand. "Stay, please" He wrapped his arms around my frame, making me sigh softly. Before I knew it, I fell into a dreamless sleep.

It was perfect, too perfect. And as I aged, I knew the consequences of perfect moments. They always came with karma.

"Alpha! Luna!"

I bolt upwards at the sudden shouting. The frantic voice got closer. Dominic looked at us with urgency. "We got another letter and this one's not good."

Dxton grabbed the letter and rubbed his face. I sleepily leant on his shoulder to look at the letter.

When the king's away, the rogues will play

"That's not all, White Crescent is under attack!"

CHAPTER SIXTEEN

DELLA

"What?" I choked out. Dxton is straight away getting his stuff together.

Dom looked to me with a grim look. "I just got off the phone with Alex. The warriors and all other capable fighters are holding them off."

I nodded and got up, quickly putting my things in a bag. "Let's go," Dxton said, walking out. Dom and I both followed him out, all three of us determined and on a mission.

"I had one of Landon's men bring the car around," Dom said just as Landon walked over to us.

"What's going on here?"

Dxton paid him no mind, which ticked the alpha off. He began to open his mouth, but I cut him off. "Back off Landon, I wouldn't piss us off with your stupid comments right now."

He looks to me with fury in his eyes. "You're in no position to order me and last I saw, you couldn't defend yourself without your oh-so-mighty mate," he bites out. Dxton's eyes snapped to his murderously. I simply shake him off.

"I'd watch that tongue of yours, it might just be the death of you" I said coldly as we approached the car.

"Coming from a weak human," he scoffed. I stopped in front of the car and let out an annoyed breath.

"We don't have time for your bullshit, so step out of the way or I'll show you how a true leader acts," I threatened, my eyes snapping directly to his in pure hot fury. He stumbled back and gulped, shaking his head. "That's what I thought," I said, getting into the car, throwing my bag to my feet. Dxton and Dom get in the front. Landon stares dumbly at the car as we drive away.

The car ride is deadly silent. Dxton drives way past the speed limit, weaving past cars that ended up honking. When we have to stop for petrol, Dxton looks more than peeved. His hand wrapped tightly around the gas pump that looks like it's about to explode.

"Maybe you should sit in the front with him," Dom mumbled, walking back from paying for the petrol. I nod numbly and hop in the front, just as Dxton slams his door shut. He sped out of the station quickly, almost crashing into a few cars, but he somehow dodges them.

I know that simply talking won't do any good, neither would putting some music on, so I go with the only thing I can do. I put a hand on his knee and softly drew circles with my thumb. He stiffens more, before he relaxes, as if he's being snapped out of a trance. He lets out a shaky breath. "Thank you," he whispered. I gave his knee an encouraging squeeze.

It's not long before we can see White Crescent. Smoke and ash floated in the sky. Dxton looks at Dom in the rear view mirror. "Dom, take Tia to a bunker with all the rest of the women and children."

"Wait. What?" I exclaimed. "I can help!"

"No, I need you safe. They want you and if they got their hands on you . . . it won't end well. I need you to look after the children and women who need you as their luna." Dxton's eyes meet mine, a look of concern crossing his face. Sighing, I slowly nodded.

"Okay, where is the bunker?"

"East side of the pack, near the forest line. There is an entryway in the pack house." We went quiet for the next few minutes. I took the time to go over everything that's been said. Whenever I get answers, I feel like I get a ton more. They get more and more complicated. Why can't everything just be easier?

"Crap!" Dom grunted out through clenched teeth. I snapped my attention to the front, where a large fire is seen. The smoke travelled high into the air, while the fire continued to eat the trees in its path. Humans are going to notice at this rate. Dxton let out a low growl, his fist clenching even more, putting indents into the poor steering wheel. The car came to an immediate stop. Dxton turned to me.

"Stay safe, and when it's over. I would like to conti—" He didn't get to finish his sentence, because rogues started surrounding our flanks. Him and Dom quickly got out of the car. "Get her to safety now!" Dxton shifted and bolted into the forest. I watched as he suddenly shifts into his lycan and then disappears.

"Be safe," I whispered. My first time seeing his lycan and it's to go to battle.

"This way, we will have to run," Dom said.

I nod and roll my shoulders. "I'll be fine, let's go" I said before I start running east. Dom runs in front of me, keeping a watchful eye for any trouble. Sadly, with my lack of lycan boost, I was practically jogging and that was killing me.

Something brown flashed passed me. Rogue.

"Your left!" I yelled to Dom. He turns and quickly grabs the rogue's neck like it was nothing. Rogues were very dangerous fighters but they were sloppy, making killing them easy. The skin on my neck shivered slightly. I jumped over the rogue and continue running. Dom had a few chasing him, but he was easily taking them all down. He shot me a few looks for safety measure, and took out the ones getting too close to me. It took everything in me not to help, but any action could raise eyebrows.

My lycan started to scratch at my brain, wanting out. I forcefully shoved her back and continued running, with my breath slightly uneven. I slowed down slightly.

Dom came back to my side and gave me a once over. "Little bit longer."

We stopped in a clearing, with trees and rocks surrounding the area. Dom walked over to a scatter of big rocks, with vines covering them. He pulls some of the thick vines away, showing the rock underneath. I look at him confused. He moves a few rocks, slowly showing cement blocks, where an opening was shown.

"Woah," I whispered.

"I've let Jade know you are here." Dom looks to me and nodded. "I'll close it up once you're in," he said in all seriousness. Slowly, I descend to the opening. I look up to Dom before I kneel to go in.

"Keep him safe for me."

"I will."

I walk into the bunker and watch Dom close the opening, all light from the outside world going with him. I hope for the sake of the pack that Dxton is okay. Maybe for mine too.

Fortunately, I can see in the dark due to my supernatural nature. I'm in a very small space that leads into a wide walkway, with dimly lit lights. Sighing, I take my hand through my messy hair stressfully, opting to tie it up, I grab my hair tie as I walk forward. I went for a high ponytail.

I walk past a few doors labelled MEDICAL and STORAGE. Soft chatter and the distinctive smell of fear wash over my senses as I get closer to the end of the hallway. I continue walking, but stop hearing more chatter coming from a double door entrance. The door is reinforced steel with a peep hole. I can smell so many different emotions and blood. A lot of blood.

Giving the door a firm knock, the chatter died down. A tall male in a guard uniform quickly lets me in. I scanned the gigantic room. Eyes looked my way, all desperate, all asking questions.

"Luna!" A middle aged lady exclaimed in relief to my left. She's seated with a group of women, children, and a few men all look at me with relief clear in their eyes, some even hopeful. I softly take her outstretched hand, giving it a soft squeeze.

The feeling I have had nonstop since I arrived in America got dramatically worse. *"This is going to get worse,"* I said to my lycan. She got up from the back of my mind and huffed out in agreement.

"Tia!" Jade waddled over to me with a few people shadowing her for support. "Tia! I-I don't know what happened. Everything was fine, then the rogues appeared. There were too many," she cried out. Her hands began shaking as they clutched her stomach. Her eyes bloodshot, they look at me desperately, "Not everyone made it down here," she whispered. I wouldn't have heard it if I wasn't listening carefully.

"Where's Alex?" I could smell his blood on her. I pulled her softly to me.

She shakily pointed above. "I can feel him getting hurt." Jade stepped back, tears in her eyes. "I'm so glad you're okay! I was so worried. They attacked out of nowhere! You and the alpha were gone, as well as the beta" Jade said, choking in the end. "Alex is up there." She was struggling to keep her composure.

I brought her back to my chest and stroke her hair. "I'm sorry I wasn't here," I whispered. I look out to the crowd of people. "I'm sorry to all of you. You needed us the most and we weren't here. I know this is a lot to ask, when I haven't proved myself worthy to be your luna. But I need you all to stand tall. We will get through this, but in the meantime we need to watch out for one another. Together." I try to listen for any movement above but we are too far down to hear anything from here. "I know it's hard, your mates, sons, daughters, parents, or siblings may be up their but we need to stay safe, for us, and them," I said towards the crowd, looking people in the eye. Some looked at me with pride and respect, others with uncertainty.

"Where are the injured?" I asked Jade. She wipes her eyes and points to the far back. A few people lay on blankets with people attending them.

"The doctors and nurses of the pack are looking into them. We have had some injured come down the ladder at the back, that's used for emergencies only. Other than that, we have food and blankets in the rooms out in the hall." She sniffs. I nod softly and pat her back.

A young female wolf, couldn't have been no more than seventeen, stood up. "My whole family is up there fighting." She starts crying slightly, "What can I do to help? Please."

I pulled away from Jade and reach my hand out to hold her cheek. "What is your name?" I wipe a few tears from her eyes.

"Monica."

"Monica, such a pretty name. I know it is hard, there is nothing more annoying than being sitting ducks while the ones we love fight for us." She nodded with more tears flowing. "Can you do me a huge favour?"

She nodded eagerly. "Yes, anything."

I turn to the gamma female. "Can you please look after the gamma? You may help wash the blood off her hands and get her comfortable, she needs someone too."

Monica nodded, wiping the tears from her eyes. "I can do that," she whispered. I kissed her forehead and let her take Jade from me.

A few more people got up too, asking what they can do to help as well. Soon almost everyone was standing, declaring their desire to help.

Turns out the bunkers are a fully functioning system, with showers, 300 bedrooms, and a fully stocked kitchen, vegetable and fruits growing in their own area down one of the many halls, even live fish that keep the plants growing naturally; altogether we would be able to live down here for about two months before running out of some rations. Even then, we would still be fine for some time.

We are currently located inside a fortified area of the bunker; a mess hall I suppose, in case enemies were to get their way through the first few security systems.

I had some pack members making soups, getting water bottles out to everyone, and even some cleaning blood off pack members. We had some members that had died down here which I had them and their families moved to bedrooms to mourn in peace. Jade and Monica also got moved to a bedroom, where I had a nurse look over them both.

I'm in an office space just off to the side of the mess space, working on a radio in hope of getting aid from any neighbouring packs. I wasn't getting any luck. I still felt something off in my system. Something still isn't right, and my gut is telling me to *run*. But that isn't very possible right now.

Changing the radio station, I sigh. "This is Luna Tia of White Crescent Moon, can anyone hear me?" I waited for a few seconds. "I repeat, this is Luna Tia of White Crescent Moon, can anyone hear me?" Static.

"No luck, Luna?"

I turn around from the table, seeing a well-built brunette male guard. "No, not yet." I sigh, putting the receiver down. I leant against the table and crossed my arms. "Is there something you need?"

The male steps forward slightly shaking his head, "I just wanted to know how you were holding up," he asked, but despite the sincerity in his voice, I felt my lycan's hackles rise.

I got myself ready to rush if needed. He wouldn't be stupid enough to do anything with so many people around, would he? "I am doing the best I can but if you don't need anything, I can give you a task if you wish to do something." I elongated my nails just slightly. "If not, I'm going to have to ask that you leave, I have much to do."

He moves closer again. "I'm going to be honest, I don't much care for you or your orders. The alpha was wrong to bring you here." He raised his hand slightly, getting ready to strike. "We don't need a human luna." He quickly swipes at my face, but just before he could, I dunked down and sweep at his legs, bringing him to the floor.

While he was down, I quickly got on top of him and brought my fist down onto his face, knocking him out instantly. *"Disappointing,"* I said to my lycan who agreed.

I swung open the door to find twelve wolves surrounding the office, the pack members being held back by more wolves.

"What is this about? Don't see me as a fit luna either?" I said calmly.

One of the members stepped forward, who I identified as Terrance. *Just when I was starting to somewhat enjoy his company,* I thought bitterly.

"We don't. The Mortem have opened our eyes to your disadvantages."

Mortem? *Are they the ones behind the rogue attacks? I don't recall reading that name in the letters. I hope Jade is okay. Mind linking would be handy right about now.*

Terrance nodded to the wolf next to him to go first. He smirks and charges straight at me. He goes in to swipe at my face very similarly to the last wolf. I duck to the right quickly and side kick his face, before quickly turning around to his back and kicking him forward. He stumbles forward into the office outside the wall, the force knocking him out. Taken back by my unsuspected reflexes, the wolves remain where they are. Terrance, annoyed, signals to another to follow suit. He unlike the others doesn't charge. He stalks me slightly, waiting for me to make the first move. He is dumb to think I'd make the first move.

I turned slightly to the left to see a wolf quickly charging at me while the one stalking remained where he is. He goes to kick at my legs but I quickly use the wall to jump off to get over him, which thankfully works. Unluckily, the stalking wolf grabbed onto my arm, while the other grabs my other arm and brings me down quickly.

Terrance leant down to be at eye level with me, his gaze sinister. "Weak," he spitted out. "You are just a weak, little human." He slapped my cheek, leaving it pounding. Terrance grabbed onto my head and got ready to snap my neck.

I look at the pack as they all scream out, some of the children crying. It's the last thing I see before I feel the snap of my neck, and my body hitting the floor.

I'm sorry, but I have to do this.

CHAPTER SEVENTEEN

DELLA

"They need us Della, get up. We can't let hundreds of people die just because we don't want to die."

I hate how much she is right. I know that it has only been a few minutes, because Terrance is yelling out to the crowd to comply or they will turn out like their luna. I am currently being held by the collar of my shirt by one of the wolves, unaware that I have woken up, or that my neck is healed.

"Who wants to be next?" Terrance said with much cockiness.

"Me."

Opening my golden eyes, I quickly rip my clawed nails through the neck of the wolf holding me up, killing him instantly. I dropped to the ground. Screams can be heard as the pack members watch in horror at my display. With my eyes gold and my lycan centred, I watched as every single person in the room fall silent. I did it. I actually revealed myself. Fuck! So much for staying out of this war.

"W-what But I-I-I ju—"

I cut off Terrance and rolled my eyes angrily. "Obviously not."

I grabbed onto his neck and let my lycan come all the way forward. I dug deeper and deeper into my bond, allowing her for the first time ever to fully expose her presence. "I would turn around if I were you." I look over my shoulder to my very terrified pack. Some turned their children around, while others turned themselves around. I smashed Terrance into the nearest wall, and then proceed to rip off both of his legs as if it was nothing.

"For attacking my pack"—I get into his screaming face—"You can watch me kill every single one of your men!"

"W-who are you?"

I flash him my fangs. "Who fucking cares." I turned towards the few men left over who are all but shitting themselves. Some attempted to hide within the pack, but no one was having it and kept pushing them away. One of them was ripping the hair of an innocent female because she wasn't allowing him to hide amongst them. Angered, I march over towards him, and pull him off the female. Not even wasting any time, I rip out his heart and threw it towards Terrance. I proceed to rip out every single traitor's heart and throw each one towards Terrance. He is going to pay for betraying this pack.

With blood covering my arms, and my lycan the happiest she has ever been, we stalked towards Terrance. We dug down into our alpha dominance, forcing whimpers out of him. "Who. Are. You. Working. For?" I grit out each word slowly to make sure he hears me clearly, because I know damn well that in my current bloodthirsty state, if he doesn't hear me I will kill him instantly and quite frankly I need answers.

"Wolfe," he whispered. Coughing up blood, he spits it out to his side. With his bloodshot eyes, he whimpers. "I don't know who he is. He said that you were the female lycan." He laughs manically. "I didn't believe him . . . It was folklore."

Grabbing his hair forcefully, I make him look me in the eye. "All folklore comes from truth." I used my other hand to grab on the socket of his left eye. "Should have stayed as a bodyguard." I pluck out his eye, earning a scream from him. I feel my lycan shiver in excitement. She has been cooped up too long. "You shouldn't have attacked my pack." I beamed, plucking out the other eye. Placing his eyes in his hand I go to reach for his ear.

"Stop!" A female voice called out. "Please!"

I clenched my hand, digging my claws into my skin. Quickly, I reached out and snapped Terrance's neck, silencing his loud cries.

I growled lowly to the pack. "Anyone else feel like betraying the pack?" Not a single person moved. Good.

"L-Luna," Jade steps forward. I feel my heart plummet at the fact she saw everything. I let my bloodlust get the best of me. "Who are you?" she whispered.

"Della Rosai. The only female lycan," I said out loud for everyone to hear. Everyone whispered amongst themselves. Horror, shock, and fear radiated within the room.

"I knew I smelt lycan blood! Wh—"

"We just got word, Jade," someone whispered behind the gamma.

Annoyed, I growl out. "What is it?" They cowered and start crying instantly, feeling something snap in me. I reel in my lycan, returning my eye colour to silver and back to a human. They visibly sighed at the lack of pressure, but still didn't say what's the matter.

Jade looks me dead in the eye. "The alpha and beta have been taken. They're gone."

CHAPTER EIGHTEEN

DELLA

They're gone . . . How . . . how did two lycans get themselves taken? My eyes twitched. "You're joking right?"

Jade continues to look dead straight into my eyes. "No."

I feel a small pang in my heart. I hate how much he has started to affect me just by being nicer. He is going to make leaving so much harder.

A soft tapping at the steel door catches everyone's attention. I get up to investigate. When Jade hurries to the door, everyone unfroze from their spot.

"Alex!" She shrieked, pulling him into the bunker. He's covered in scratches and blood. Some of it isn't his. I winced when I smelt his wounds. They were laced with silver. They must have dipped their claws in it before attacking White Crescent Moon. Jade frets over him.

"What's happening out there? I know about Dom and Dxton." I didn't want it to be repeated to me.

"The surviving members are in the pack house waiting for treatment or their family, but we managed to take out quite a few of the rogues. Once they drugged the alpha and beta, they disappeared." Alex moves in a little closer, whispering, "You know what they want right?"

I nodded, I know very well what they want. "They want me to come out as the female lycan," I said out loud. Alex instantly stiffens, quickly looking around to see everyone listening intently. "They know. Terrance betrayed us and I was left cornered. If I had taken them out as a human it would have looked suspicious anyway." I sighed, pointing over to his corpse behind me. "I didn't have too many options."

"Wait . . . you knew?" Jade looked between the two of us, horrified.

Alex stuttered out a yes. "He caught me in my lycan form. I threatened him and his pup if he didn't keep his trap shut," I said. Jade's hands instantly went for her belly.

"You wouldn't have actually killed our pup," she breathed out.

I gave her a sharp look. "Yes, I would have."

"Wha—"

"We live in a kill or be killed world, Jade. I am not a kind person. I am a survivor." I get in her face a little bit. "And you don't live to my age without some risks." I lied, I never would have killed the pup. There are reasons that hit too close to home for me. Ignoring her shocked, disgusted looks, I turned to Alex. "Is it safe to go up?"

"Yes, they're gone."

All the innocent eyes of the pack looked to me for guidance. How terrifying. "Let's go."

Wordlessly, the pack followed me out of the bunker. For the first time in over twenty-four hours, we felt the sun kissing our skin. Some members started crying instantly, the sight of our pack too sickening for them. The entire pack was deserted. A few bodies were on the ground, some rogues, some ours. An eerie silence surrounded the area. It smelt foul, of death, blood, and faeces. I reeled my lycan back in to keep my stomach from emptying its contents. I look over to Jade who wasn't so lucky. Alex rubs her back softly.

A few pack members follow suit, but not too many. The sad thing about being a wolf is that you get very quickly used to death. It's too common of an occurrence and fights are natural amongst surrounding packs. It's safe to say this is a royal shit show.

Now what? What should I do? What do I do, Dxton?

Almost all at once, every pack member fell to the ground, agonising, screaming bloody murder. I felt a pricking sensation all the way up my arm with a burning sensation. Not enough for me to be on the ground with them, but enough to have me wince at the sensation. Jade gasped, putting her hands to her mouth. "What's happening to them?" She hurried over to some of the ones screaming.

"They are being tortured," I said, looking towards the forest line. I felt myself wince again; a rush of blood forming in my cheeks. "They are torturing our mates." Dxton, I hope you're okay. For your pack's sake. And for mine.

CHAPTER NINETEEN

Dxton

"*Poderoso lobo*. What a joke."

She threw her wine bottle at my head. It landed on my face, some of the shards sticking into my skin. "If you really were, you would have saved your father!" She screams. Pointing a finger to the girl, she screams at the top of her lungs. "You weak bitch! We never should have taken you in! You bring bad luck everywhere you go!" She gets right up into her face. "Look at your real parents, they are dead! They were with you too!"

She spat at Lucia's face. "I wish you were the one who died," she venomously said, going in to kick her in the gut. Quickly pushing her aside, I took the full extent of her kicks. Lucia cried, begging for Mom to stop, but she keeps kicking. "Now you want to play hero?"

She kicks me square across the jaw, snapping it. Her blazing eyes glared into my soul. "You are such a disappointment." Turning to Lucia, she raised her hand and started clawing at her back, causing Lucia to scream the most blood curdling scream I had ever heard.

"Please," I beg softly, my jaw aching and my heart tearing into two. "Please stop."

"Mom!"

"Lucia!"

Lucia looks at me for a split second, her eyes always soulless. Mom is going to kill her. No, no, no, no, no please, please don't kill her!

"Don't kill my sister!" My voice sounded more commanding. I suddenly got up. My eyes burned. My skin ripped. My bones were displacing. My senses increased. For the first time ever, I shift into my lycan, and I rip into my pleading mom. I killed her.

I quickly looked around for my mother, but only found Dom lying on the ground. I've woken from a nightmare, only to awake in one.

It's been a few days. I know that much. Dominic believes we are somewhere in the mountains based on the smell of the soil surrounding us and the slight difficulty in breathing. There is a mountain range not too far from White Crescent Moon. Hopefully that's where we are.

I looked down at the needles embedded into my arms. I have every drug known to harm the supernatural going into my veins. Silver, mistletoe, wolfsbane and even more silver.

I can hear my pack being tortured. I can feel their pain on top of my own. When they were dying back home, I felt a stab at my heart in every death. It's a pain I have never been able to get used to over the years. It was for the best that Della hadn't joined the pack. I wouldn't want her to feel the pack's pain on top of my own. *I hope you can't feel this, Della.*

Della. I hope she is okay. I know she can keep her own, but she's about to be forced to be a leader of a pack she doesn't accept. She was right. I shouldn't have forced her into my pack. She needs to run, get as far away as possible from these rogue groups and from me. This was a trap from the beginning to bring her out of hiding. She even said that and I just shook her words away. She's been right the whole time. I just never listened. *I'm sorry,* I whispered to our bond. *I'm sorry I never listened. I hope you can forgive me.*

If she still accepts me as her mate, even after everything I have done to her, I will take her to France, to England. I will be her everything. I would even step down as alpha if she really doesn't want to be an alpha. I have so much I want to do with her and for her; Sit in a bath with her, while I massage her soft shoulders from all of her stress. Cook her the most amazing meal she has ever eaten. Play with her hair as she reads. Tell her every day how much I love her. Go for a run as our lycans. Bring her breakfast in bed. Go on dates. I would even write her a song. If she stays, I would do everything, anything for her.

"*She will,*" my lycan whispered. "*Our snowflake is scared, but she will never be able to properly withstand the mate bond. I can feel her now, she's saddened by our capture.*" He tugs on our small bond, caressing it. "*She will stay.*"

"*I think you're trying to convince yourself more,*" I softly said to him. In response, he withdrew to the back of my mind. For your sake and mine, I hope she does.

I miss her. Her angry looks, her irritated eyebrows, her puffed up chest when she's proud, her laugh, her toes curling up when her book gets interesting, her over-the-top sighs, her unknowing need to be close to me, when she claims not to like me even when she's practically sitting on my lap on the couch. Her. I always wanted her. I never did not want her. I just didn't want her to die. One year would feel like one second for me. But she isn't going to die. She could stay with me till the end of time. We could be together.

"What are we going to do, Alpha?" a soft voice asks in the darkness. I can't see the pack, but I can hear them in the room next to me. Dominic has been in and out of consciousness majority of our capture, he isn't on as high of a dosage, but it was enough to render him immobile.

I can barely move with all the poison in my system being administered twenty-four hours by a drip within the chains and the bullets they were shooting when they captured us. I'm too drugged to do anything.

"We wait. That's all we can do, for now," I reply.

"What about the Luna?" Someone pipes up.

A few murmurs could be heard. "With all due respect, Alpha, but she's only a human," a voice said, her tone kind but scared.

"She may only be a human, but she's much stronger than you think," Dom answers for me. "She can take care of herself, the pack is in good hands with her."

"But . . . they want the female lycan. What do they want with us?" A female voice whispers hurriedly, her tone scared.

"We're the bait. They want to draw her out." Someone whispers back. I try to keep my eyes open, the poison getting to me slowly. I shook my head to remain awake.

"Why would they think she would save us?" she asked. "She's not even from our pack."

"Because the rogues think she's hiding in our pack," I called out, earning some gasps from around the room. And I will do everything I can to make sure that will never happen. I can only hope that she is safe. "They believe I am hiding her."

"Are you?" Someone whispered across the room. I look at Dominic. He's lying on the ground, staring at me weakly. I nodded.

He looks ready to rip into me, but holds back. "That's the dumbest move you could have made." I shook my head, but feel myself losing consciousness.

"I'll explain when we aren't here," I whisper. The will to keep my eyes open fades, and soon I'm drifting back off to sleep.

CHAPTER TWENTY

DELLA

"What do we do about Terrence? And all the other wolves that lost their lives?"

Terrence, I should have kept a better eye on him, can't believe I let him get away with this under my nose. "I'll leave it for Dxton to decide, for now, leave them in the cells" Why did the dumb male have to get captured, leaving me with his pack. I'm not ready to be the luna, I wasn't even planning on being his Luna. I swear he better have been drugged to no end to get captured, because if this was his plan to draw me out of hiding, I'll kill him.

"With all due respect Luna, that could be weeks." Fuck, Alex is right.

"I know, but . . . this isn't really my pack." Alex sighs, running a hand through his hair. I'm driving him mad, I can tell. But I can't just stop being insecure overnight, it can take months, years even to get over your insecurities. He can't expect me to change my tune just because everyone knows who I am now. That won't stop me from leaving.

Getting up from my chair frustratingly I look at the damage done to the pack. They do need us.

"I'll have a ceremony made for the fallen. The traitors can be hung on our border towards where the rogues came from." I look over my shoulder to Alex. "Hopefully they will get the message." I can't help but smirk slightly.

Alex nods, his eyes blurring over, no doubt going about my orders., "How is Jade?" She's been ignoring me. Understandable, I did give her an empty threat on her pup.

Alex shrugs. "She's as good as she can be."

"And you?" He appears to have fully healed now, but just because you look fine, doesn't mean you are.

He nods. "I'm fine." He crossed his arms, flexing them slightly. "Want this war to be over?" I nod. *Don't we all?* "How about you? How are you holding up Luna?"

Conflicted, very, very conflicted. Not really wanting to answer his question, I do what I'm good at. Running away from my problems. "I'm going for a run." I leave before Alex could really say too much.

My run ends up with me going to Dxton's house. My eyes glued to the handle of his room door. I keep finding myself coming here, going back and forth with my lycan on whether we should enter the room or not. He will smell us in there, but he will also smell us outside of his door. *What were you going to say before you ran off?*

Sitting against the door, I put my head against it, closing my eyes. I try to tap into our bond. It's alive, but it's in pain from Dxton's torturing. There is no end too. I can also feel our lack of attention to the bond. I can't feel him, or communicate with him. I can't when we haven't marked each other.

I can feel fire burning my arms, traveling down my body and stinging at my heart. He's being poisoned with something heavy if it's hurting him. Lycans have a very high tolerance for typical supernatural poisons. We have to ingest the same amount of liquid in our bodies for silver to kill us. When our entire system is made of silver, then our bodies will shut down.

"We have to find mate," my lycan whined softly.

"I know. We will."

* * *

Alex and Jade cuddling on the couch sent a pang through my heart.

"Oh Luna." Alex raised his head. "How was your run?"

Sitting on the pack house couch, I nod softly. "Yeah it was good."

Alex looks between Jade and I. "I'm going to go check the border, I'll be back." He kisses a dumbfounded Jade on the cheek and leaves out the door before she can get a word in.

Not even a second after he leaves, "I might go do some laundry" Jade weakly excuses herself, but before she can leave the room, I command her, "Sit down"

She does as I ask, but fidgets with her fingers in her lap. "What's wrong Jade?" I ask softly. She opens and closes her mouth a few times before muttering nothing. "What is the matter Jade? I can't read minds." I snap slightly. I wish she would just go out with how she feels. I can't handle this suffocating small talk.

She looks down at her lap, a mixture of anger and sadness on her face. "I was grown up to fear you, and despite your threats I don't. I don't know how I feel about it."

Sighing I lean back into the couch. "If you don't then what's the issue?"

"Is my baby going to be safe with you here?" She whispers, a look of shame enveloping her features.

"I honestly don't know Jade, that's why I didn't want to stay here." I look to the few pack members near us. They are listening in on the conversation, I know they are. "I never wanted to join a pack for this exact reason. I can't guarantee your safety or theirs. But I will try my hardest to keep you, your pup, and everyone else safe. Not because I'm your luna, but because I refuse to let people die because of me."

She goes silent for a few minutes. Assuming that we are done, I got up to leave when she asks abruptly. "Why do people want you so badly? No offense."

Slowly sitting back fully in the chair, I cross my legs. "Have you ever noticed how much weaker Dom is to the alpha?"

"Actually yeah." She nods, absentmindedly rubbing her belly.

"As the next generations of lycans are being born, they get weaker. They are turning into ordinary werewolves. This is because the moon goddess regretted her creations so much that she decided to naturally wipe them out, except for one. Only one line of lycans will remain with their original lycan power, the females. Soon only my line will give birth to lycans as long as each child has a female, the line will continue." I had planned to never have children fearing I'd have a female. But I have a sinking feeling that isn't going to happen, not with Dxton wanting an heir.

"The moon goddess turned her back to lycans after Franz Wolfe. She wants them gone. She gave the power to procreate lycans to her favourite child, her daughter. Alvery Fambre, my mother. As an added bonus, on nights of a full moon, I can communicate with her."

Jade quickly turns to face me. "Shouldn't we use that? She might be able to help us find the pack members, the alpha."

I shake my head. "No, I hate the bitch. I'd rather talk to a rogue" Getting up, I look over my shoulder slightly. "Besides, she never meddles in our business. The 'gift' is useless."

Jade gets up quickly following me into the kitchen despite my obvious attempt to get away from the question, "But wouldn't it help?"

Sighing, I place my hands on the counter, taking in a deep breath. "Look I know why you want me to, but it wouldn't do anything. She does not help people. This ability is a waste. I have tried asking for her help before, she doesn't help."

"What did she do to you?" Jade jokes half-heartedly.

"Everything and nothing."

CHAPTER TWENTY-ONE

Della

I didn't think I would feel this attached to the alpha at all. But being in this big house on my own is depressing. How could he live in this house alone for all these years?

I keep finding myself trying to look for his scent, trying to get a feel of our connection, but always coming up blank. We aren't mated, we have no connection. For the first time ever I regret not mating him, just so that I could find him sooner and so I wouldn't feel this lonely. Do I actually like him?

I've been passing the hallway to his room and to his study nonstop all morning. I went in there to get a whiff of his scent to calm my nerves. To feel some sense of sanity. What's stopping me from bursting in right now, is that my scent would be everywhere and he will know. But he will smell my constant movement outside both doors.

I now stand in front of my Dxton's room, the door knob in my hand. I debated whether to go in or not, while my lycan softly but firmly urged me in. It was cut off by a phone ringing in the distance. I quickly jumped back, my eyes blinking rapidly from my daze. "What am I doing?" I muttered before quickly running to the phone. Please be news, please be anything.

"Hello?"

"Tia! Are you okay? I heard your pack was attacked and that your mate was kidnapped an—"

"Ness! Calm down, I'm fine," I said softly with a sigh. It's not news, but it's what I needed right now.

She lets out a relieved breath. "Thank goodness, I can't imagine you hurt. I didn't want to think you'd gotten hurt, I need you in my life you know."

Tears well up in my eyes. "Oh Ness, I need you too, you're my sister." Ness lets out a small choked sob, muttering how much of a sap she is.

"I'm so glad you're okay. I don't know what I would have done if you were hurt." The tears I've been trying so hard to keep in, break through, in silent streams. I let myself cry. "How are you really? Please don't give me the bullshit answer of 'fine' because I know you're not."

And I don't. I tell her everything. "I hate how affected I am. I hate how much I want to stay, how much I have grown to like the people here, how much I enjoy pack life. I feel like a part of me is coming back to me. My lycan is the happiest she's ever been and I hate how much happier I am." I wail out, my back sliding against the wall as I dissolve into a depressed heap on the floor.

"I wish I hadn't meet him, but I am so happy I did too. I am starting to like him and that's scaring the shit out of me. I hate him, I hate him so much for trying to be my mate then getting kidnapped straight after. He is such an asshole, and I just want him back so we can talk again, he didn't finish what he was going to say." I just want to know if he is okay. I want to stay . . . Holy shit, I want to stay and I genuinely want to get to know Dxton.

"Della," Ness whispers softly. "You don't know this but you deserve everything. Happiness, a mate, a pack, and friends." I can hear her need to comfort me, her words feel like a warm hug. "I want you to have all of that. It might be time that you did. It's all Henry and I wanted for you. A family, a pack to lead. You might not think you deserve it, but you have a strong mate, and pack to help protect you now. You have everything you need to have. The life you deserve. Your lycan is out, you don't have much to lose now. You are strong, you can fight anyone who threatens you or anyone you love." She stops hearing my loud cries, soothingly she whispers sweet words, before long I've started to fall asleep, but just before I do I hear her say what I needed to hear.

"It's time to stop running."

* * *

The ceremony went relatively well. I spoke with the mourning families, talked with a few wolves unsure of my legitimacy. But I didn't speak about Dxton. I don't want to give the pack false hope, not when we don't even know where he is yet. And today was about the loss of pack members, not Dxton. Hopefully we won't have one for Dxton, or the beta. I hate how much history is repeating. I don't want to do this again. I don't want to see more loved ones dying. I can only take so much pain in a lifetime. Immortal or not I still have a heart, a fragile heart.

"Luna, please come quick." A wolf I don't recognize rushed through the crowd of mourners, stopping abruptly in front of me. He urged me to follow him.

Did they find them? Are they okay? "What is it? Is everything okay? Have you found any news?"

The guard gave me an apologetic look. "It's the gamma female, she's about to have the baby."

CHAPTER TWENTY-TWO

DELLA

"Right now?"

"Yes luna." The guard nods enthusiastically. "They are at the pack hospital."

Good timing little one. "Okay, can you please let Alex know I will be there shortly?" I said over my shoulder as I run towards the pack hospital. It takes me no less than five minutes to get there with my lycan speed.

"Luna!" A nurse quickly pops her head out of nowhere. "The gammas are this way." She gestured to a hallway to our left.

"Thank you," I huffed out. I can't believe it's time. I'm nervous and excited. I love babies, even though they also terrify me.

"So Luna." I look at the nurse's name tag—Abigail. "When will we expect a baby from you and the alpha?" Tripping over my feet, I land headfirst into the floor. "Omg, are you okay?"

Groaning, I got up and nodded. She starts fussing over me, asking over and over if I'm okay and started to examine me. Putting my hand up, I showed her the grazes healing over. "I'm fine Abigail, you just surprised me."

"I'm sorry," she said with a giggle. "I just can't wait to see a little alpha, it would be an absolute honour to be here helping with the delivery." Her cheeks went bright red in embarrassment.

"We will see, Abigail," I said as I spot Alex in the hallway pacing back and forth. "Alex! How is she?"

He stopped pacing to look over to me. "Um, good, good, I think." He started pacing again, eyes on the ground. "I hope they both will be okay. I can't believe I'm about to be a dad." He looks up to me. "I've always wanted to be a dad and now I will be—"

"Alex," I said softly. "Don't you think Jade needs you now more than ever?"

He stops his pacing. His eyes went wide. Slapping his forehead, he muttered, "Right," and dashes into the delivery room. Laughing softly, I took a seat in the hallway. I wonder what Dxton will be like. Would he have the same kind of reaction or— *Stop it, don't go down that rabbit hole, Della.* For now, just wait for the baby to arrive.

And I did, thirteen hours of it, and thirteen hours later, in the late hours of the night, Jade gave birth to her first child.

"Omg!!!" A distant voice hollered. I laughed slightly when the owner of the voice came charging out of the doors. "I'm a dad! I have a daughter!" Alex exclaimed before dashing back inside. He rushed back outside to usher me in when I remained outside the room.

Laughing softly, I got up. "Congratulations," I said, walking in through the door. He beamed widely at me. I look over to Jade who was lying on the bed. She carried her daughter in her arms, with the softest smile on her face. She looked up at us and smiled weakly. She waved Alex over. Carefully, Jade placed their daughter in his arms.

"I-I'm a father," he slowly said. "Oh good God," he groans.

I laugh at him and put my hand on his shoulders. Giving it a pat, I said, "You're going to be fine and you're going to be an amazing father." I smile softly at him.

"Thank you," he said.

I stop momentarily, seeing a small part of the old Alex, the one I met when I first got here. The happy-go-lucky person. I'm so sorry I destroyed that, but I hope your daughter brings a little bit of that back. I can't help but smile seeing him so happy. Looking at the little baby in Alex's arms, I can't help but think what would Dxton look like with our own in his arms.

"What's her name?" I ask, not taking my eyes off the baby.

"Madison Thea McGavin."

I am definitely calling you Mads. "She's gorgeous."

Her tiny tuft of hair is a soft blonde. She hasn't yet opened her eyes, but she's one of the most quiet babies I've ever seen.

"Would you like to hold her?" Jade calls out softly from her bed.

Shocked, I turn to her. "M-me? You are okay with me holding your baby?"

"I know you would never hurt her."

I could feel myself tearing up slightly. "Okay," I whispered as Alex hands me Madison gently. Looking down at the small warm bundle, I feel myself getting emotional. "Hello, little one." I softly touched her tiny hand, which she grabbed back. My heart exploded.

But I start to feel the faint anxiety over children, softly handing her back to Alex. I excuse myself out into the corridor. I tried to relax my breathing. *That was a long time ago Della,* I repeated over and over in my head. I feel suffocated by memories that I started to get a panic attack.

"LUNA! Luna!" The young guard from before huffed out in a fit. "We found him." Standing up straighter, the wolf took on a hopeful, proud gaze. "The group sent to track down the rogue's activities and their movement found an abandoned warehouse just off human territories, in the mountains. They found the alpha's scent."

I grabbed his shoulders roughly. "They found him?" He nodded frantically.

"The trackers are there awaiting your orders now, Luna."

We found him. We actually found him. "Get all of our warriors together, we leave now." *Don't worry I'm on my way.*

Popping my head back into the room, I look to Alex who is passionately kissing Jade. "OI." I said, startling them. "Bit earlier for baby number two, don't you think?" Alex tried to protest but I wave him off. "That doesn't matter," I said. He rolled his eyes, but asks me to go on. "They found them, and I know the plan was that you would come with me and lead the trackers, but change of plans. I need you to stay here, in case they attack again. I want everyone in the bunkers now. You're in charge of making sure everyone is down there, and I need you to be safe."

Alex got up. "I can fight." He shook his head and started grabbing his things. I looked over to little Mads, who's sleeping peacefully.

"You need to stay for her and your mate." I look to Jade. He stops and looks over to a worried Jade.

"I would feel safer if you were here." Jade added.

Sighing, he drops his stuff onto a chair. "Sorry, of course."

"If I'm not back within forty-eight hours, call for everyone you can," I said as I start to walk towards the door.

"Hey Luna." I turned around to see Alex and Jade smiling softly. "Be safe," Alex said. Giving them a soft smile, I nod.

"Of course."

CHAPTER TWENTY-THREE

DELLA

Word quickly travelled of my reappearance. Before long, I had every pack in America calling Dxton's phone. Everyone demanded answers, wanting verbal proof. It got so overwhelming to the point where I changed the voicemail to "This is Luna Bosque. We are very busy at this time, so we kindly request that you call us another time. Thank you." My worst nightmare has become a reality. I am now in the open, exposed. Everyone knows I am alive, that I am at White Crescent Moon. We are going to have a rough couple of months. Maybe even years. This isn't something that will just blow over in a few hours.

After days of waiting for any news, the trackers finally reported back. They could hear the pack and smell them within the walls. They are still alive, just badly drugged and broken. I had the hospital get beds prepared and every pack doctor and nurse to get ready for a nasty few weeks of whiny wolves. I will have to buy them all lunch at some time as a thank you.

Vanessa was right though. It's time to stop running. I am a lycan. I need to start acting like one. I am the daughter of Alvery Fambre and George Rosai, the two greatest lycans of their time. It is time I made them proud. No matter how scared I am, I need to be there for these people, these good people. It's time I act my part.

According to Alex, the trackers said the compound is two hours from the pack, up in the mountains. Hopefully this won't take too long. I can feel Dxton getting weaker and weaker as the days go by. They must be raising his dosage every day. Any longer and he might not make it.

I stared out to the twenty warriors with me. "Everyone ready?"

"Yes Luna!"

"Good, let's go get our loved ones and Alpha back!" I said, shifting into my white lycan. Throwing my head up to the sky, I howled. The warriors all shifted and howled too, before we all darted into the forest.

I wanted to howl more, not to the moon, but in pure joy. I can't believe I've gone this long without shifting properly. I wanted to badly run forever and never stop, but the sound of paws smashing onto the earth's floor behind us was a constant reminder of why we were here. To save our pack members and our alpha. The reminder echoed into our ears, our inner beast snarling and baring their teeth. The excitement of the hunt grew more, as we got closer to our enemy.

My wolf licked her lips hungrily, more than pleased to be unleashed. Her claws dug deeper into the dirt floor after every leap. I can't remember the last time we properly let ourselves out. Our scent carried out into the air protecting our pack from those around us, but most of all it revealed that I am alive. I'm not a folktale. I might not fully accept this pack or male, but my lycan has, and she's feeling more than proud to be running with them.

Our form is monstrous compared to theirs. We've slowed down for their sake, but we want nothing more but to run with them. Bolting ahead is not ideal right now. There will be plenty of times in the future for that. I'm a lycan and it was about damn time I acted like one. I have the pack behind me every step of the way and I have their loyalty. I don't have everyone's trust, but the fact they are here is more than enough. Everyone here is risking their lives to save the others and wipe out the enemy.

This group was all chosen by myself and Alex. These are strong warriors and trackers. We're the leading group. Our job is to take out the leader and find Dxton and Dom. The second group is our stealth and speed, they are taking out the guards without anyone noticing, letting us through.

I pull in my lycan to a normal wolf so I don't catch too many people's attention. My scent isn't too overwhelming, but it's still noticeable up close. The only issue will be communication. I don't have a mind link with the pack yet, but if everyone sticks to the plan we should hopefully be able to get everyone out safely. I hope so.

I stopped when I saw two wolves in the distance. I can smell that they are from our pack. Every wolf will smell a little like their alpha once bonded into the pack. It acts as a safety net of protection to let other wolves know who their alpha is. They came barrelling towards us and shifted into their human forms. "Luna." They bowed. "The compound is just up ahead, this way." Shifting back, they darted further into the forest and stopped at the base of the mountain. You can see a guarded compound with a wire fence and cameras lining it.

This is easy. Too easy. Which then only goes to prove this whole setup was just to draw me out. This wasn't about hurting Dxton, it was to confirm my whereabouts amongst White Crescent Moon. *Stay strong just a little longer, we are almost there,* I whispered into the void of our bond.

Shifting back into my human form, I look to the twenty wolves with me. "Is the van on its way?" One of the wolves shifts back, his name is Christan I believe. He is the head male warrior.

"Yes Luna." He nodded. "Morgan is in position now, waiting for orders."

Nodding, I looked over to the compound. "Okay I want you five"—I signal to a group of wolves—"to go in and take out the guards. You five will go find Morgan and guard the vans. The rest of you are with me." Each group quickly darted off as soon as they received my orders.

* * *

"Luna?"

I softly grabbed her shaking hand. "It's okay, you are safe now." I said, then looked at the rest of the starstruck eyes. "All of you."

Helping her up, I pass her onto one of the warriors I came with. "Christan, follow me. I'll need help getting Dominic. The rest, grab someone and go."

"Yes Luna."

Following the scent of Dxton, I walked back out into the hallway, stopping at a door not too far from the room we were just in. The bloodstains were a mixture of people's blood, ranging from different species and ages. I try not to vomit at the smell, and walk into the door I hope Dxton is in.

Dxton lay against a bloodstained wall, chains and tubes sticking out of everywhere. His body was considerably thinner in just a few days he has been here. His eyes were closed and he's completely naked. His skin's scarred and covered in his blood. A few cuts across his arms and torso aren't healing, and based off the smell, those were recently cut open with a silver knife.

I looked up to him and put my hand on his cheek, sparks softly buzzing beneath my skin. "Dxton?" His eyes blink open. He looks up at me and moves away from my hands slightly. He moans a no, trying to get away from my touch. "Dxton it's me."

"Della?" He blinks at me, his vision clearing up. I place my hands back onto his cheeks.

"It's okay, I'm here," I gently said.

"What are you doing here? Your eyes," he said, shocked. I smile slightly as my eyes shine a brighter gold.

"Long story short, I had to," I said, ripping the chain in two, then proceeding to the next chain. I winced at the small sting of silver.

"Luna?" a voice said on the other wall. I turn over to see Dominic, his eyes wide and mouth agape. "Y-you're—"

"A lycan?" I said with a small smile allowing my lycan to come through to sniff at his. "I'll explain when we get home."

Dominic stares down Dxton, who gives him a look. Christan helps pull Dominic up, putting an arm around him. "Is this okay, Beta Dominic?" He nods.

"Let's go."

Picking up Dxton bridal style, he groans, his face going just slightly flush. It's then that I smelt it, arousal. "Really? Now?" I was shocked to say the least. I expected him to put up a big fuss.

"Just go," he groans. His eyes shut. I smile at him softly. His face is covered in dirt and specks of blood. I bet this does look weird. I laugh slightly. I am after all 5'6, carrying this giant of a man.

Christan and I get to the vans, helping Dxton inside the back. I place a blanket over him. "Are you okay?" he whispers.

Scoffing, I roll my eyes. "I think you should be more worried about yourself, any more silver and you might not have made it." I tuck the blanket in, and then do so for Dominic, who gives me a small nod.

"Worry about yourself right now," I said.

"Luna." I turn around as Christan approaches me. "The area has been secured, no sign of anyone that could be in charge. Doesn't look like the leader has been here either. An office that could have been his hasn't been touched. The only thing found was another letter. Addressed to yourself and the alpha." He hands me the letter, but I shake my head.

"I'm going to run alongside the van. Can you hold onto it for me until we get home please?" He bows his head.

"Yes Luna." He jumps into the passenger's side of the van. I quickly do a head count to ensure we had everyone accounted for.

"Are all the guards locked in the basement?" I ask one of the nearby warriors.

"Yes Luna."

Alright, let's get out of here.

"Leaving so soon?" A voice calls out from the roof of the building, A tall burly man with bright blonde hair stood with his arms crossed and a smirk. "So rude of you to leave without saying goodbye, Della."

The pack all get around the vans. "Who are you?" I ask, letting my eyes shine gold.

He just smirks in response. "Oh yes of course, I am Beta Ezra of Dunkler Wolf." I feel my lycan shifting within my skin. Franz's pack is active after all. Feeling uncontrollable anger, I jumped up to the roof. Bolting after him, he laughs out loud and runs. He stopped suddenly, only to backflip over me. "I have been so eager to meet you, Luna."

Taking a swing at him, he just dodges, but before he can blink too much I punch him square in the jaw, instantly breaking it. He broke it again so it'll heal properly then quickly jumps away from me, giving us some space.

"Why?" I ask.

He smirked. "Because, I wanted to see you in your prime before my alpha kills you. Tsk, you have done a real number on him."

"Who—"

"That is a question for another time" he said, getting closer to the ledge, almost close to falling off it.

"What? Not going to stop me?" I asked angrily. He shook his head.

"No, we got what we wanted," he said before shifting into a grey wolf and jumping off the building. I don't know why I didn't run after him. I feel defeated, we might have gotten the pack back, but at the cost of my visibility. Dunkler Wolf is active. I knew I should have double checked to make sure it stayed in the ground. I can't believe I was so stupid to think Franz didn't have followers still running his pack.

Jumping down from the roof, I glance at Dxton once more, finding he is already looking back at me. He is sharing the same look as me, worried. With a strained smile I turn around and shifted. I let out a long howl up to the sky. The pack followed my lead, before dashing into the forest beside me. Time to go home. I sighed. This is going to be a hellish few months.

CHAPTER TWENTY-FOUR

Della

"In all the years I've lived, I've tasted and eaten some weird stuff but I'll have to admit the inventor that made this disgusting mess is a genius." I mutter to Alex. He laughs in agreement. Lucky charms, who would have thought.

"I guess this generation just knows what's better to eat," Alex said rather smugly, but teasingly.

In the last two days a lot has happened. We rescued the captured and got them straight back to their old heathy selves. Well some. Dominic is currently healing from internal damage to his organs and muscles. His ribs are almost healed and his collar bone that was fractured is also healing. The mistletoe and sliver took quite the beating, but he'll be fine in the next twenty-four hours. Some of the wolves were unable to shift for a certain time period due to physical damage in their wolf forms. If they shift back, they could possibly die or cause a problem that could be life changing. Dxton is in and out of consciousness, but the doctors said that's to be expected with all the poison he had in his veins. It'll take some time for it all to leave his system. As for Jade she's out of the hospital, resting with the little one.

"You should go," I said, nodding to his foot. He stops tapping and placed another spoon of lucky charms in his mouth.

He looks at his feet. "No it's okay." Not a second later, his feet start tapping away again.

Rolling my eyes, I take both of our bowls and call out from over my shoulder. "Just go, I'm fine. I'm going to the hospital today. I don't need a babysitter Alex."

He wanted to say something but I give him a go-away look. Sighing, he got up and grabbed his things. "Thank you," he calls over his shoulder before he leaves.

"Thank the goddess he's gone. That tapping was getting annoying," Roxanna muttered. "But I must admit his pup is a cute one." She added.

I nodded in agreement. "I'm off to the hospital, I'll be home later." I call out to Roxanna as I put my white Converse shoes on.

"Okay dearie, be safe." I think this woman forgets how much older I am than her, but I'll admit I don't exactly hate it. It's nice sometimes. She's just showing that she cares.

When I got to the hospital, the doctor went over how he's been sleeping practically the entire time. The poison's working its way out but it's draining him in the process. He looks so peaceful sleeping, face slightly flush and hair a messy heap despite me washing it for him yesterday. Softly moving it out of his face, I gently trace his jaw, then ears, then nose. *What are you doing to me?*

Prepared to wait a while, I had some books brought over from our little library at home. I'm currently in the middle of a book called *Acid* by Emma Pass. It's surprising good. I look over to Dxton when I hear him groan and shift in his bed.

"You're up," I coolly said, flipping the page. Despite my emotions becoming haywire and rather hormonal, I keep my composure solid and emotionless. But Dxton of course. Even in his state he saw straight through it.

"How long ha—"

"A while."

"How is th—"

"Up and running and very safe."

"What about Dom—"

"Awake and will be fully healed in a few hours," I responded looking up from my book. "Anything else?"

"No. Thank you," he said with a glimpse of pride in his eyes.

"Woah! Wait a min what do you think you're doing?" I exclaimed. Dxton's feet touched the ground and he swiftly stands up. His eyes on mine. "You can't get up yet. You've just woken up, you idiot." I go to push him back down but he pulled to his chest. He wraps his arms around me, holding me like he's afraid to let go. Like I would disappear. I find myself wrapping my arms around his torso, soaking in his warmth.

"Don't do anything like that again." I sighed into his chest. He nodded against my head, his nose in my hair.

"Your turning out to be quite the luna," he said softly.

I pulled away and smiled softly. "I guess I am. Now go back to your bed." I helped him into his bed, pulling the covers over him.

"Can we put the wall away?" He was referring to the wall between his room and Dom's. A little feature the hospital has is that all of the walls between rooms can be pulled down, so if the patients were related or mates, they won't freak out wondering if they are okay. I nodded and brought a nurse in to bring the wall down. Dominic stared at us, his mouth attached to a tall handsome nurse.

"Well you seem better," I mused as Dominic went bright red. I look to his male friend and saw Christan, his face being covered by his hands. "Christan," I acknowledged.

He bowed and muttered, "Hello," before quickly leaving. Interesting. I didn't push the subject while Dxton and him are clearly mind linking.

Dxton and Dom have been bedridden for two days, and they were already being pains in the arses. Dxton kept claiming to have work to do and Dom complained about needing to get into better shape. They're made to be horrible patients. I feared for their poor nurse and doctor.

"How are you two feeling?" Jade asked from the door, little Maddy in her arms. I looked up from my staring match with Dominic. I took a seat next to Dxton, where I have been the whole time. The two males grunted out replies, ranging from *fine* to *get me out of here.*

"Any news?" Dxton asked, sitting up from his bed, getting straight to business as usual. He is a good alpha, but for fuck's sake he was just captured and tortured. Can't he take a few days to deal with himself?

Alex shook his head. "No new letters yet, we are still as clueless as before I'm afraid."

We all remained silent for a few minutes, before Dominic interrupted that silence. "Can you please explain why 'Wolfe' is after you? You know something, and you've kept it to yourself this whole time." The nerve of this male, but Dom isn't wrong. I do know more than I am letting on. I know a lot more.

Dxton softly grabbed my hand and gave it a squeeze. No one knows this. This is a secret that died with my parents and Ivan Bosque.

"Our history isn't written down in books because of me. Your line of lycans tried to document it and I destroyed it." I play with Dxton's fingers, feeling everyone's eyes on me I grow anxious. "I didn't want the world to know my story, I wanted it to all die. It was better if the world thought I was dead with it, but it's coming back to haunt me."

I look into the eyes of Alex, Jade, Dominic, and lastly Dxton, who was looking on encouragingly.

"My parents left frequently when I was growing up. They were on the front lines taking out Franz's forces, his rogue armies." I paused to look into everyone's eyes again, my anxiety building. With a soft squeeze from Dxton, I continue. "They were saving the world, just doing their duties as lycans, as the moon goddess planned. But I was naive and so stupid. I wanted to help them. So one night when they left to fight, I followed them using everything my mother had taught me. I was able to stay amongst them undetected. I wanted to help them fight so they could be home more. So I wouldn't have to see them tired and hurt. But I just ended up getting in their way, an—" *In and out, Della.*

"Franz ended up capturing me. I was only fifteen. He had me in his capture for two years w-where he raped me repeatedly. I-I gave him two sons. I-I . . ." My throat tightened, causing me to choke on my sobs. "I killed both of them." Dxton's hand held mine tighter at the mention of my rape, his lycan growling, causing the others to whimper, but he calms seeing my state, taking in his own deep breaths he softly strokes circles on my hand.

"I killed them, I had to, I couldn't let him raise them into monsters

I should have just stayed put at home, as they had said, because this moment haunted me forever. "My mother ended up making a trade with Franz, behind my father's back. Her life for mine. Franz agreed, but he didn't follow through with his plans. He kept both of us in his capture. I spent another year listening to him repeatedly rape and torture my mother. When she gave birth to a son, he went blind with rage. He tortured her for months, and his . . . raping got worse.

"By the time my father saved us, she was barely alive. She ended up committing suicide a month after her escape. She couldn't hold it together anymore. Her lycan went feral and she was borderline becoming a lusus naturae. Years of being the female lycan had taken its toll on my mother. Franz wasn't the first person to have raped her." I burst out crying. I haven't told anyone this. I've never talked about what happened all those years ago, I've kept to myself. Not even Ness or Henry knew, and I didn't even talk to Ivan about it.

"My father was driven mad from her loss that he turned into a lusus naturae. With his mind gone, he attacked me" I lift up my dress to reveal a scar along my inner thigh running all the way down to my knee.

"I had to kill him." I whispered. "Not long later, I tried to kill myself, but the moon goddess always brought me back. I would die, only to wake up tomorrow healed like nothing had happened. I would beg and beg her to let me die but she wouldn't answer my calls. She left me alone! In a world against me!" I could feel my lycan coming out. We were finally saying what we've wanted to for years, and we could feel the weight being lifted from our shoulders, but I badly wanted to punch something, anything. To just cry.

"Della," Dxton whispered, pulling me into his lap. He held me softly as I cried into his shoulder. Everyone else kept quiet, letting the events sink in fully.

"Do you think that the Wolfe sending us these letters is one of the children?" Jade whispered, bouncing little Maddy in her arms. I can smell the fear on her, fear for her child in this cruel world. Looking to her from Dxton's lap, I nodded weakly.

"It has to be. Franz is dead. I checked so many times after Ivan killed him. I watched him burn his corpse. Ivan was my father's best friend. He made sure to avenge the pain he caused on us. Then a hundred years later, Ivan found his mate"— I looked to Dxton—"then had Dxton."

Ivan offered me sanctuary in White Crescent Moon, but I vowed that I wouldn't rely on the help from others. I wasn't going to bring anyone into my death course. Unknowingly I would end up straight back here, only this time with his son. I miss Ivan, he was like a father to me.

"I believe the Wolfe we are dealing with is the child my mother gave to him. My father though he had killed him, but Franz had many loyal followers; they could have tried to bring him back." My half-brother. It has to be, it's the only thing that could explain the notes.

CHAPTER TWENTY-FIVE

DELLA

"Are you okay?"

I look up from my book to look at Dxton. He is looking considerably better but still confined to his bed, unlike Dominic who was discharged today after a week in the hospital. However, the salty male managed to pull some strings and persuaded the doctors to allow him to bed rest at home, with a doctor coming by to visit every now and then.

Pulling him closer to my chest, I sighed. "I don't know." He gave me a raised eyebrow. "I honestly don't," I said, rolling my eyes. "I am really confused at the moment."

"With?"

"Everything."

"Oh my," Roxanna said, her hands going to her mouth to cover her smirk. "How lovely to see you Alpha."

"Roxanna," he mumbles, trying to wiggle his way out of my arms. I bit his cheek, surprising him greatly.

"I don't think so, I am not putting you down," I said sternly. He rubs at his cheek softly, a blush forming on his face. He mumbles fine, but I knew he wasn't that bothered by me holding him bridal. I reckon based on the blush and arousal, he rather likes it. I giggle quietly. Who would have thought, the big bad alpha likes being dominated. Interesting.

Giggling, I take him up stairs to his room. He sniffs dramatically. "Why do I smell you? It's very strong up here."

"No reason," I said a little too quickly.

"Okay . . ." Dxton said suspiciously.

His room is about the same size as mine, his view is out towards the forest, showing a nice view of the trees softly swaying in the wind, and the animals going about their business. His bed, much too big for just him, has a dark blue quilt, with million pillows lining the bed's frame. All of his furniture is black, with the wall behind his bed being a natural wooden blank mural.

Putting him down on the bed, he slides under the covers. After checking his temperature and his wounds, I nodded, satisfied.

His room, much like his office, is littered with things everywhere, a whole wall with shelving filled with personal items. Upon closer inspection, I can see a few photo albums, labelled, PACK OVER THE YEARS, PREVIOUS GAMMAS, TRAVEL and one not yet labelled. He is quite sentimental.

I found a few nick knacks he has collected from traveling, a proclaimed vase with some symbols of the Taiwanese language and even a fossil. I don't know what it was. Picking it up, I turn it over.

"I found that with my sister," Dxton softly replied from his bed. "We were digging holes, determined to find groundhogs, but we ended up finding the fossil instead. I had it looked at not that long ago, it's a bit of coprolite, in other words poop" Cheeky shit. Literally. And I'm holding it. Placing it back down gently, I go into the bathroom, causing Dxton to laugh.

"Okay, I'll go get you some food."

Dxton shakes his head. "No need." And just in time, Roxanna knocks on the door.

"I have some ham sandwiches, pretzels and orange juice, is there anything else you would like?"

Stunned that they both read my mind, I shook my head. "No, no, thank you, Roxanna." She hands me the tray and takes her leave for the day. Dxton and I remain in soft silence, eating the food.

When we were done eating, I got up to put the platter in the kitchen but before I could grab it, Dxton grabbed my hips and pulled me in onto the bed. "You know Miss Nurse, you need to rest too," he whispered to my ear.

I tried to wriggle out of his grip, but he holds onto me even tighter. Huffing, I bit his shoulder, but he just looks down at me with darkened eyes. "I wouldn't do that if I were you."

Blushing, I scold myself for my stupid mistake. What did I think that would do? "I don't have time to rest."

"Yes you do."

Sighing, I give in. I am tired, and I doubt Dxton is going to let me leave. Pulling me in tightly, he rests his head on top of mine. I will admit this does feel nice. I feel warm, and protected.

"How are you feeling?"

"Dxton—"

"No how are you actually feeling?"

Sighing, I play with the hem of his shirt. "Confused, and scared."

"With?"

"You, the pack, everything," I whisper. He remains silent, waiting for me to elaborate. "I am so sick and tired of feeling lonely. I want to be with you, I just don't know how. I want a future where I can finally go to a populated area and not look over my shoulder every second fearing that someone might be behind me. I want to feel safe, and I do with you and that terrifies me." I softly trace my fingers over his scars, feeling him shiver slightly. "I know I won't leave. I've become too invested in the pack, and maybe you. But that doesn't mean everything you pulled while I was 'human' was okay. I won't just forgive you because you are being nicer and tolerable. You need to earn that."

He pulls me closer. "That's fair, and I'm sorry."

Yawning, I mumble out, "I know."

"I'll do whatever I can to give you the life you want, a safe one." He runs his hand through my hair softly. "One free of worry, and danger."

I know. I know you will try.

We looked at each other. I feel my heart rate spike slightly, which he hears because he starts to smirk just a little. He grabbed my hips then pulled me up so we're face to face.

"Can I kiss you?"

Breathless, I nod slightly.

He moves in closer, his lips just barely grazing mine. Then, they softly touch, moving them against my own softly. It's nothing like I thought it would be. I expected Dxton to be rough and forceful, but he was soft and sweet. He pulls away and kisses my forehead, each cheek, and my nose softly. "I have wanted to do that for so long," he whispers, peppering kisses on my face. Giggling softly, he pulls me into a hug. I feel my lycan go berserk within my mind.

Mate just kissed us." She sighs love sick. "*I want another.*" I laugh softly at her antics.

"*We have forever.*" I gently remind her

I let my mind wander to everything that has happened in these last few weeks. So much has changed, a lot I didn't think would ever happen. Some I wish hadn't been forced, but there wasn't much I could have done about it. It's happened, now I need to accept it and move on. After a few minutes of silence, just when I was about to fall asleep.

"We need to go see Quinn."

"Who's Quinn?" I mumbled, feeling my eyes getting heavier.

"Our oracle, she's been driving us mad for weeks now. She claims she needs to speak with you."

Sighing I nod and mumbled later. "We can do that when you are better and out of bed."

He said something but I ended up not hearing it, because for the first time in a long time, I fall asleep dream free, and it was the best sleep I have ever had.

CHAPTER TWENTY-SIX

DELLA

There was a soft sigh before Dom spoke. "What's on the schedule today?"

"Well we had Alex visit all the kidnapped victims this morning and see what they might know that we need. So far we don't have anything. I'm going to visit the oracle once Dxton gets back. Apparently she is a bit of a nut and I have been warned that I might get harmed. So Dxton's coming also," I replied, looking over her file once again.

"She is a little bit special." Dom agrees.

Oracles don't mix together potions and make spells like most think. They are no witches. They are a portal into the world beyond if you will. They are highly respected amongst most packs or considered to be crazy.

I look over her file. She's only twenty-four, been the oracle for five years this year and has apparently tried to break into mine and Dxton's house more times since my arrival. Her entire family going back seven generations has been gifted with the ability to contact the dead and speak the goddess's wishes through visions they have, and have the gift of future sight.

Some powerful oracles can have the moon goddess take over their body and tell them the future. For Quinn, she can have her body taken over for ten minutes. Any longer and she could die or go onto a week long coma, making her one of today's more powerful oracles. It's something that is rather rare these days, majority of the bloodlines have died out.

My mother was able to talk to the moon goddess at will. I remember her talking to the mood goddess regularly for guidance. That's what makes a female lycan special. We can talk to the moon goddess. I'm quite happy to not speak to the goddess, but Dxton thinks it might be a good idea to get the oracle's insight.

"Be careful then, doesn't matter if you're a lycan. Never underestimate someone's ability to harm others." Dom and I walk up the steps to the pack house.

"You think she could harm me?"

Dom holds the door open for me and nodded. "Potentially." I was about to reply when arms wrap around my waist. I look over my shoulder to see Dxton. He dug his head into my neck, his warm breath and nose tickling me.

"Well aren't you cuddly today," I mused, pulling away slightly so I can see his face. He smiled softly, a small yes escaping his lips.

"Come on, best to get this over and done with." Dxton grabs my hand and pulls me away from the pack house. He gave Dom a few instructions.

We walked hand in hand to Quinn's house, which is on the other side of the pack not far from the entrance. It's a small wooden cabin with lots of different flowers and plants around her house. The smell of rosemary and lavender is a little too strong for my nose. Dxton has guards all around the house. A little over cautious but we will see what makes this wolf so anxious. Before Dxton could even knock, the door opens. It was so fast, the air around us shifted quickly.

"My luna!" she exclaims with an overly high pitch. Quinn's appearance is soft, with a crazed smile and very baggy eyes. Her blonde hair was cut short with many piercings on her ears. She was dressed in a light purple crop top and high waist jeans shorts. She waved us in. "Please come. I've been expecting you, the goddess has been going crazy with your arrival. She has been bothersome, keeping me up all night long." As she speaks, her hand starts to twitch. She immediately sinks her nails into her other arm and mutters. She shoots her head up to the sky her eyes slits. "Not yet! Please let me talk to her first, you are making this very difficult."

Dxton grabs my arm about ready to start walking away.

"We need to talk to her. We can't leave yet," I whispered.

"I don't like this. She is crazy, her whole family has been. They always made me uncomfortable."

"What's wrong?" I ask Quinn.

"The goddess is trying to take over my body. She has much to tell you. Much too much. I have control, we must talk," she said, walking into her house with a bright smile, completely ignoring what just happened. I squeeze Dxton's arm and walk in.

Quinn's home is a lot nicer than I thought it would be. I'll admit I expected wind charms, dream catchers, rugs, and everything stereotypical. But she had soft scents everywhere with lots of homey objects and inspirational words covering her walls.

"We must begin with the moon goddess talking to you so she'll have peace over what she wants to talk to you about and there is also the spiritual ailment of our souls—" Quinn begins to ramble, getting some teacups and fresh ingredients.

I put my hand up stopping her, "I'm sorry Quinn but we are not here to talk about the goddess. We are here to ask questions about your kidnapping and if there is anything you can tell us. Any information would be helpful"

She looks at me with sadness and dismay.

"No, no, no" she shakes her head gripping her arm again. "She won't leave me alone. You don't understand. You've shut her out and now she has turned to me to deliver her news. I've tried getting his guards to let me tell you," she said, pointing to Dxton. "That's why they kidnapped me. They wanted to talk to the goddess. They knew about talking to her and wanted to know so badly how to do it," Quinn exclaimed, horrified.

Quinn looked very crazed and I couldn't help but want to help her. She looked so mentally drained and hurt, and it was all my fault. I approached her slowly as she twitched. "Quinn" I whisper softly. She looks at me disoriented. "What did they want to now?" I ask as calmly as I could.

"How to bring him back."

"Him?" I asked calmly. But my heart was anything but calm. There are a million different people she could be talking about. But there is only one *him* I have on my mind now.

"Franz Wolfe."

What happened in the next few minutes become a bit of a blur. While my mind is screaming in agony, my body stiffened. I couldn't move, my mind trying to reassure myself that she got it wrong, that I heard wrong. I dreaded she would say it so I think I heard it. It was just gaslighting myself. But, deep down, I know I heard correctly. If not by the words screaming in my head but the fact my lycan was acting up. It happened so suddenly. My lycan shot through the surface in a blood thirsty rage. My eyes were now her bright gold. I couldn't control her, but I wasn't in any state to stop her.

"He is to remain dead," she growls to Quinn who's on her knees whimpering for her life. The power radiating off my lycan now fogged over the area. The guards outside were on their feet whimpering. She growls out angrily, but seeing the look Dxton gives us, she stops.

"He's caused enough pain," she said more to herself. The pain of our past was now too clear on our minds. The beatings, sexual assaults and nightmares we've tried so desperately to ignore were all coming back. We haven't gotten one in a while but they still linger deep within our mind. Dxton grabs hold of our arm and softly rubs circles. "You will protect us right?" my lycan whispers softly.

Dxton cups our face and soothingly runs a hand through our hair. "Always." He kisses our forehead, then rests his own on ours.

"*We must be in control,*" I said shakily to my lycan.

"*He hurt us, we cannot let this happen.*"

"*We won't. But we need to move on,*" I whisper to her softly. She sighs, mumbling a small okay.

I pull her in gently and retook control. Taking in a deep breath I look at Dxton. He glares daggers at Quinn, both eyes a swirl of dark and gold. They are both on edge, both in control. But one wrong move and Dxton's lycan will have full control. His control over his lycan isn't as strong as mine. It's clear they have a strong bond but they haven't bonded like my wolf and I. He really does dislike Quinn though.

I said, "We need a clear head if we're going to get any answers," as softly as I could I take his hand and give it a squeeze. He in return takes it in his. He reins in his wolf, but won't hesitate to bring him back.

"Quinn, I believe we need to talk to the goddess."

Quinn gets to her very wobbly feet and shakes her head quickly. Probably getting whiplash. She grips onto the nearest item for dear life, helping to support her. I offer her my hand but she gives me a small smile and gets up herself.

"I-I of course." Her eyes twitching ever so slightly.

I look to Dxton and pull him into the direction of the chairs. "How do we do this?" I asked Quinn, turning to her. I could wait till tonight to ask the moon goddess myself, but we're here anyway, might as well give Quinn the rest she needs.

"I pray for her visit," she mumbled, not daring to look at our eyes. Quinn sits in front of us at the table, her hands a fidgety mess. She softly started chanting shakily. "Please grant us your presence moon goddess. We are in need of your wisdom and guidance," she faintly said. She breathed in loudly and out softly. Her eyes flutter close.

The air feels heavier, but also somehow calming. It was almost as if it's caressing me. Momentarily, I close my eyes, a sigh escaping my lips. My wolf relaxes greatly. I even felt Dxton's hand relax within mine.

"Della. Dxton." It was a voice so soft, like that of an angel's. I look at Quinn wearily. Her face was now a soft glow, eyes wide and shiny. Her posture was now straight and a beautiful smile graced her face.

"Hello my children."

"Moon Goddess," Dxton whispered, quickly bowing his head. I stayed how I am, not even bothering to show her respect. She reaches over and lifts up his head. "There is no need for that my dear." She looks to me and smiles brightly.

"Della." A look of excitement glows within her eyes. She then frowns, a look that doesn't suit her beautiful glowing complexion. "You have been ignoring my callings. I am quite disappointed . . . But that is a lecture for another day. We have more important matters to discuss."

"Like him," I said, finding my voice.

"Yes, him." The moon goddess looks out the window with a distant look in her eyes. "He was my most promising son. I had so much hope for him. He was just like your father, full of new ideas to improve his share of the lycan treaty." She signs softly. "Now he lies within hell. He brought me much shame. But I'm not here to talk about Franz, you my dear, face a grave future if you don't stop it now."

She looks between us and stops on me. "Wolfe had a child who survived, and he is the alpha of Dunkler Wolf pack—"

"So it is true then, I figured as much." I got ready to leave. "If you aren't going to give me any new information, I'll be on my way then." I tug on Dxton's arm. "Come on, this was a waste of our time." I look to the moon goddess. My expression was blank. I went to walk out the door.

"Wait, Della." I pause at the door, giving her a moment to speak. "Please answer my calls, I just wanted to talk to you." Hypocritical bitch.

"I would have, if you had ever answered any of mine."

"Please believe me Della, I would have brought back Alvery if I could have."

"But you could bring me back continuously."

"You are the hero of this story. It wasn't your mother's destiny." The glow fades from Quinn's face. "I'm sorry that I have disappointed you, my child." Quinn's body sags down onto the table. She groans at the impact.

I look at Dxton, who is mirroring my expressions. What now. "We have to go come up with a real plan" I said as we walk out of the house, the guards tailing us.

"We just need to find him" Comes Dxton's response, as he grabs onto my hand, "What are we going to do with him?" Dxton looks at me with a look in his eyes. A look that could put the fear of the gods into anyone's heart. But I can see the small concern within them.

"Kill him."

He stops us momentarily, "Do you think you could kill your brother?"

"A few weeks ago, I didn't even know I had a brother. Besides, if I can kill my own children as a teenager, I would hate to think of what I could do to Wolfe now." Dxton's expression sours over slightly at the mention of my previous children. I can't blame him. I wouldn't have been happy with any children if he had some either. But what do we do about this issue? How do we bring the fight to us, but also keep our pack safe? There's the bunkers but that would only hold for so long. Is there a way to hide an entire pack?

"Omg! I am such a dumbass." I slapped my palm to my forehead and laughed out loud.

Dxton pulls his hand from mine and used it to pull my hand from my reddening face. "I don't think you're a dumbass, but why?"

"I have a plan, and we are going to need the others for this one"

CHAPTER TWENTY-SEVEN

Della

I mind link Jade and Alex, plus made sure to tell them to leave little Maddy with someone reliable for some hours. Dom was being handled by Dxton. We meet them all in the meeting room at the pack house, where they were already waiting for us.

"What's this big plan you've come up with, my luna?" Dxton said pulling my chair out for me. I kissed his cheek and sat down at the front of the table.

I smirked at the four of them, feeling beyond dumb for not thinking of this sooner, and for the bomb shell I'm about to give them. "You guys know that each lycan had their own country to rule right?"

"Yes," they all mumbled, unsure where I'm going with this.

"As you are all so obviously aware, White Crescent Moon is on American soil per Dxton's birthright." I pause as they all look at me as if I've gone a tad mad.

"Luna where are you going with this?" Dom interrupts me suddenly.

"Yeah I hate to bring this to your attention but we are aware of the lycan country ruling," Alex added in, with Jade nodding next to him.

I sigh out annoyed and tightly ground my nails into the palm of my hand. "If you are done being rude, may I continue?"

The three of them nod. Dxton was still at my side, giving me a questioning look that I ignore. "As per the lycan agreement, each was given a country, that also meant my mother with France." Alex looks ready to interrupt me again but I quickly glared at him. "Interrupt me again and I am ripping your tongue out." He closes it immediately. "My mother also had a pack, one kept secret in Étretat, France." Home, I miss it. Last time I was there was because I was borderline becoming a lusus naturae, after almost two years of not shifting. It caused a lot of damage to our bond. After shifting, I was out cold for a month.

"So my plan, is we go to France and get help from my witch friends." I got excited. Home, I miss it so much and the people. Home . . . is it home? No. I look at Dxton and smiled. I'm already home.

"Lunar Moon has two witches whom my mother saved, who in return made her a barrier around some lands, one that could keep her safe from the world. It's designed to teleport people who might step into our pack line to the other side, but they don't notice a thing. It's heavily charmed, and the three sisters even decided to stay at the pack as they are hunted just as much as lycans. My mother then turned the land into a pack. A pack for the hunted, endangered and the rare. The current alpha that I have placed is actually of the werewolf royalty line. Her family has served me since the monarchy fell." That was a dark time.

"Why didn't you just stay there?" I look to Jade with an eyebrow raised slightly. "Why didn't you stay at the pack? It seems like your best option for safety."

"I did. I was the alpha for a little over a hundred years, but my lycan was drawing people to the pack. Even with the witches's barriers, we almost got caught a few times because of me. The pack is built into the cliffs, with my house being far underground so that I could shift and be a bit freer, but even then you could still sense my presence. I was putting my people in danger, so I stepped down, and opted to travel. If I was going to get caught, it was when I was on my own, far away from anyone I cared for.

"I am more powerful than my mother, it worked for her for many decades, but I had a much more prominent aura compared to hers. Do you trust me?" I asked Dxton.

He looks at me as if I've grown another head. "Of course I do."

I grab out my phone from my back pocket and dialled a memorised number. "Hello, you bag it, we bury it, how can I help you today?" An overly sweet voice came through. It made me smile. Jaclyn, always the jokester.

"Hello, can I please get the home delivery package please?"

"Della. What are you doing?" Alex asked, then I hear him mumble to Jade. "We can't bury a body we haven't killed yet."

"Okie dokies, and how many packages will that be today?"

"I'll take five please."

She hums on the other side of the line. "That will be with you shortly. Thank you for picking Bag 'Em."

"Awesome, thank you."

Dxton gave me yet another questioning look and got ready to say something but I mouthed, "Trust me."

"What the fuck was that?" Jade was slightly outraged. I was more shocked that she swore.

A beam of white light shines on all five of us. "You'll see," is all I said as we teleported away. We land in a room I recognize as the alpha's office in the pack house. It still looks the same as ever. A family portrait of myself and my parents hung over a fireplace with a wall littered in photographs, all of the previous alpha and her families.

"Welcome to Lunar Moon."

I look up and see Florence, my current alpha. Lunar Moon is an all-female ranked pack. No males allowed, unless it's to be a normal member.

She is built like a tank with arms much bigger than any of the males in the room right now, but she has a smile so bright and sweet. Her blonde hair was pulled into a braided bun. She stretched out her arms, already pulling me straight into a bear hug.

"Alpha. It's so good to see you." Her French accent is so strong, it's hard to understand a word she is saying.

"Florence," I wheezed out. "It's good to see you too."

I turn to my starstruck pack and smiled out brightly. "This is Alpha Florence of Lunar Moon, my mother's pack, which is where we currently are. This is Alpha Dxton, my mate." I gestured to Dxton, who nodded in greeting. "And our beta, Dominic, and gammas, Alex and Jade."

She bows slightly. "It's a pleasure to meet you." The pack does the same. "What brings you here, Alpha?"

I have asked her so many times to stop calling me that, but she never listens. I look over to Florence. "We need help. The magical kind." Dxton walked up and grabs my hand.

"Ah I see. Shall we go to the drawing room? The witches will meet us there," Florence said softly, her hand outstretched to the door she's holding open.

* * *

"Does anyone want a coffee? Some biscuits?" Florence asked, bringing over a tray with some sweets, coffee, and a pot of tea. We all grab a plate and cup each, helping ourselves. I have some tea and a lime sugar madeleine.

"Luna. If I may ask," Dom said hesitantly.

"You can ask whatever you want to know Dom," I said, popping the biscuit in my mouth.

"Is your father's pack still yours?" Timberjack Pack. People for so long thought I was hiding there, but I haven't stepped foot in that pack in so long. I haven't even met the current alpha, we've only talked briefly.

"At the moment, it's like Lunar Moon, only more independent. I have more to do with Lunar Moon since it's my inheritance pack. I was never to be the alpha of Timberjack. My father wanted to give the pack over to his beta, Nickson Timberjack, since my mother refused to have more children, after all I wasn't even meant to happen. But Nickson died from rogue attacks, so in his honour, father named his pack after him.

"I choose who stands in to be the alpha here, I don't at Timberjack. I picked the first family but they took it from there. I'm technically their true alpha but I never will uphold the title as my father didn't wish upon it. But if Dxton and I were to have children, one of them could then inherit the packs from me and the current alphas of both packs will have no choice. I had a treaty signed before I left them to their first alphas," I said, looking at Dxton for that last part.

"If we were to have children, our first born would of course be alpha to White Crescent."

"Of course," I said to him. "That's how it was always meant to be." I grab onto Dxton's hand and give it a squeeze. "But if our children don't want my packs, I'm not going to force it upon them," I said, kissing his cheek.

Florence gets up. "Alpha, the witch sisters are here."

I got up and looked to the door, seeing two almost identical women walk in. A deadly power radiated off them in waves, along with a very prominent burnt sugar scent. The smell of witches. The two sisters have heart shaped faces, with colourful make-up that makes their hazel eyes glow. They had button noses and long wavy hair. One has black while the other has blonde.

The blonde haired witch squeals in delight, which makes the wolves in the room cringe and cover their ears. She runs into my arms and yells, "Della!" She hugs me so tight I thought my lungs would explode. She pulls my face back and examines it. "Omg, it's been way too long!" she said, peppering my face with kisses like an aunt would to their niece. She pulls me into a hug again.

A light-hearted laugh pulls the witch away from me. "Careful Jaclyn, you'll scare her away."

"I just miss her so much," Jaclyn exclaimed. "Though you need to eat more, you look rather skinny." I pulled back and laugh softly.

"I miss you too," I said to Jaclyn. I look at Daphne and smiled.

Daphne hugs me and whispers in my ear softly. "It's nice to see you embracing who you are." She kisses my forehead. "Your mother would be so proud of you."

"Thank you," I whispered back, smiling.

I turn to introduce the two but Jaclyn is already bouncing around introducing herself to everyone. Daphne goes around and does the same.

When they sit themselves down, everyone looks at me expectantly, but I turn to the two witch sisters. "Shall we tell our story first to get a better idea of why witches are in a werewolf pack?" Daphne asked. I nod, taking a seat next to Dxton, placing my hand into his.

"I gave them a brief summary before we got here but feel free to."

Daphne looked to my pack members with a kind smile on her face. She licks her fingers to bring up a small orb of light. She flicked it to the table to enlarge and show the memories Daphne will be talking about.

"Jaclyn and I are descendants of the first witch, which doesn't do a lot for us power wise. But that's not what people believed," Daphne said. Jaclyn interrupts to add her part of the story.

"We were running from some hunters, when our youngest sister got caught. She was badly hurt and none of our healing spells were strong enough at the time. That's when Alvery came and saved us, She tried everything to help us get our sister back, but it was too late. Rose-Mary wasn't meant to continue with us. But we owe our life to Alvery. We help protect her pack for helping us. We have a home here thanks to her. She was in our eyes our very own goddess." Jaclyn and Daphne both laugh softly with tears in their eyes as they looked back at the memory fondly.

"We miss her every day, both of them." Daphne said softly with a smile. A slight pang hits my heart at her words. Alvery might very well be alive if not for me, but I must move on from the past. I can't run from it anymore. I have packs to protect.

"But, a bit more exciting news, we have charms all over the pack and the surrounding highlands. This is the safest place on earth, even for the Luna," Jaclyn said excitingly. "We have made more durable spells, so that Della could one day come back home, but you have found your own home."

I have, haven't I? I look at the gammas who are both smiling happily. Dom gives a small smile. I turn to Dxton who has a soft look on his face. "Yeah, I have. Where's Harold?" I asked, referring to Daphne's mate.

"Oh you know my sweet Harold. I'm sorry he couldn't come and meet you all. My mate doesn't take too well to others. He was tortured by vampires most of his life and it's made it hard for him to talk to others."

"That's horrible," Jade said.

Daphne nods. "Yes, but my Harold is getting better. Slowly, he is showing some social skills," she beamed proudly. "So, what do you need help with?" Daphne sat up in her chair to grab another biscuit.

I tell her everything to the note. The moon goddess, how I met Dxton, and how I had to come out. They listened the whole time, scolded Dxton a fair amount and then when it came time to think of a plan, they thought it over. The room goes silent again as they think over everything I have said.

"We could do the same as what we have done here essentially. A barrier surrounding your pack. That way, it can also remain there when we leave. It'll definitely help with your rogue issue, but you aren't trying to hide, so we can take it back down if you wish," Daphne said.

Jaclyn adds in a comment. "We could charm your bunker. Anyone who tries to touch it without a sigil will be electrocuted, burned, well you know . . . harmed. Could even work out a way to better advance your forces, but the charms will help keep your pack safe, and I can try to figure out a way to make it so that you can activate them in case you have a time in the future where you require your bunker again."

That could work, and if they can figure out a way to make them reusable, that would be a handy arsenal to have. From the corner of my eye, I see Jade trying to hold in a yawn. Looking at the time on the wall, I see that it would be pretty late in America right now. "Maybe we should sleep on it."

Dom stands up and bows his head. "Yes, Luna." He yawns.

Jade and Alex get up and bow their head as well. "We will see you tomorrow. Good night Luna, Alpha."

Alex stops and looks to the witches. "Don't witches have familiars?"

Jaclyn and Daphne nod at the same time. "Yes," they said together. Clicking their fingers, a panther appears by Daphne's side, and a red panda on Jaclyn's shoulder.

"We usually keep them at home," Jaclyn explains.

The panther, whose name is Raine, rubs her body against my leg, purring. I scratch behind her ear softly where I know she likes it. I used to shift and play with her outside. It was fun. She would try so hard to bring me down, even though I was much bigger than her. Daphne's mate has a panther too. Mated witches always have the same animal. His name is Link. He would give it his best shot to take me down too.

The red panda's name is Flick. He only really likes Jaclyn. Grumpy thing.

Florence quickly waves Alex to continue walking towards the door. "Please follow me, I'll show you all to your rooms and feel free to help yourself. What's mine is now yours," she said instantly, playing hostess.

I get up to leave myself when the two witch sisters stop me. "So when do we expect children?" They both coyly smiled at me.

Oh boy.

CHAPTER TWENTY-EIGHT

Della

"Not anytime soon with this war brewing." I try to move around them with Dxton's hand in mine when Jaclyn steps in front of the door.

"You know Jaclyn is a great name."

Daphne rolls her eyes and steps in front of her. "She means Daphne is a great name."

"I am not naming my children after you two." I quickly picked them both up and set them aside, making them both giggle. "Come on, let's go before they ask more questions."

"I can't believe our little Della is growing up." I hear Daphne whisper to Jaclyn. Rolling my eyes, I take Dxton out of the pack house. A few of the members bow their heads to us, saying welcome back and hellos. I politely greet them back.

"Is it okay if we take a quick detour?" I asked as we leave the pack house.

"Sure." Dxton smiles down at me.

It's early morning in France, and the sun looks so pretty over the ocean. Our pack is on a cliff near the ocean, and it's a view I can never get tired of. We walked up a path that goes off in two directions. One goes off to my house, and the other to where I want to go. Stopping at a rose bush, I pick a few of the flowers. Florence has always made sure to keep white roses around in honour of my mother as they were her favourite. A very sweet touch of hers, one of the many reasons why she is one of the best alphas I've had here so far. She even planted an English oak tree near my house in honour of my father.

We stop at a cliff, where a monument is. On it is written IN HONOUR OF ALVERY FAMBRE, FIRST ALPHA OF LUNAR MOON, AND HER MATE GEORGE ROSAI, ALPHA OF TIMBERJACK. It is tradition to be cremated in werewolf society, so that they can be a part of the earth they once walked. This is where I set their ashes free. Putting the roses by the stone, I bow slightly. I smile at the stone, running my finger over their name. I give it a small kiss.

I miss you guys. Dad's endless jokes, his purposely made attempts to make Mum annoyed. He made every day fun, even the days where we weren't safe, the days we were scared. He never failed to put a smile on my face. Mum was overbearing but what protective mother isn't? She was more serious, but she told the best stories, of her first day alive, her journey to find herself, and how she met Dad. She was always cooking sweet cakes, when she wasn't being an alpha. Luckily with the witches's help, Mum and Dad were able to successfully alpha their own packs, and live here in the meantime.

"I'm sorry it's been so long since I came by, you wouldn't believe my month," I whisper, softly tracing their names. "The world knows I'm alive, that I'm not a myth. Shit is about to hit the fan, big time . . . I think he survived, one of the little boys. Mum's one." I feel myself tear up slightly. I hated killing them so much. Franz's baby or not, it was still mine. I have their blood on my hands, and I will always feel that stain. "I'll do what I have to."

I feel Dxton put his hand on my shoulder, giving it a soft squeeze. I gave it a squeeze of my own. "But I found someone." I sniffed. "My mate. Who would have thought, after all these years, I finally found him." Turning, I look up at Dxton, who is already looking at me. "Dxton Bosque, Ivan's boy. He's alright."

"Only alright?" he said. I giggled and hummed. "How do I make it more than alright?" he said. I tap my mouth. Chuckling, he pulls me to my feet. "If that's what the lady wants," he mumbled, leaning in to press his lips to mine softly, moving them in rhythm with each other. He slides his tongue against my lips. Smirking, I allow him access, where he dominates my mouth and explores every corner. Lifting me up so I'm strangling his hips, I pull away slightly.

"Are we going to do this here?" I whisper, looking over to the stone.

Dxton looks and nods. "No." He puts me down and bows. "Sorry, it's nice to meet you. I'm Dxton Bosque, Della's mate." He side eyes me, with a raised eyebrow. I do a thumbs up and laugh softly.

"Alright, let's go. My house is this way. It was built into the mountain." I grab onto his hand and lead him away.

He pauses slightly. "The mountain?" He gives me a doubtful look. I pull him to continue walking.

"It was an idea my mum came up with actually. She had hoped the extra layers of dirt would help mask our lycans. It worked, for her and Dad. But not me."

"That's why you didn't stay." I nod.

"When they died, and I was too young to go off on my own, we extended the house further into the mountain, but we were still getting supernatural creatures attracted to my aura. So I played human, only letting her out in my house once a month. But I wasn't used to keeping her in for long periods and it started to badly affect our mental health and our bond. I almost turned into a lusus naturae a few times. If it weren't for Daphne and Jaclyn, I might have.

"Eventually I got used to it, and can go almost over a year without shifting. But I couldn't stay. Even if I was better at hiding my lycan, I had still drawn too much attention to them while I was learning. We ended up getting flooded with creatures of all kinds, wanting to see a female lycan, or get some kind of body part thinking it would make them immortal."

"That was the most stupid rumour I had ever heard. I remember when I first heard it, I couldn't stop laughing. Of course it does nothing for anyone else," Dxton interrupts.

"They never saw the pack, thanks to the witches. But they still came because of me. I vowed to protect them by leaving. When I needed to shift, I went to a remote island I brought. It's actually where I've been most of this time." I laugh softly, playing with the hem of my t-shirt. "But it got very lonely, so I would take on human identities when I needed a break. I had just spent a few years in England before we met. I wanted to visit Ness and Henry then I was planning on going back to the island." I give him a pointed look and poke his chest. "But then someone had to get in my way."

"So if you didn't stay, you would have gone to the island?" I nod, "So I literally never would have found you." I nod again. Definitely not, I am after all good at blending in.

I point to the big double doors made into the mountain, with a few of the rose bushes around the entryway. I look over to the oak and smile.

The door has been carved into the stone, making a small undercover area, and stone carved stairs to the door. Swinging the rather loud doors open, we walk into the main room or lounge room of the house. A big black leather L-shaped couch is seated in front of a rather ancient TV, with a red Persian rug underneath. Nestled in the corner is the kitchen, which is also rather ancient, but still in working condition.

The space isn't very big, but down the hallway off in the corner lies three bedrooms, two bathrooms, a study that also is a library with rows of bookshelves, and a basement that goes far down into the mountain, for when I needed to shift.

The walls and floor are sanded down, but I kept the roof the natural stone. It made the place look more like a cave, which definitely sparked my imagination as a child. I loved this house so much. I thought it was cool how unique it was, and who can say they live in a mountain? Not a lot of people.

Dxton walks around admiring the architecture. "This is nice, very cosy for a cave. Did your parents help make it?" he asked, walking into the kitchen area. It's not too big but big enough for just me at the time.

I ran my hand over the rock wall. "Yeah, my dad helped. Mum kept losing her temper when the tools broke on her, so she ended up getting kicked off the team." I giggled. I wasn't alive then, or even thought of. My mum was dead set on never having children. She didn't want any children to go through continuous rape attempts. She also didn't want superstitious people coming to check if consuming us makes them immortal. Plus, Franz was very active. But I accidentally came into the world. She ran away from my dad, because she had planned to kill me at birth, but the moment she picked me up, she started crying and she couldn't do it. She went home with me in her arms. My Dad didn't even know she was pregnant. She ended up stabbing her uterus to make sure they didn't have any more accidents, since modern medicine wasn't a thing back then.

"She sounds like quite the character," Dxton said, looking at the ancient stove top, which miraculously still works.

"She was." I show him how to turn the stove on, seeing his obvious uncertainty. "Anyway let's go to bed." I grab his hand and pull him down the hall towards my room. I never took the main bedroom. I was going to but it felt wrong to move their stuff. So I've remained in my childhood bedroom. Obviously, I've made it more mature as I've gotten older. It's located down the hall, in the very last room. I motion him in. The room has a little step near the bed to bring the bed on a different level, with the top tier being my bed, and the bottom my living space. There's a large chest with blankets at the foot of the bed, with a set of draws to the side of the room and another chest, filled with childhood items. I have a

Persian rug under my double couch, and a much bigger blue one under my bed.

My living safe has two double couches that face each other and a coffee table between them. There's also a few books and coasters on the table with a few coffee ring stains.

I smile seeing the bed has been freshly made. Florence must have gotten that done during our meeting. I'll have to thank her for that.

I go into my walk-in closet and put on an oversized t-shirt, while Dxton gets undressed into just his boxers. We were both too tired to stay up to talk like what we have been doing lately. We hop under the covers. Dxton pulls me into his chest, kissing my forehead. "Night," he mumbled, already falling asleep. Laughing softly, I say it back. Soon, I too fall asleep.

CHAPTER TWENTY-NINE

DELLA

I was sitting in bed, enjoying my book *Six Crimson Cranes* while drinking some tea. Suddenly, he came and dropped this bombshell.

"Let's go on a date."

I choked on my tea. Did I hear right? Did he ask us on a date?

"I think he did," my lycan whispered giddily. Dxton quickly smacks on my back lightly.

"I'm sorry, pardon?" I said while coughing.

"Let's go on a date." He turned my attention to him. I put my book in my lap. I took in a deep breath to calm my racing heart and my nerves.

"Why?"

"I want to make it up to you, and we are in your hometown. You could show me all of your favourite spots."

"We are in the middle of a war though?"

He sits up straighter in the bed, turning to look at me properly. "Alex, Jade and Dom already went back to White Crescent Moon. If he attacks before we get there, then we will go back instantly. We will be going home tomorrow. Why not unwind with this small chance we have?"

". . . What do you have in mind then?"

"I was thinking we could go to your favourite restaurant here and then go for a run in our lycan forms."

That doesn't sound too bad of an idea actually. "Any food I want?" He nods.

Thinking it over some more I grin devilishly. We are in France. Home of some quite unusual dishes. He really shouldn't have left the option to me. "Okay."

His eyes widened a little. "Really?"

"Yeah. It doesn't seem like a bad idea, why not? When?"

He immediately looks at the time, 10:56 AM. "What about today? We are having a day in already."

The witches are working on making a few charms to place around our pack lines. At the moment, we are just waiting for them to be ready to leave, which could take some time. And I do miss France.

I look at him from head to toe. "Are you sure?"

He nods. What's the harm? It would probably be good for us. I nod excitedly. "Okay, let's do it." I can't remember the last time I went on a date. Last time it was with my past lover, Alison. I get up and quickly go to my walk-in wardrobe. Luckily I still have clothes here, just in case I ever came back.

I went with a nice blue mini dress, with straps and some see-through lace running up the sides. I tied my hair up into a high ponytail, with some black heels with straps wrapping around my leg, ending just below my knee. For the make-up, I went with just a very simple look.

Dxton has the same clothes he was wearing yesterday, consisting of a button-up white shirt and a nice expensive jacket over it. He also wore some block dress pants and stylish Oxford shoes.

"Beautiful," Dxton whispered, putting a kiss on my cheek. Giggling, I take Dxton to one of my favourite restaurants in Étretat. *Printemps sur le lac.*

I grinned. Oh, how I am going to love this? Dxton reaches over and grabs my hand, giving it a soft kiss. He winks. "Bill is on me, order anything you want and the best wine they have."

The waiter comes up to us. I smirked and explained to him in French how I want to prank my "American boyfriend" with all of the French delicacies. The waiter smirks and nods along to my orders before leaving.

"What was that about?" He raised an eyebrow.

"Nothing," I said sweetly.

He goes with what I said. "You sound very sexy when you speak French too by the way." I feel my cheeks go bright red, but I feel a small smirk cover my lips. Luckily I was saved by the waiter returning with our glasses and their best wine in a bucket of ice.

"*Merci*," Dom said, causing my brows to raise.

I shook my head. "No, no."

"I think you mean *non*." Dxton sits back in his chair, arms crossed looking at me very cockily.

"Promise me you will never do that again." I tried to erase his pronunciation from my head.

He leans forward. "Why?"

"The accent, the pronunciation, just no." I laugh, but quickly change the subject. "What are your hobbies?"

Dxton rolls his eyes rather immaturely. "Really?" I nod and motion for him to answer. "Hunting. I rather enjoy it, and fishing." I remember him having a picture of him and Dom in his office. "Oh, and I like cooking."

Cooking? But he doesn't cook. "If you like cooking why do you have Roxanna?" He smirks slightly, then looks off to the city, taking in the roaring streets of Étretat. "You're too lazy, aren't you?" He gives me a sly look from the corner of his eye.

"Maybe. Yourself?"

I have had so many over the years, I wouldn't know where to start. "Painting, though it's been a while. Learning a new language—"

"How many do you know" He rudely interrupts, feeling my eye twitch, which I knew he saw because he started to smirk.

"Roughly twelve I—"

"*Entiendes la profundidad de tu importancia para Mí?*" Feeling my eyes twitch again, I grab onto his hand and squeeze it tightly.

"*Dejar de interrumpirme.*" I squeeze harder. "*Te arrancaré la mano, estamos claros?*" He laughs, but nods. "Jade didn't think you knew another language." I said as the waiter starts putting our food onto the table. The waiter winks, placing the exciting dishes in front of Dxton.

He gives me a lopsided smile. "My last name is Spanish. My mother was Mexican, of course I know Spanish." That is true. I look at the arrangement of food in front of us and can't keep the smile planted off my face.

"*Cuisses de grenouille*," I said, pointing to the dish in front of him. I try to keep in my giggles. He gives me a hesitant look, and picks up one of the legs.

"Why does this chicken taste like fish?" He whispers slowly. I burst out laughing and shrug.

"Maybe because it isn't chicken?"

He looks at the leg, then me, then back to the leg. "What am I eating Della?"

I grab one of the legs and bite into it. "Frog." He pauses, and puts the half eaten leg in front of him. He looks at it for a while before shrugging and continuing to eat it. Giggling, I grab a fork and have some of the goose cassoulet.

He continues to eat the frog when he looks at one of the dishes to his left, then looks me dead in the eye. "Snails, really Della." I giggle and grabbed a spoon to pick one of the snails up.

"Escargot is not that bad," I said, eating the contents. Dxton visibly stutters. Smirking, I grab one and hand it to him. "How do you know if you don't like it? It might end up being your favourite," I sweetly said.

Hesitantly, he takes the snail and scoops some of it from out of the shell, and puts it in his mouth. Almost instantly, he spit it out. I start laughing my head off, causing more than a few people to look over at me.

"I love your laugh." Dxton smiles at me. I grinned and gesture to the snail. "Don't want another one?"

He shakes his head. "Hell no." Pushing the plate away, he takes a bite out of the cassoulet instead. "This is a lot better." He hums. "I do like this one."

"It's pretty alright." I couldn't help smiling. Hell, I couldn't stop. All day I smiled. At him. My mate. I didn't even think I could smile this much. He was kind, gentle, and very patient with me. He even laughed a few times.

He didn't enjoy our side dishes, but he did like the rest of the food, even said we should go back again one day. After we had lunch, we walked around the city for a while, enjoying each other's company and the views of the city. We found ourselves asking each other questions back and forth while we walked around.

"Which country is your favourite to visit?" Dxton said.

I don't even have to think on this question. "New Zealand. The nature is breath taking." I sigh. It was easier to get by there as well. Not many werewolves live in New Zealand since no packs are in the oceanic areas. Most werewolves prefer to be under the protection of an alpha.

"I can't say I've been," Dxton said.

"Well one day I might take you," I counter.

We continue our talking and walking for a while before Dxton says it's time to go back home.

The walk back is a calm one. We listen to the sounds of nature and ask our questions every now and then. When the pack starts to come into sight, I find myself smiling, happy to be back to my home.

But just before I get up to the porch, I got an idea. Quickly turning away, I shift straight into my lycan, shredding my clothes in the process. Taking Dxton by surprise, he quickly gets defensive thinking something was happening, but he sees my tail wagging and laughs softly.

He scratches behind my ear, but I push him slightly and yipped, before dashing into the forest. I heard a low laugh from behind me and not even two seconds later, he was chasing after us in his own lycan form. I tried to weave in and out of trees as much as I could to throw him off, but the male was onto us. He growled behind us, almost onto our tail.

Coming up to a rocky ledge, I shifted midair and rolled onto the grass below. Before getting back up, I shift. I hear Dxton's growls from up on the ledge. He didn't jump. I giggle to myself as my lycan and I quickly run towards some trees. Quickly shifting, I climb up and sat on one of the higher branches.

Luckily our male didn't keep us waiting long. With his nose to the ground and growling every now and then, he sniffed his way to the tree and then proceeded to look up. I waved my fingers teasingly. "Hello down there." Laughing to myself, I quickly get to my feet and jump into the next tree. He follows me as I jump from tree to tree, shifting midair. I land on the ground and book it in the opposite direction.

Determined to outrun him, I run as fast as I can, letting my lycan take momentary control. Feeling him flanking our left, we stop suddenly to nip at his legs, catching him off guard. We pin him down and nip at his sides, causing him to squirm. While he is distracted, we book it into the forest, but we look up at the sky feeling ourselves. We were loving the feeling of the run, the chase, being us. The stars look so pretty tonight. I look up as I run, eventually slowing down to a jog.

I stop to look up at the stars, momentarily distracted. They do look much prettier here than in America. Then I feel someone barrel into me, causing us to roll around. With his teeth to our neck, the bastard got us when we were busy looking at the stars. Trying and failing to wiggle out of his hold, I sigh and accept defeat. Shifting back, I look at Dxton and smile.

"Okay you win, now get off me." He shifts, chuckling, and lies down next to me. We lie next to each other and enjoyed the stars. I point out a few constellations, and so does he.

"Have you ever been in love before?" he asked me softly, eyes still trained to the sky.

I nod, smiling at the memories. "Yes." I giggled. "She was amazing. Her name was Alison. I met her in the city actually." I looked over to him, expecting to see him react negatively, but instead he smiles softly at me.

"What was she like?"

"Funny, and so clumsy. She use to trip over her own two feet so much. This one time, we were just walking and I looked away for one second, and next thing I know she is head first in the city centre's wishing fountain."

Dxton laughs softly. "She sounded interesting."

I nodded. "She was." Turning to face him, I rest my head in my hand. "How about you? Did you have past lovers?"

"Once, her name was Laura." He grabs my hand and starts to play with it. "She was a human. She didn't know about our kind, but hunters knew I wasn't human. I refused to leave the land White Crescent Moon is on now, which they didn't like. They killed her. I still didn't move."

That would explain a few things. His father and his ex-girlfriend was murdered by hunters. "I'm sorry Dxton."

He smiles, and rubs my palm. "It's in the past now." He gives my hand a small kiss. "Alright let's go back." Dxton gets up from the ground, and offers out his hand. We walked hand in hand towards my little house in the mountains.

I smile, the entire time, feeling happy, very, very happy. Today was amazing, being with Dxton, shifting into my lycan form, and actually being able to go for a proper run.

"Della."

My heart beats faster at my name. I stop my hand from reaching the handle and look up at him. "Yes?" I stepped into the house, closing the door behind him. He stares at me while I just smile at him. What's gotten into him?

He looks at me with the most love struck look I've ever seen, taking my breath away by the rawness of it.

"I love you."

CHAPTER THIRTY

DELLA

"I love you."

My heart skips a beat. He has said it before, but this time, this time is different. Feeling our mate bond swell in pride, I smile at him lovingly, pulling him into a hug. I dig my head into his chest, nuzzling it. My lycan sighs like the love sick fool she is. It's then that it hits me. I love him. I have for a while, I've just been too stubborn to admit it. I want to spend forever with this male. I want him in my life. I want him by my side. I can't imagine a future without him now.

"I love you too."

He stiffens, pulling me away from him softly. "Really?" he whispered.

I nod, tucking some of my white hair behind my ear. "Yes."

He smashes his lips to mine. I quickly kiss him back and wrap my arms around him. Dxton wraps one of his arms around my waist and uses his other hand to hold onto my neck. "Say it again" he said in between kisses.

"I love you."

"Again."

"I love you, Dxton."

He tenderly traces over my jaw in circles, drawing me closer to him. I kiss him harder, making him growl and bite my lip. Gasping, I bite his tongue that dared to enter my mouth. Dxton growls competitively. Our tongues fought for domination. Our lycans were close to the surface, wanting so badly to take control.

Dxton pushes me against the wall, his grip tightening. His touch burned in my skin, the mate bond aching but almost purring in happiness.

"It makes me so happy to hear you say that," Dxton said breathlessly, placing his forehead on mine. He looked at my eyes. Desire, pride, and happiness all swirled in his eyes hazily.

"Makes me happy saying it." I sighed softly, eyes traveling to his lips.

Dxton closes his eyes, almost pained. "We should stop. I won't be able to stop myself or my lycan soon," Dxton said softly with a sudden huskiness in his tone.

Looking up at him slyly, I push away, grabbing his hand and walking over to my bedroom door, swinging it open.

"Then don't."

And he doesn't, because he instantly lifted me up into his arms. His lips were on mine again. His hands went all over me, leaving not an inch of skin untouched. He then laid me onto the bed. Our mate bond swirls happily in our mind. Tugging on our bonds, he lets out another moan, causing me to smirk at him sensually.

Grabbing his neck, I force him closer to me, licking all the way up from the base of his neck to the lobe of his ear. I bit and tugged at his ear. "Are you just going to lie there?" I whispered.

Unlocking something feral in him, he starts growling lowly. "Oh you want me to do something?" He starts to travel his fingers downwards. "What do you want?" he whispers, causing me to shiver.

"I want you."

He chuckles and does as I wish. For hours he does my wishes. His lips were ruthlessly punishing mine, attacking and sucking at everything. His hands were constantly finding skin to tease.

His fangs start to grow, as we move together. As we reach our end his mouth finds its way to my neck, sucking at the skin. His fangs grazed it. "Say it again," he breathed out. "Tell me again."

My own fangs started to ache. "I love you." With a pained moan, his teeth bit down onto my skin, and just as I reach my climax, I bit down hard onto his neck, claiming him as mine forever, and me his.

Sparks fly, and memories flash before my eyes. I could see him as a child playing with his father's lycan, him being a good big brother to Lucia, and I saw his father's death. I can feel the pain he felt the day he found him, and the sadness over killing his mother. His loneliness in his pack as the only lycan, until he met Dominic. And then the day he met me. How he wanted nothing more than to claim me as his own, right then and there. His fear over me being a human, and the agony he felt turning me away time and time again.

I could see his entire life. And I can feel all of his emotions, his happiness, his tiredness, and his love for his pack, and for me.

"Mine," I whisper.

"Yours," he whispers back.

Exhausted, we both smiled at each other. "Sleep," Dxton whispers, pulling me close to him.

And I do just that.

CHAPTER THIRTY-ONE

DELLA

I wake up to the feeling of someone running a finger up and down my back, causing goosebumps to cover my skin. "Morning," I whisper out, turning over to face the goosebumps maker. Dxton smiles and kisses my forehead.

Tucking some hair behind my ear, he kisses my cheek. "How did you sleep?"

"Good," I whisper as he kisses my other cheek.

"Oh that's good" he whispers, kissing my neck, then trailing down to my fresh new mark. Kissing it softly, I feel my arousal and squirmed under his gaze and touch. Laughing at my reaction, he then proceeds to flip me under him, where he continues to kiss and lick at my new mark. I moan softly. Wrapping my arms around him, I pull him closer.

When me phone rang, I tried to grab it off the bedside table, but Dxton hits my hand away. "Leave it." He growls out.

"It could be important." Sighing, he moves away so that I can grab the phone., "Hello?" I said cheerfully. Meanwhile, Dxton frowns at the intrusion of our moment.

"Rogues have been seen approaching the pack, they are being led by a lycan."

Dxton, having heard what Jade said, immediately gets up to put on some clothes he brought yesterday while we were out. I followed suit. "We are on our way." I quickly call Florence.

"Yes, Alpha?"

"I need you and the witches to meet me at my house," I quickly hung up, not letting her say much and put some clothes on.

Of course he is coming, now when we weren't at the pack. Did he know we weren't there? I look to Dxton who is already looking at me grimly. He's eyes were dark gold. He looks very pissed. He looks like he is about to kill the nearest living thing next to him.

Florence and the witches burst into the house. "Florence, we need to leave now. Sorry for the rudeness, but we need to take the witches if that's fine."

"Yes of course, call when you have killed the bastard," she said, bowing then turning to the witches. "Return the moment you are in danger. Stay safe all of you."

I turn to Daphne. "Are you ready?"

She looks to Jaclyn who nods. "Yes, we have what we need."

Daphne and Jaclyn approach Dxton and I, holding a wand each. "Where do you want to land?"

"Same spot you picked us up at," Dxton said through gritted teeth.

Daphne nods and with a flick of her hand, she opened a purple and blue swirling vortex—a portal. "Get in now, if a witch is nearby they could trace us back to here."

Stepping through the portal and arrived into our meeting room in the pack house. "Okay, I'll take the witches to the bunker to seal it shut and I'll have Jade with them, so that they can put a barrier around the pack without anyone bothering them."

Dxton nods. "Good plan. I'll take the warriors to the clearing just outside of the pack, hopefully I can buy you enough time to get the barrier up. Dom already has the warriors together out the front." I grab his hand and quickly run down the stairs, Daphne, and Jaclyn hot on my tail.

Seeing Dominic waiting for us out the front, I quickly walk up to him. "Is everyone in the bunker?" Dominic nods.

"I evacuated them just before you got here." Good, that's one less thing to worry about. I need the seals and charms set and the barrier, now.

I look over the witches. "You two will be with me and Jade." They both nod.

"Oh." Daphne quickly digs through her bag. "I can show you a spell you can write on everyone's arm, it'll help you blend in. You'll smell like your surroundings instead of a wolf."

"Okay do you have a pen?" I asked quickly.

Jaclyn digs around in her bag and pulls out a black marker. "Okay, this is how you do it." Daphne drew a symbol on my left forearm. I've seen this before in one of the books Jaclyn has back in France. She called it a sigil.

As Daphne draws it on my arm, I motioned for Dominic to come pay attention. "I need you to make sure that every warrior has this drawn on their arm." He pulls out his phone and takes a quick photo of mine, and starts going around drawing it on people's arms.

Dxton walks over to me and looks at me seriously. "Once everyone is inside and safe, get to the meeting room straight away. We can face them head on together. Don't make a move on the enemy without me Della, we work as a team." I nod my head in agreement and get ready to leave but Dxton grabs my arm tightly. "I mean it Della, I don't want you fighting without me. If I can't see you, I can't protect you."

We don't have time for this. I sigh softly, I appreciate the concern, I really do, but he still hasn't changed. He still views me as something that needs protecting. I'm the only one who can beat the lycan. If he really is my brother, only I can match his strength.

"For you I will, but remember I'm the one who will be protecting you," I said with a small smile.

Dxton growls at my stubbornness. "Just be safe." He kisses my forehead, holding me tightly.

"You too," I whispered. He is about to leave when I quickly stop him. "Wait." I grab his hand. "I know this is bad timing, but I want to join your pack."

Stunned, he grabs both of my hands. "Now?" I nod. "But we would need to plan a ceremony. It's traditional." He rambles on. I shake my head and grab his face softly.

"Why not?" I look over the pack. "When has anything we've done been traditional so far? Besides, a ceremony is an opportunity for them to attack us." I smile softly. "I'm ready Dxton, I want to be your luna."

"Really?" he said. I nod, grinning.

"This is a life bond. You won't be able to back down this time, not until we hand over the reins to our children," he quickly stutters out with a red face. Placing my hands back into his, I smile genuinely, placing a kiss onto his forehead. I lean against it and nod.

"I'm ready Dxton."

He peppers kisses over my face, earning a giggle from me. He grins the biggest grin he can that I have grown to dearly love.

"Respond after me."

Slicing my palm, I place mine in his free hand palm up. He then sliced his own palm then placed it on top of mine. "Do you, Della Rosai, promise to protect White Crescent Moon pack as our luna, our alpha and as my equal?"

"I, Della Rosai, promise to protect White Crescent Moon as your luna, alpha and equal." I feel rock candy popping away in my mind softly, eventually getting louder and louder.

"I, Alpha Dxton Bosque, pronounce you, Luna Della Rosai of White Crescent Moon."

"Actually it's Luna Della Rosai-Bosque." I wink, with a small grimace at the pressure in my mind. Hundreds of voices flooded my mind. Hundreds of thoughts. It's been so long since I had a mind link. Imagining a barrier in my mind, I place it between my thoughts and the pack's, clearing their thoughts from my head. I sighed as I feel the pressure leaving.

Dxton grins at me. "I love you."

I place my forehead back onto his. "And I love you," I whisper back. The pack went crazy, some congratulating me through the bond. I quickly put up a barrier in my mind to block them out.

I stepped away from him and turned to the witches as I start to walk over to find Jade. I look over my shoulder to Dxton and winked. "Be safe."

I see Jade already outside shifted, her jaw to the ground. She yips, wagging her tail. *"Welcome Luna, I see you guys finally mated."* I scratched behind her ear.

"Thank you." I mind linked back, leaning down to her level. *"I don't want you fighting. You need to stay safe for Maddy, so I need you to help the witches. The other wolves aren't going to be too accepting of them, don't let them kill them."* She growls lowly in understanding. I look to see the witches ready. "Let's go."

Shifting in my lycan, I kneel down so that the witches can get on my back. I ran towards the bunkers with Jade close to my flanks. I can't help but notice how much smaller her wolf form is to mine, she's so tiny.

Stopping at the bunker's entrance, I shift back into a human. "Will you be able to do the barrier inside the bunkers?"

Jaclyn starts chanting, shifting her fingers in odd angles. Daphne sighs. "We will handle it Della, don't worry get back to Dxton." She grabs my face gently and kisses my forehead. "And please be safe." Daphne's face reflected so many emotions at the moment. It was too much. She was worried that much was clear, she's like my aunty after all. Family.

"I will, you stay safe too." I kiss her check back and turn to Jade "Make sure everyone has the sigil on their forearm. It's also what makes us immune to the witches's barrier and what protects us from their charms."

She shifts. "Got it." I check her forearm to see she already has one. "Be safe, and keep my mate safe too please."

I gave her a small hug. "Of course." Jade shifts back into her wolf, and takes guard over the witches as they start putting hexes on the bunker entry.

'I'm on my way." I linked Dxton as I shift into my lycan. He replies back not too soon after.

"Okay, see you soon."

With everyone safely in the bunker and Dxton waiting with our warriors, I quickly ran towards the clearing. But what I wasn't expecting were the hundreds of warriors all waiting. Everyone stops and stares as I approach the group, whispering amongst themselves. Dxton must have called in reinforcements when I wasn't paying attention.

"Della!" I turn to my left to see Vanessa waving besides Dxton. Shifting, I quickly engulfed her in a bear hug. Coming to my senses, I quickly push her away.

"What are you doing here? What were you thinking? This is the feeling I've been having! You can't be here!" I grab her shoulders and start shaking her frantically. "I told you to run, not join the fight!"

"Della, I'm not like you. I don't run from my problems." Ouch. This bitch. "Nice mark," she said, smirking.

"Do not change the subject," I hissed.

She rolled her eyes, sighing. I look behind me to see a faint glow starting to surround the pack. The barrier. *'How is everything going?"* I mind link Jade.

"They are finished with the charms. The barrier is almost done."

"Della, this is Alpha Gavin, and Luna Malia Naught. They helped bring down some of the rogue camps," Dxton said. I shake their hands. They are both of a native American decent. Their names ring a bell. If I'm correct, their pack is in Idaho. They are a very brutal pack, but they alpha it very well.

"Pleasure to meet you, female lycan." They both bow their heads. I bow in return.

"You obviously already know Alpha Moore." I nod and turn to the star struck male.

"Who would have thought, you were under my nose this whole time."

I can't help but smirk. "Crafty little trick, isn't it?" I said, pulling my lycan all the way in to appear human.

He nods, flabbergasted. "Very crafty."

"And this is Alpha Donovan Knight." Dxton motions to a very young male. *Why is this teenager on my battle field*, I wanted to ask.

"Luna." Donovan bows his head, not a trace of malice, but not a trace of any emotion coming from him at all. He may as well be the tin man from the Wizard of Oz. This male needs a heart, because it is very obvious his has been taken.

"I don't care how strong this pup is, why is he here?" I mind link Dxton.

Knowing I'm mind linking about him, Donovan looks me dead in the eye. "This operation is being led by the Mortem. It said so in your letters. They are a supernatural terrorist group and they killed my parents. I want answers from this lycan. I am staying here, whether you like it or not. I don't care if you're a rare powerful species. I want answers."

Not liking his attitude, I let my lycan come forward all the way, causing him to stumble back slightly. "You need to learn some respect. I will allow you to stay but only because I know what it feels like to lose your parents young. Next time I see you, your manners better have improved pup." I let my lycan snarl at him, she lets herself be known to everyone around us. She does not like being belittled, especially by a pup. Causing a whimper to escape his lips, he falls to the ground. A few of the wolves around us also stagger to the ground.

I stop when I see Vanessa fall to the ground from the intensity of my lycan's aura, drawing her in to just be a noticeable hum. Everyone relaxes around me.

"He's just hurt Della," Dxton said softly.

"I know, but he needs to hear it. It's what I wish someone had said to me. If you let your grief get the better of you, you're going to find yourself very lonely." I said softly, leaning down to Donovan's level on the ground. "I admire your will to find answers, but you need to respect that other people have it rough too. You might be hurting, but don't ever take that out on someone else. One day it could get you killed. Am I understood?"

He nods softly. "Yes Luna." I helped him up. I might have just wasted time scolding him, but I don't want to deal with him being a pain in the arse. Besides, this is his chance to gain allies, and where he is right now, he isn't gaining anyone.

"Does everyone have the sigil on their arm?" I asked all of the alphas.

Alpha Naught nods. "That Beta of yours made sure of it." He showed his forearm, where the sigil is.

"Good, whatever you do make sure it doesn't rub off. That's your only way back into the pack's barrier and the only way for all of the charms to not be set off." I look out into the field. They should be here soon. "It will also help mask your smell." I look around. "Where is the beta?" I grabbed on to Dxton's hand.

"Jade needed help, some rogues are trying to get into the bunker, he's dealing with it."

We stand at the front of the four packs. "Let's kill a lycan."

CHAPTER THIRTY-TWO

DELLA

"Alpha, Luna, they have crossed onto our border"

I look over to Dxton, who is already looking to me. "Everyone get into position, but remember the lycan is mine," I said. Everyone except for our pack go off into their position. Our main goal is to ambush. If everyone can get the rogues under control, then I can deal with Wolfe.

I see them, rows and rows of rogues, all filling the air with a toxic stench. You can smell their minds rotting. Without a proper pack, they will wither away until they become mindless beasts. Some have already become one based on how many are shifted and attacking their own. A disgustingly sad sight.

At the head of the army is Wolfe. He stops a few yards ahead of us, already shifted

"Why does he look like that?" I heard a wolf to my left ask.

His lycan form resembles that of the old folklore lycan shifters. The one where they are on their hind legs, standing like a man. It's the version of the werewolf that so many thought to be what we actually looked like for so many years. A myth that came from truth.

"Lycans can take another form," I said loud enough for anyone to hear. "We call it lusus naturae, when our lycans and human sides don't coexist, when we have reached a stage of insanity. Much like a rogue."

Shifting, he stands quite tall, possibly taller than Dxton. His hair was a dark shade of black. He looks lanky for a lycan, and even worse he is twitching like mad. This lycan isn't sane. He is going to be unpredictable to fight. Standing to his left is the wolf I saw at the compound when I saved the pack and Dxton. I think he said his name was Ezra.

"Hello, Sister."

His voice deep and velvety, echoing across the open space. His eyes are crazed with murderous intent. He has scars on his neck from claw scratches. Stressful self-harm from the looks of it. He hasn't looked after himself, that much is plain to see, but what shakes me to my core is the fact that he looks like a splitting image of Franz. The only difference is that he has my mother's eyes. My eyes.

"Who are you?" Dxton calls out. Wolfe snarls at Dxton.

"I don't wish to speak with you!" He looks ready to shift and attack Dxton.

I squeezed Dxton's hand then let go. "What is your name?"

"Afron. Afron Wolfe."

"Afron . . . so we finally meet." I cross my arms and let my lycan come forward. She snarls, snapping her jaws at the male. Afron remains quiet. He looks me over. I use this as an opportunity. "What do you want?"

Afron smirks when he meets my eyes, but then scratches at his neck which tells me that he isn't as calm as he is letting on. He is borderline about to shift. "It's because of you, I never got to meet my mother and because of you, my father is dead. I will avenge them."

What? Because of me? I wish I had been the one to kill him. Franz died by Ivan's hand, but it was because of Franz that my—our mother—is dead. Who has been brainwashing him? Has Dunkler been more active than I thought?

"Afron, where have you been this whole time?" I asked. He pauses, starstruck. He scratches at his neck. "Have you been in Dunkler Wolf pack this whole time? Are you trying to bring Franz back to life?"

Ezra whispers something into his ear, causing Afron to look at me deadly, his eyes changing to gold. "You are not worthy to speak his name." He shakes his head in dismay. "You might have this pack fooled but you can't fool me. You are the evil in this world, and I will kill you. I will make my parents proud, and end the one that has caused so much suffering."

I look away from him. Worthy? Speaking his name is nothing but venom in my mouth. I tightened my folded arms. Annoyed, I look back at him. This is childish. "Afron, you've been brainwashed by Dunkler. Franz was not a good man. You are the product of rape, of all of his bad deeds. He was not a man worthy of your revenge." I put my hand out to him. "I'll show you." Ezra whispers into his ear. "I'll show you what Franz has done and I'll help you."

He looks at my hand, confusion written on his face. Then he shook his head. He looks at me with determination. "No, I've been looking for you for years. I know how you work. I will not let you get to me. I will not let you get into my head."

I sigh softly and lower my hand. "If you know me as well as you say, then you know you're not going to leave victorious."

"Jade how is the barrier coming along?"
"Done Luna, we are onto phase two."

He scoffs, hands scratching at his neck. "Stop acting as if you're the hero or the victim. Your father brainwashed my mother into thinking they were mates. When she had me, he killed her for wanting to be with her true mate."

What else has he been told? What lies has the leftover wolves of Dunkler been feeding him? Has he really lived his whole life just to fulfil a dream that isn't even real?

"That's not true! Alvery Fabre and George Rosai were mates. Franz kidnapped my mother and raped her. They weren't mates. You talk of being brainwashed, but it's you that's the one brainwashed." My wolf starts to growl lowly at the false claims being thrown at us. "Franz was not a hero, Afron. He tortured people, murdered families, raped innocent girls. If you call that a hero, then you are as twisted as him."

He looks at me angrily, ready to murder me and everyone else that dares to go near him. "Liar!" He screams. He was shaking, both hands scratching at his neck.

I look at him desperately. He's in turmoil, I want to try and help him. He is my family whether I like it or not. "No Afron . . . Please just let me help you. I don't want to kill you. We might have different fathers but we had the same mother. I can help you see. Please, just let me." I stepped forward slightly.

"No, I know the truth." He looks up, hands still at his neck. "I will avenge the ones you took from me." He looks back at me threateningly, his eyes dark and lycan bloodthirsty. "I will kill you, and everyone you love." He shifts into his lusus naturae lycan.

You leave me with no choice. If you won't let me help you, I will have to kill you. Even if we aren't close by any means, I can't help but feel a pang at the thought of killing another blood relative. I look over to the tree line on either side of Afron's army.

"Now."

On cue, Alpha Moore's pack comes charging forward from the left and Alpha Naught's pack from the right. Surrounding the rogues, Dxton and our pack charge in from the front. Staying where I am, I turn around and walk away moving towards my charging pack. *"Jade is phase two done?"*

"Almost," she said rather breathlessly.

"Almost needs to be now, I'm on my way," I said quickly as I moved.

* * *

Just as I had hoped, Afron followed me into a clearing, hidden away from everyone else. If I'm going to fight him, I don't want any of his rogues getting in the way.

I turned to him. "Last chance. We can still work this out, all you have to do is surrender."

"I have waited too long to kill you, Della Rosai. My parents can sleep peacefully when your line is gone, and so can I. I will not surrender to you." He sighs in relief at the very thought of my death, scratching at his neck slightly.

"If I have to, I will kill you Afron, don't let it come to that." I warned, flashing my fangs.

He growls lowly, flashing his own fangs. "Don't go threatening me here, you're the one surrounded." He puts his arms out to a few of the rogue pack that followed us here.

They all roared in agreement, some throwing profanities at me, some yelling for us to fight. They get louder and louder, to the point I get annoyed. I let out a loud roar, silencing everyone, bringing all the rogues to their feet. I let my lycan come all the way out, effectively bringing out the wolves's flight sense and they quickly leave us alone.

I turn to Afron angrily. "This is between you and me, brother. Don't bring your rogues into this." I spit. I start to circle around Afron looking for a weak spot. He makes the first move, by charging at me head on in his shifted form. I step aside and grab Afron by the tuff of his neck then threw him straight into a tree.

"I need that spell Jade!"

"Sorry, it's almost done, we're just to your left, roughly a yard away in the trees."

"Hurry up!"

Afron gets up and bolts at me again, but this time pounces around me like a boxer in a ring. He roars out.

He punched me square in the face, breaking my jaw. Momentarily stunned, he kicks me. I landed a few metres away from him. Shaking it off, I run towards him and shift midair, letting my lycan have more control over the situation. She growls out in anger, snarling at Afron. We jump onto his back then sank my teeth into the back of his neck. He growls out and tries to swipe us away. We don't let go until we hear the bones in his neck snapping. Howling out in pain, he stumbles. We quickly lock onto one of his hind legs, bringing him down, snapping it. Afron tries to swipe at our face with his free leg, but I quickly moved before he could, and locked onto his other leg. We've effectively snapped both of them.

I hear the snap of his neck healing. Shifting back midair, I wrap my legs around his neck and quickly brought him down. I squeeze tighter and tighter, effectively cutting off his breathing. He is about to pass out when he manages to find enough strength to stand up on his knees despite his broken legs. Still in my choke hold, he digs his claws into both sides of my hips. Screaming, I let go and kick him away.

He was coughing and wheezing while I breathe in as evenly as possible, waiting for it to heal over. I feel a stinging and I could smell something metallic. I didn't notice before, but the scratches on my skin aren't healing as quickly. His claws are all laced with silver. "Are you ready to talk about this?" He growls in response. "Be that that way." I snarl just as Afron's about to charge back at me.

A voice soft as an angel filled the space around us. "Della." Momentarily taken off guard, Afron looks up, completely stunned.

"Mother?"

CHAPTER THIRTY-THREE

Della

There standing in the field is my mum. She's smiling at the both of us, her white hair flowing in the wind. I feel myself tearing up slightly. I haven't seen her since she died, when I watched her burn at her funeral.

"Mother?" I whispered. I know it isn't her. This is phase two.

Afron quickly rushes over to her, but he phases through her, like she's a ghost. "What, what's happening?"

"It's a memory." On cue, six-year-old me rushes towards her, giggling hysterically as she picked me up. "My memories." I look over to Afron. "If I can't persuade you, I'll show you the truth."

He looks pained. "That's her?"

I nod. "She was beautiful, wasn't she?" I said, looking at the projection. She's playing with me at the beach, and we're building a sandcastle. It's one of my better memories. Another projection appears next to it. This one is of mum going over battle strategies on how to take down Franz. She's exhausted. Another one appears but it's one that makes me look away. Franz appears with a malicious smile plastered on his face as he rapes fifteen-year-old me. Chained to a bed, he ruthlessly doesn't stop despite my continuous screams and pleas for it to end. He kept going, harder, faster until he came. Then he would come back and do it all over again within the hour. The next projection to appear is one where he rapes my mother. Franz had a sick, twisted mind. He loved having me watch everything he did to her. And then have her watch whatever he did to me. He was forcing me to watch, threatening to kill her, harm her. He would get me to help him torture her with the same threats. I learned he wasn't bluffing when he ripped her ear off, and had me rip one of her eyes out.

    The last one is also a memory I turned away from. I just feel sick just seeing everything else, but this one makes me vomit. Her suicide. She ripped out her own heart in front of her daughter and her mate. She said she was sorry.

    I killed my mother, and my father. If I hadn't gotten kidnapped, she wouldn't have been taken by Franz. She wouldn't have lost her mind. She wouldn't have killed herself. I wouldn't have had to kill my father from the loss. Afron has every right to kill me, but he needs to know the truth behind Franz.

    We are surrounded by projections of my memories. I wiped my mouth. "I'm telling the truth," I whispered hoarsely. "He wasn't a good man."

    "No, no this is just a trick!" He scratches at his neck painfully, drawing blood. "You're lying to me." He looks over at the sounds of my agony. "You have to be," he whispers.

    "She is!" Ezra appears out of the forest line. "It's all a cheap trick to get you to be her next slave. So she can get to your heart and rip it out." He stands next to Afron, smirking at me, as he puts a "comforting hand" on Afron. "She's trying to get into your head."

    I point to the projection of Franz laughing over my defeated body, as he pulls his pants up, after continuously raping me. "Does that look like something I would lie about? Do you really think I would lie about something so serious, something so devastating?" I shake my head, feeling tears leave my eyes, as I hear the sounds of the projection, of another rape. "Rape isn't a joke." I look at Afron pleadingly. "Please, I just want to help you."

Afron opens and closes his mouth. "Listen to my heart," I said placing my hand there. "You tell me if I've been lying"

"She's just trying to get into your head Alpha," Ezra said, getting in Afron's face. "Are you really going to trust a girl you've just met over me? I've been by your side my whole life! Kill her Alpha! Avenge your parents!"

"Do what you want," I said softly, seeing him get overwhelmed by Ezra's yelling, as his scratching gets worse.

"KILL HER!"

Afron slowly starts walking towards me. "It doesn't have to end this way! He was a monster! It's his fault so many wolves have lost their lives, and how so many have turn to his light. He believed that only lycans can stand victorious, only lycans could live on in this new world. His influence caused mayhem. His followers have been causing wars in human society for years. They had hoped it would spark the humans to kill each other off so that it would make one less species for them to wipe out."

Afron looks at me hesitantly, and turns to look at the projection of our mother. "Franz Wolfe was not a good man, Afron. You can still walk away. You can still walk away from him, we could be a family." His face drops slowly, contemplating my proposal.

"No!" Ezra gets in Afron's face, punching it. "You are the son of the all mighty Franz Wolfe. My family didn't dedicate their lives to your father so you could turn around and decide not to fulfil your purpose! You get your ass over there and you kill her! Make your father proud!" Ezra goes to punch him but I quickly grab his hand, snapping it. He screams out and grabs his hand.

"He is wrong!" Why can't he see that? Even after seeing my memories, he still wants to believe that Franz was good. Afron ignores me. He looks at Ezra's broken hand, and something inside of him snaps. His eyes turn back to their diluted gold. "No."

"Ezra's right, I refuse to believe you. You're using magic to get me to see what you want." He shakes his head and gets into a fighting stance. "No. No, I refuse to trust you." He starts sobbing. "I can't trust you." He charges at me.

Shifting in my lycan, I sigh. *"We have to,"* she whispers to me softly, hoping it makes the blow to kill him easier.

"I know, but a part of me had hoped he would see the truth."

This is for the best, it would be better and easier on Afron to put him out of his misery. At least this way, he can find out the truth through mother with the moon goddess.

"You leave me no choice." Pinning him down, I glaze my teeth along his throat, clamping them down, I tighten my hold with the intent to kill.

"WAIT!"

Because of the distraction, Afron threw me to the ground with a painful crack. Momentarily winded, Afron quickly slashed the side of my head causing me to let out a cry.

"Stop!" Dom quickly runs towards us.

"Della!" Dxton mind links me. I look over to Dxton who puts his hand through my fur. He gently pulls me back from Afron and gestures for me to look. Dom is on his knees frantically asking if he is okay. Afron stares on disgusted and flabbergasted, shifting his weight away from Dom.

No way . . . they're . . . they're . . .

"Mates."

I look straight up to the faint moon. You fucking bitch. You couldn't have made this easy for me, made it so that he had a quick painless death so that he could live in peace, and not be in pain. But no you had to make them mates. Give him the confusion of being gay, give him the pain of living amongst his enemies.

We haven't solved this war, just worsened it. Him being mates mean that they are either going to both live here or move away. And I can tell you right now if Afron stays here that's going to cause nothing but pain, confusion, and a whole lot of drama

Shifting back, I lightly move Dxton's hand away. "Fuck you," I seethed up to the moon. I don't care if that will take me to hell. I'd rather talk to Satan than go to her when I die.

A low growl fills the field. I look over to see Dxton fuming and grabs my head where Afron swiped at me. "Are you okay?" He was in panic and anger.

A warrior rushes over and passes Dxton a shirt for me. He covers me quickly before his eyes dart back and forth between my face and the cut. He grabs my face again, this time more softly.

"Shit Della, that's going to scar," he said, looking at the wound carefully. That's the last of my issues right now.

"What are we going to do?" I asked quietly. Dxton sighs. He buries his head in my neck.

"I don't know, but we will figure it out."

Some of the guards surrounded Afron, Dom in the middle fuming and panicking at the same time. So many emotions for a very emotionless person. Mates. They're mates. I can't help but to look up at the sky and send the goddess a thousand uncensored words. What are you doing?

I turned to Alex. "Take him to the cells." He nods, helping a few guards pick him up, along with a few others. Dominic tailed after them.

Oh Dom, I'm so sorry.

"Luna Bosque."

Alpha Donovan approaches me. "Yes?" He nods with a bow.

"I think you might want to see this." He pulls out a phone. "I placed trackers on a few rogues. They are running back to the rogue camps being rumoured in Idaho. I think this will suffice as the proof you need to get into the packs. I have also sent some of my pack members to follow them."

I take the phone to see about twenty blinking red dots. "Thank you Donovan."

He nods. "I thought it would be a good start towards my apology for the way I behaved." He bows his head. "I am sorry, I let my grief get the better of me, you were right."

"Well it's a very good start." I said softly. "I'm glad what I said sunk in. I know it was harsh, and I apologise for doing that in front of so many people. But I know it's something I needed to be told a very long time ago."

"Thank you for your wisdom," he said before he walked away.

Dxton approaches me and softly places a blanket around my naked body. "What did the pup want?"

I hand him the tracker. "Proof."

The trackers proved to be more than helpful. With the weeks to come, Dxton and the neighbouring alphas would use it to take down rogue camps around the states. But we knew there were still plenty more around the world. I just hope that Dominic can get through to Afron. If he proves to be helpful, hopefully he can tell me more about the Mortem that he mentioned too.

Hopefully the hardest part has happened. Hopefully I can have the peaceful life I've always wanted. Hopefully.

CHAPTER THIRTY-FOUR

DELLA

I wiped my forehead in an aggravated manner. Dxton was trying to speak to Afron, after so many failed attempts. He refused to talk to anyone, especially Dominic, which was breaking his poor heart. It's not going to be easy for them. It's going to take a long time to get him on his feet. Years even. But Rome wasn't built in a day. I'll help anyway I can, but if I sense he is a danger to anyone I'll do what I need to do, even if he is Dominic's mate.

"Della?" I look up from the couch to see Daphne and Jaclyn walk in.

I waved. "Hey, what's up?" I asked, fanning my face a little. Man, it's hot in here, I'll have to open a window, or put the aircon on.

"We are going to head off, we've added a few features for extra protection to the pack," Jalyn said.

I wipe my forehead and nod. "Thank you so much, for everything, you two are life savers." I get up and head into the kitchen. "I made these for you two actually, as a thank you." I pull out a strawberry shortcake roll, and some blueberry madeleines.

"Oh Della those look amazing." Daphne gushes. "I can't wait to have some."

"Make sure Florence gets some too of course."

"Oh yes of course," Jaclyn said with a wink. "If there is some leftover." I rolled my eyes.

Daphne claps her hands together. "So," she said as she puts the food in a tote bag.

"I have deactivated the charms, oh and . . ." She goes through her bag. "I've set up the barrier so that it's a permanent thing, but if you want to deactivate it, break this talisman," Daphne said, handing me a piece of paper from her bag. *Break the talisman, got it.*

I feel my heart start beating a tad bit faster and my body growing a little hotter.

"Are . . . are you okay Della?" Jaclyn said, eyeing me softly. "You look very flushed."

I wave her off. "It's probably nothing." I wave my hand in front of my face. It's very hot.

"Honey, it's not hot," Daphne said, putting her hand to my forehead. She immediately hisses and brings it back as far away from me as possible. "Shit Della, you are like really burning up." She shows me the burn mark on her hand.

Then it hits me. "Fuck. I'm on heat."

Daphne and Jaclyn formed an O with their mouths. "She really is growing up." Jaclyn gushes. "What do we do?"

I wave them off. "It's all good. I'm just going to run an ice bath. I'll let Dxton know."

They nod. "Okay we will get out of your hair," Daphne said. I mumble a thank you, as Jaclyn blows me a kiss.

"Bye sweetie, visit us soon!" Daphne said as a light beams onto them, Jaclyn throws in a quick, "Toodles."

Quickly running up to Dxton's—our—room, I strip my clothes off and run the cold water. Feeling overheated and humid, I get straight under the running water, causing a sigh to escape my lips.

"Dxton."

Soon the cold water wasn't enough. It's not cold enough. I need something else. Someone else.

"Dxton!"

"Yes Della? Is everything ok?"

"No, I'm in heat! I need you to come home now!" He doesn't say anything, but I can feel our bond shifting excitingly. Please hurry.

I feel my heart beat picking up. I turned the water off. I can see steam coming off my body, with the water now boiling. I was about to get out when I hear the front door being slammed open. Loud footsteps ran up the stairs. "Dxton?" I called out just as he burst through the bathroom door, his eyes very dark.

"You smell amazing!" He breathes out in a huff, quickly grabbing my back, causing instant relief. I moan at the brief relief, he grabs under my legs and picks me up outta the tub.

"You smell really, really good," he said, digging his face in my neck.

"That's nice" I huff out, meanwhile I'm feeling like I'm on fire, "I feel like shit right now, it hurts" I grit out. My below region is aching so painfully I want to scream. I wish it was snowing right now so I could lay in it.

Putting me on the bed, he smirks. "What do you want me to do?" His fingers trailed up my leg. I whimpered when it "misses" my aching core. "What do you want?" He trailed his other hand up. Growing impatient, I grabbed his hand and put it where I want it.

"What part of 'I'm in pain' aren't you getting?" I growl out.

"Tsk. You need to learn some patience and manners, my love."

I glared up at him. "You try being internally on fire and then we will see who's talking". I snapped. He laughs softly, but obliges to all of my wishes.

My heat lasted a week, and what a hellish week it was.

On the last day, I woke up, and when I don't feel like I'm burning up, I sigh happily. Doesn't matter if the activities were fun, that was still hell. I can't believe I'm going to be going through that for the rest of my life now, once a year at least.

"How are you feeling?" Dxton asked, looking down at me, head resting on his propped up arm. I hum and move away from him as a response. He laughs. "Aw don't be like that." He pulls me into his chest, and starts tickling my sides. I scream out and try to wiggle away but he just laughs and keeps me glued to his side. "As much as I am enjoying this, I have to go," Dxton said softly, still giggling.

"Go where?" I asked, taken back by his sudden news. Turning around to face him, I find myself pouting.

"I'm in charge of the hunt for the rogue camps." He brushes a piece of hair away from my eyes. "Are you going to be okay on your own?" He whispers softly.

I grab his hand, bringing it to my lips. "I've done it before." I mused. "How long is it going to take?" I don't want him to leave, it feels like we haven't had a proper moment alone in a long time. I still have so much to know about him, so much to learn.

"Two weeks tops." He looks over to the time on his bedside table. "I guess I should start packing. Good thing your heat came now and not while I has gone."

"Yeah," I mumbled. He smiles softly and kisses my cheek. "Two weeks isn't very long. I'll be back before you know it. You'll probably end up kicking me out of the house." He attempts to joke. He gets up and packs his bags, while I stay in bed watching him. I don't want him to go.

"I put it off a week, I gotta go at some point, Dee." Did he just call me Dee? "Come on, walk me to the door?" Nodding slowly and wrapped in the blanket, I follow him to the front door.

"Do you have to go?"

He nods, kissing my forehead, left then right cheek, and then my nose.

I start having this gut feeling that he shouldn't go because something was about to happen. "Be careful," I said as he brings me in for a hug. He nods and kisses my forehead.

"You too, I'll be back soon."

I watch him shift into his lycan and run off into the forest. I didn't go back inside until I couldn't see him anymore. I felt my hand rest onto my stomach. I can't shake the feeling. Either I'm being paranoid or something is about to happen. I look down to my stomach. Something did happen.

CHAPTER THIRTY-FIVE

DELLA

"Luna?"

He is going to kill himself before we even get a chance to ask our questions. *"He needs us."*

"He needs professional help," I counter to my lycan softly.

"We are all he has, he isn't going to accept Dominic for a long time."

"I don't see how he is our responsibility. Brother or not he tried to kill us."

"You know he isn't mentally stable Della, besides it's not his fault how he was raised, he was just a pawn in Franz's game." She comes forward slightly to meet Afron's lycan who cowers away instantly. *"He doesn't know any better."*

I place a hand on my stomach softly. *"I think we have better issues at the moment."*

It's been three weeks since Afron's attack, and during those weeks, I ended up going into heat. It was to be expected since we had been marked, but I knew the moment the heat ended, we were pregnant. It was just a gut feeling, but one test later, it was true. I'm pregnant.

"Luna?"

"I have his lycan under control, the human side is up to you to deal with." My lycan looks on longingly to our brother. His lycan and

human sides are at odds. You could tell the moment we meet him that they weren't in sync. A naturally born lusus naturae.

"*Leaving the hardest part to me, I see.*" Of course she decides to go back to her part of our mind.

"Della?"

"Hmm?" I turn to Alex, an eyebrow raised. "Yes? How long have you been there?" He looks at me frustratingly. "When did you start calling me Della?" He has always been refusing, despite all we've been through. And *finally*. Titles are still not something I'm used to.

Alex's facepalms himself, maybe a little too hard if you ask me, because he instantly made his face red with his hand outlining it. What a dumbass. "Was that really necessary?" I said.

He looks at me with his eyes twitching slightly. "Yes! I've been calling your name for five minutes now!" I roll my eyes at his theatrics, turning my attention back to Afron. He is currently in a full body harness, screaming, struggling, and desperately to escape while the doctors all surround him trying to keep the lycan still for a dose of medication.

Dom. He is trying to help the doctors keep him still, but his company only seems to be causing Afron more discomfort. However, he refuses to leave him. The mate bond would be keeping him attached to him. It's going to kill them both at this rate. Afron is going to stop at nothing to kill me. I can't help but not blame him. I might not like him, but a small part of me wants to kill him just to put him out of his misery. But with Dom being his mate, it has complicated things greatly. I will kill him if he dares touch my little one.

"My lycan and I are arguing over who should be helping Afron." Alex said "ahhh" with a nod. He too looks to my estranged brother.

"Quite the predicament."

I nod. "Quite."

What are we going to do? This isn't the outcome I had foreseen. Fucking moon goddess, she is always ruining everything. She couldn't have just made our lives easier. No, she had to make them mates. I know his lineage isn't his fault, but it would have been so much easier if I could just kill him. Now we are stuck together forever, with the constant reminder that we are related. If I'm being honest, I don't even know if he is my mother's child or mine. He could very well be mine. I know I killed my offsprings, but so did my father for my mothers. One of them has obviously survived. Just which one. I don't even know how to test that to be honest, if I even want to. Both relative titles make me feel sick, but if I was actually his mother . . . I don't even want to think of that option. For now, he is my brother, that is the only answer I am willing to accept at this time. One day I'll do a DNA test. Today . . . I just want to get by the day.

"Have you told him yet?" I don't need to ask to know what Alex is talking about. I shook my head.

Sighing, I turn around to leave. "I haven't exactly had any good opportunities to tell him." I can't smell them yet, but I know they are there. After two pregnancies, you can tell the pattern. "I had a test this morning. I am definitely pregnant." I smile softly. The timing isn't great. I would have liked to have spent a few years with Dxton first. We have forever to have children, but we also have forever to just be us. If Dxton isn't ready . . . I will have an abortion, but I hope he is. I don't think I can kill another baby.

"How is Maddison?" I asked to change the subject. Alex, ever the most observant, notices but thankfully allows the subject to change.

"Good." He smiles. Heading out of the cells, we take a moment to appreciate the fresh air. The cells smell stale and there's too much blood. It's suffocating to say the least. "She definitely keeps us busy. Barely even a month old, and she's taken all of our sleep," he mused softly.

I smile out into the distance. "I can't imagine, but if you two ever need a moment to get some sleep, let me know.'" I turn to him and smiled. "I'd be more than happy to look after her."

Alex smiles back. "I'll have to take you up on that soon."

We've come a long way, all of us. I take in a deep breath. I no longer have the feeling bugging me anymore. I can finally think.

* * *

Ness went home not long after I came back from the cells. Ness heard that her mate had finally come home from his home pack. It's safe to say she was ecstatic to have him home. I didn't tell her about the baby, it would have been wrong of me to tell her before Dxton after all. Dxton, who hasn't come home yet. He is still helping the neighbouring pack with rogues and with taking down the camps. Last I heard he was in a pack in Dakota, taking down a camp and appointing someone as alpha from our own pack. He hasn't said when he would get back. Hopefully it's before the baby can be smelt.

"Roxanna." I called out from the kitchen. I'm currently making a cake. Nothing too special, just a vanilla sponge cake. It's the decorating I'm looking forward to. I picked up some Kit Kats and wanted to cover the outside with them, then smash some honeycomb to put in the middle. I bit like a bowl I suppose.

Roxanna pops her head into the kitchen, reading glasses on the tip of her nose. "Yes dear?"

I put my cake tin into the oven and give her a stern look. "Last I checked, I asked you to go home young lady."

She raised her eyebrow. "You expect me to stand idly by while you are in my kitchen?" She scoffs. "I would like to see this through, I don't want my kitchen burning into flames." I put a hand onto my chest in mock hurt.

"You wound me Roxanna, utterly gut me." I stand back to put my hands onto my hips. "Besides, if you really must know, I actually happen to be a very good cook, thank you." I smile slightly at the memory. "There really isn't much I haven't done. You would be surprised how many jobs you can do in one human lifetime."

Roxanna hums. "Most bizarre?"

I instantly laugh at the memory. "I would have to say a snake milker." Roxanna's face dissolves hysterically. "I was hired to milk venom out of poisonous snakes for research. I definitely got bitten a few times."

"You must have many memorable stories to tell." Roxanna smiles. "I can't imagine the lives you've had. It would have been quite the adventure." She picks up her things from the counter. "Okay well if you're confident in keeping my kitchen clean, I'll be off then. Link me if you need anything dear, toodle peep." She hollered as she left.

I never really thought about it that way . . . I do have many good memories. So many of my lives as a human were fun. I . . . I think I'm happy. This feels good.

Pulling the cake out, I get to decorating, and before I know it time has flown by. The cakes were now in a little glass holder. I debated taking a slice, but thought against it, deciding I'd wait for company to share it with. Otherwise, I might end up eating the whole thing. There is nothing wrong with that, it's just I would feel like a glutton.

Growing bored, I went to take a seat on the couch, deciding I'd spend the remainder of my day reading, when I hear the door opening.

"Della?"

"Dxton?" I look over to the door, and there is Dxton dripping wet, soaking our poor floor.

"Dxton!" I jump straight into his outstretched arms, allowing him to spin me around in his arms. I laugh out loud. He showers my face with kisses causing me to giggle. I, in return, kiss him deeply.

"Dxton. I missed you," I murmured. He brushes hair out of my face.

"I missed you too, mate."

Putting me down, I pull him to the couch. "How did it go? Did you solve all the issues?" He nods, saying a quick "most," before pulling me to sit on his lap. He asked me about Afron and Dom and how I was. Then we smooth into a flowing conversation when the matter of my pregnancy slipped over my mind.

I should tell him. I have too. I definitely need to. So why won't I?

"Della?" Dxton gets up to kneel in front of me. "I was talking to you," he softly said, catching my attention. I took in a deep breath.

"Dxton, I . . . I'm pregnant." He does what I had hoped he wouldn't do. He remains silent, just looking at me.

I was about ready to run off crying when he started talking so softly I almost didn't hear him. "I'm going to be a father?"

"Yes, I understand if you aren't ready, I didn't even think about a baby . . . I'm sorry." I start crying, every possible scenario going through my mind as I sink deeper and deeper into a rabbit hole. He's going to ask me to get an abortion . . . It'll be another baby I have to kill. I . . . I don't know if I can do that again. I might have killed them, but that doesn't mean it wasn't hard. It was the hardest thing I have ever done. It was never their fault who their father was, but I had no choice.

"Della." He brings his hand to caress mine. "This is the best news I could have come home to." He kisses my forehead softly, pulling back with the biggest smile possible.

"Really?" I asked, shell-shocked.

"I love you," he whispered, then he puts a hand on my stomach, "And you." He . . . he isn't mad. I . . . I'm keeping it? He puts his nose to my stomach, inhaling deeply. "Smells like . . . a boy."

"Can you really smell them?" I asked, tears escaping my eyes.

He nodded. "When I am up close." He looks up to me with the biggest grin on his face. Lifting my shirt up, he gives my belly a soft kiss.

A little boy. We are having a son. I teared up, causing Dxton to smile and pull me in for a hug, allowing me to burst into tears. I refuse to let anything happen to him. I won't let this one go.

Dxton picks me up suddenly, causing me to squeal slightly, "I'm so happy!" He had the biggest smile I have ever seen on his face, causing me to blush and smile back just as big. "This feels right." He announced, taking us to our room.

"Dxton!" I slap his shoulder. "What do you think are you doing?"

"Wooing you," was his quick response that instantly made me go red. "Because you make me so goddamn happy and I plan on showing you."

I leant my forehead against his and smiled into his eyes. I don't think I could feel any happier right now.

CHAPTER THIRTY-SIX

Della

Dxton came back not even a week ago, and he has already organised everything. He is currently in the middle of renovating one of our spare bedrooms into a nursery for our son, and he has organised a pack meeting.

I look at the pack members around the pack house. Dxton has just called the meeting, and it's safe to say that everyone is buzzing to know what is going on.

"Hello everyone." Dxton calls out to the crowd who all murmur their own hellos back respectfully. "I wanted to give you all some background on what has been happening lately." He grabs my hand softly. "Firstly we wanted to tell you that it is true, Beta Dominic has found his mate—" Everyone scatters out into whispers, mildly irritating Dxton, who growls out lowly. "His mate's name is Afron. Yes he is a lycan. He isn't very stable at the moment, and we ask that you treat him with kindness. He is after all your Luna's brother."

Dxton had a DNA test done yesterday afternoon and it came back just before our meeting. We are siblings. Thankfully, I didn't want to be his mother. It would have complicated things so much and I want to enjoy this pregnancy without worrying about the past.

Pulling my hand from Dxton's, I place it on his shoulder to let him know I'm taking over. "I ask that you step lightly around him. He hasn't been around a proper werewolf society before and he isn't even 100 percent sure where he stands right now. He's just found out his entire world isn't real. I'm sure he would be having an identity crisis, and would be feeling very alone. This is a big scary world and the last thing you want is to walk it alone." I step forward slightly, feeling the emotions towards what I'm saying strongly. "But we are all in this together, not just because he is my brother but because, he needs some good people in his life right now. And you are those good people," I said with a proud smile.

"Della is right as usual," Dxton said, causing a few people to laugh, "Afron needs all of us." Dxton pulls me back to him. "We are White Crescent Moon, we never turn our back on those that need our aid." The pack hollered to Dxton's words, even howled.

While they cheer out, Dxton whispers into my ear. "He's going to take a lot of work." I nod in agreement.

"He will."

"But we won't give up on him," he said. Everyone deserves redemption. Maybe not everyone, but Afron hasn't been leading his own life, he has been living Franz's. It's time he led his own life.

"Oh yes." Dxton catches everyone's attention, silence fills the air. Dxton smirks at me before turning to the crowd.

"Della is pregnant."

EPILOGUE

DELLA

"When do you think you would be ready to leave little one?" Dxton asked my oversized belly. I am due any day now. I have a deep gut feeling that it's going to be tomorrow, but Dxton believes it's the day after. Then the two gammas believe it'll be today. Dom believed it was yesterday, he was obviously wrong. Afron hasn't put in too much input but he went along with Dom.

He is doing better, Afron that is. He isn't 100 percent, nowhere near but he has moved from the cells to Dom's house. They aren't really mates yet, but slow and steady wins the race. They have forever to be mates.

"I'm going to quickly duck out, you said you wanted gherkins and crackers right?" Dxton calls out from the kitchen. I yell out yes from the couch. The fire softly burns, keeping me nice and cosy as I read my book. "Okay, mind link me if there is anything else you want or if you feel that our son is on his way."

Waving him off, I continue on with my book, but I find myself with too much of a baby brain to really focus. Instead, I find myself staring outside, just off into the distance. I love how the forest looks in winter and I love how peaceful I feel. I feel genuinely happy for the first time in a really long time.

Huh imagine that. "Who would have thought?" I said out loud to myself.

I have everything I swore I never would have. A mate, a pack, and love. Then, I looked down to my stomach and softly rubbed the surface. "And I have you." It's then that it hits me. *Because I want you to look back on this day, and know how wrong you were to even think about abandoning us. You'll stay because you want to.* That bastard gamma, he was right. I laughed out loud. *"You were right."* I mind link the gamma.

He responded back not too long later. *"I am always right but why now?"* I laughed as a response and put up my mind barrier.

I'm here to stay. I'm here, because I want to. I am the female lycan, I know I can't change that. Whether I like it or not, being a lycan made me the person I am today and gave me the people I have in my life now. I never should have ran. I should have faced the world head on from the beginning. I deserve happiness. I realise that now. And I am going to do everything in my power to continue this happiness and to have a life worth living with Dxton, with White Crescent Moon. I am going to be me, and I won't let anyone tell me otherwise. I wasn't born into a world of happy endings, but I will do everything in my power to get mine. I am Della Rosai-Bosque. I am free, and . . . I am the female lycan.

And I grab my stomach suddenly, feeling a sudden wetness between my legs. I am about to be a mother.

"Dxton, it's time. Adrien Bosque is ready."

Do you like werewolf stories?
Here are samples of other stories
you might enjoy!

MY SECOND CHANCE MATE

ANNA GONZALES

CHAPTER ONE
Rejected but Moving On

HARMONY

Waking up in the morning has never been easy for me and now it feels as if there's no point in doing it at all. I didn't always feel this way. I used to love life. I enjoyed hanging out with friends and even going to school. That changed the day I met my mate. What is a mate? It's supposed to be the best part of being a werewolf, which is what I am. We are born in human form and can transform into a wolf at the age of twelve. From that point on, it's a waiting game until we find our mate. A mate is a special someone who completes you; the one you was made for and vice versa. I should be happy to have found mine. Unfortunately, my story is unique and I don't mean that in a good way.

* * *

One Year Ago . . .

I met him at the age of sixteen. He was everything I could've hoped for. Seventeen years old, 6"1', gorgeous gray eyes, dark black hair, nicely tanned skin, washboard abs, and strong long legs. Perfect, right? I thought so too. We found each other outside the airport baggage claim area. Our eyes met and it was electrifying. We moved towards one another as if pulled by some force until we were only a foot away.

"Mate," we both whispered. He reached out to touch my cheek and I leant into his palm. It felt right; like home. I was so happy that I closed my eyes to savor the moment when he suddenly tensed and dropped his hand. I opened my eyes to ask what was wrong just as he took a big step back. I stared at him in confusion and was about to ask what made him move away when the sound of a familiar voice made the words freeze on my lips.

"Babe, I see you've met my sister. Isn't she adorable?" My older sister, Megan, gushed as she gave me her usual too-tight, can't breathe type of hug.

"Did you say babe?" I asked.

"Yes, silly! Aiden, you didn't introduce yourself?" She laughed while playfully swatting his chest. "Harmony, meet the best thing to come out of this whole mandatory wolf camp that mom and dad sent me to. My boyfriend, Aiden James," she announced happily while grabbing his arm.

My wolf growled at the sight of her touching my mate, but I couldn't say anything right now. I love my sister. She's my best friend and she looked so happy. I couldn't do anything to ruin that. Don't get me wrong;I had some serious questions to ask but I would get my answers when the time was right. Even if I had to tie Aiden to a chair to do it. There was a satisfactory rumble from my wolf just by picturing it. I couldn't believe that, out of all people my sister could have met at this camp, she had to meet and fall in love with the one wolf meant for me.

The camp they attended was a first of it's kind. It was created for two types of wolves. The first was for someone like Aiden, a future alpha. These types of wolves would one day be the leaders of their pack and had to be taught to control their added power and authority so that it wouldn't be misused. The second was for wolves born from two werewolf parents who both carry the recessive gene. It causes their child to be born completely human, and my sister was one of those children. The whole thing was complicated enough as it is, and finding out I was the mate of a future alpha my sister was currently dating only added to the complication.

Aiden and I quickly exchanged hellos as if the spine tingling encounter between us never happened. We grabbed their bags and headed to the car. The ride was uncomfortable mainly because the love birds decided to share the back seat and cuddle. I exchanged looks with Aiden a couple times in the mirror, and though he would smile at my sister, the looks he gave me seemed sad and resigned. His mood confused me but I expected to get an explanation soon.

We made it to our pack house where they were having a big barbeque to welcome my sister and Aiden back. Aiden is the only nephew of our alpha, and because our alpha's mate is human, she could not conceive a child. Our law states that the next male in line would be the alpha's younger brother, Aiden's dad. However, he was killed by rogues when Aiden was thirteen so by law, Aiden is the next heir. It is strange that we never had the opportunity to meet before but that's due to the fact that Aiden's mother took him back to her pack shortly after his father's death. She was unable to deal with the memories of her lost mate that surrounded her wherever she went. Her story was sad and was still used today to teach young pups the ups and downs of mating.

After about an hour into the barbeque, my sister made a run to the store with our mom, and it finally gave me a chance to get Aiden alone. I dragged him to a clearing, a little far down from our pack house, and laid above him.

"So, what are we going to do? I love my sister to death but we're mates. We can't deny that. I don't want to hurt her but the pull I feel for you is so strong I can't ignore it," I started rambling.

"I can," he said.

I continued, not quite hearing him. "I mean, I know this is going to be difficult and create a lot of drama but I'm so happy I've found you a—"

He cut me off and repeated those two words, loud enough so I could hear them. "I can."

"You can? Can what?" I asked, confused.

"I can ignore it. This pull between us," he stated. He proceeded to rip my heart out of my chest with the rest of his words. "I never had a choice in many things in my life. I didn't choose to lose my dad, or have to leave my pack, or be put into the role of alpha but I chose your sister. I fell in love with her all on my own with no influence from anyone. I refuse to change how I feel just because my wolf wants me to. I want to be with the one I love because I say so and not because a bond is forcing me to."

I stared at him. I was shocked and hurt. "Are you saying what I'm thinking? Are you rejecting our bond?"

He sighed. "Look, I don't want to hurt you, Harmony. I spent time with your sister, and I got to know her and fell in love all on my own. If I'm with you, it's not by choice anymore but by fate. I refuse to let fate control anything else in my life. I'm sorry but that's just how it has to be."

To say I was hurt was an understatement. What came next was just anger. "You refuse? What about me? Do you know how long I've dreamed of meeting my mate and finally feeling the love only he can give me? Only you can give me? And now you tell me I can never feel that because fate has dealt you a cruel hand and you're rebelling? And so I'm the one who has to pay for your misfortune? I have never done anything in my sixteen years of life to deserve that, but does it matter to you? Obviously not!" I cried out.

"Look, Harmony. I—"

"No, you look. I'm sorry you had to go through all that but that's what I can be here for. I can help heal the pain you've been through and support you through the role that was forced onto you. No one will be able to understand you like I, your mate, can. Let me do this for you. For us," I pleaded.

"I just can't, Harmony. I've already chosen the future I want, and that future is with your sister," he replied firmly.

"What about our bond? It's going to be hard to fight it. My wolf is trying to get through, and I'm sure so is yours. How are you going to deny him?" I questioned.

Nothing. And I meant nothing could have saved me from the pain his answer caused. "Well, I'll fight him off until I completely mate with Megan. Once I mark her, he will be easier to control, and as more time passes, our bond will eventually weaken."

"True, but you forgot one important detail. Or maybe it's not so important to you since you won't be affected but what happens to the rejected mate, Aiden? What will happen to me? Let me remind you, being that I don't have a choice in the rejection," I lashed out in anger, "my wolf will weaken. When you mark Megan, I will feel as if my chest has been ripped open. You will have your love for Megan to help get you through the weakened bond, but I won't be able to find another wolf mate since we are only given one in our

lifetime. Even though the bond will deteriorate, I will still hurt every day. I will have to see you together and be reminded of my rejection time and time again. Is that really what you want for me? I know you feel something for me. I saw it at the airport. Are you absolutely sure this is what you want to do?"
"It's what I want," he whispered. "I've thought about this my whole life."
I tried one last plea."What about kids, Aiden? Megan is human. You won't be able to have a pup with her. How will you carry on your alpha line?"
"I'll deal with that when the problem arises."
"So you'll give up your mate and any future blood children just to spite fate?" I asked, hurt and shocked.
He nodded. "Yes. I'm really sorry. I just can't be with you." There was a hint of sadness in his voice.
"It's not that you can't. You just chose not to," I whispered in defeat. "So you're finally getting to choose for yourself, and that choice forces me into a life of pain and misery," I said as I looked him in the eyes. I thought I saw some indecision and pain, but it was quickly replaced by resignation and determination. I looked away as the tears started to fall. "Fine." I turned back to face him. "I will accept your rejection of the bond but only because like a mate should; I only want your happiness. You see, that's what mates are supposed to do: Protect each other, care for one another, and put each other first. I will endure the pain of the future for you, and I hope that it haunts you every night while you live your happily ever after with my sister." And with that said, I shifted into my light brown wolf and ran further into the darkness of the woods.

* * *

Shaking my head of the unwanted memories, I think about my life since then. I haven't done anything drastic to my appearance. I still wear my brown hair long and straight, no contacts cover my light green eyes, my full lips are still only covered in clear lip gloss, and I haven't changed from skinnys and tanks to ripped jeans and grungy t-shirts. No, the only change is my attitude.

The sweet carefree nature is gone. I now know how real life can be and it isn't a fairytale. My enthusiasm for life is gone. When you look into my eyes, you'll see emptiness that hides the constant pain.

I no longer live with my pack. Six months after my rejection, Aiden marked my sister and the pain was unbearable. I couldn't be around him and see him happy anymore. Yes, there were times when I was near him and could feel his wolf fighting for control but Aiden always pushed him back. I begged my parents to let me leave the pack and join my maternal aunt's pack— Her mate's pack in Hawaii, to be specific. My parents didn't understand why at first because I never told anyone about my rejection. I made up the excuse of it being hard to be around Aiden and Megan knowing I haven't found my mate yet. At least it was half true.

That's where I am now. A new pack, a new school, and hopefully, a new life. I should have an optimistic attitude, but I no longer have the illusion of happily ever after. Hope is something I seriously lack in the present. There is one good thing to come from all this.

"Harmony, get your lazy ass up so we can get to school. I don't want to miss all the fresh meat awaiting me. My game is on fire today. Just don't stare too hard at me 'cause you might be blinded by all this hotness."

There it is. My cousin Jared. He's the only one who knows about my rejection because, unlike my aunt and uncle, I can't hide the pain from him. He knows me too well, and it took all of my wolf strength to stop him from jumping on a plane to beat the crap out of Aiden. It's good though because he constantly takes my mind off of things with his crazy man whorish ways and wise remarks. His friends are awesome too. And are total eye candies. A few tried hitting on me when I was first introduced to the pack, but Jared gave all them death glares. He warned his player friends that I was completely hands off unless any of them were planning on putting a ring on my finger. I laughed at all the deathly ill expressions in the room after that announcement. Commitment is equal to a bad case of crabs in their minds. I can't wait 'til they meet their mates. It'll be fun watching them get tamed.

I get dressed in some black skinnys and an off-shoulder white top with a black tank underneath. I put my hair in a loose bun, gloss my lips, and slip into a pair of black gladiator sandals. As I'm tucking a fly away hair behind my ear, the opening of the front door announces Jace, Nate, and Brad's arrival. I make my way to their voices and find them in the kitchen as usual.

"Bro, I'm telling you. This year we're gonna score so much pu—"

"Lady in the room!" I shout, interrupting what I'm sure was gonna be one of Nate's more colorful terms for *vajayjay*.

"Right. Sorry, Harm. As I was saying, we're gonna score so much chicks because we're now seniors," Nate corrects himself excitedly.

"Well, I know I will, but I'm not too sure about you ugly mutts. Just don't stand too close to me and you'll have a chance since my sex appeal is just too massive," Jared boasts, a l in his usual arrogant self.

"Really, Jared? I know what's massive about you, and it's not your sex appeal or your weiner. Don't try to deny it. Our moms showered us together when we were little, and if I remember correctly, which I do, it was very, very, very tiny," I say, making sure I emphasized the size with my thumb and pointer fingers.

"Hey, that's because I haven't changed yet. Trust me. Massive isn't even a big enough word to describe it now," he argues, a tiny bit offended.

I cringe. "First of all, gross. And second, your ego is the only thing that's massive. I'm worried if you don't bring it down you might not be able to fit your fat head out the door."

"She's right. Besides, we all know my sexiness outshines all of you," Brad informs them.

"No way. I score the most ass . . . I mean chicks every year," Jace argues.

"That's only cause you don't have standards and will screw anything with two sets of lips," says Nate with a raised brow.

This sets off a whole new conversation about what's doable and what's not, followed by pushing and headlocks. These boys are too much and, even though I'm not excited about the day ahead, it promises to be entertaining.

If you enjoyed this sample, look for
My Second Chance Mate
on Amazon.

CATCHING GENESIS

NICOLE RIDDLEY

CHAPTER I
Worst Birthday Ever

"Happy birthday!!!" They chorus as soon as I step into the kitchen.

Mom is beaming, carrying a stack of pancakes dripping with maple syrup to the breakfast table. A single candle is burning right on top of it. Dad is already sitting at the table, smiling wide.

"Hyaaaahhhh!!!" I hear my sister yells as she bounds down the stairs behind me.

I huff the candle out before she even reaches the bottom of the stairs.

"Genesis! Damn it!!!" she yells in frustration.

"Autumn Harmony Fairchild! Language!" Mom admonishes her.

I flash my sister a victorious grin before I turn back around and give mom and dad an angelic, innocent smile.

My sister Autumn is two years younger than I am. Last week was her birthday, and I blew out the candle on her special birthday pancakes. I knew she would try to seek revenge. Unfortunately for her, I came downstairs early today, and just like that, I've foiled her evil plan of revenge.

Mom disappears into the living room and I give my sister another mischievous grin. She takes her seat beside me at the breakfast table and scowls at me.

Not only are our birthdays close together, Autumn and I look almost the same. Sometimes people thought that we were twins. From our light hazel eyes to our red hair. The only difference is that Autumn's face is a little bit rounder than mine and my red hair is a darker red, closer to Auburn, while Autumn is more of a strawberry blond. I'm also a bit taller than she is. I'm 5'11" which is just a little over the average height of most she-wolves, and Autumn is 5'9".

"Happy Birthday, by the way," says Autumn "Are you excited yet?"

"Excited about going to school on my birthday?" I ask back, sharing my stack of pancakes with her. Mom gave me too much.

"No, silly! About possibly meeting your mate today!" she replies, looking at me as if I've lost my marbles.

"I don't know...I'd be more excited if I don't have to be stuck in school the whole day on my birthday." I am, but I'm not going to admit that to her.

Yeah, we're the regular werewolf family, and as werewolves, we get the gift to sense out our mate as soon as we turn eighteen. That means for me, sometime during lunchtime today, if my mate is already eighteen and he's living somewhere around here.

"I had to go to school on my birthday too," she reminds me. "I can't wait to turn 18 so I can meet my mate already." She sighs. "Oh, I bet he's so hot. Hotter than your mate. The hottest guy in the whole pack."

"My baby girl might be meeting her mate today!" mom exclaims as she comes back from the living room where she hid my birthday gift. She places my gift on the table and says, "You're excited, right?"

I'm going to be asked this question over and over again today, it seems.

"No, she's not. She's not going to let any boys near her until she's at least 40," announces dad.

I resist the urge to roll my eyes at both of them as I rip open the wrapper. I already knew what's inside. It's a new airbrush paint set and mediums. I'd been giving obvious hints about wanting it for months.

"Thanks, mom, dad! I can't wait to try it out." I give them both a hug.

Actually, I am very excited about meeting my mate. I can feel my wolf, Ezra, being restless and excited the whole night.

My Ezra is excited, which makes me even more excited. That's why I'm all dressed up today. Well okay, so I'm dressed the same way I always dressed for school every day. Jeans and t-shirt. Nothing special, but yeah, I am very excited about possibly meeting my mate today. Not that I would ever admit that to my parents. Goddess, no! That would be so embarrassing.

Autumn and I walk to school. It's just a 15-minute walk. The weather is mild and I always enjoy the short walk.

When we get to school, Autumn heads off to where her friends are waiting, while I stroll inside to where my friends usually hang out.

Penny, Reese, and River are hanging out by our lockers as usual. Reese and River are mates. Penny hasn't turned 18, so she hasn't found her mate yet.

"Happy birthday, girl!" yells Penny as soon as she spots me, drawing the attention of most other students loitering the hallway.

She pulls me into a hug and soon after, Reese and River do the same.

"You're going to have to wait until after school for your gift," says Reese excitedly.

"You're going to be 18! Finally. Are you excited?" asks Penny.

"I don't know. I think I'm a bit nervous," I admit.

"Yeah, I'd probably be nervous too, meeting our mates for the first time...but it's exciting too!" shrieks Penny, clapping her hands excitedly.

"Don't be nervous, Genesis. It'll be okay," soothes Reese.

"It's better than okay. It's the best thing that's ever happened to me," says River, wrapping his arms around Reese.

"Awww...isn't he sweet?" coos Reese with that look in her eyes as she stares up at River. "Anyway, we'll see you losers at lunch!" she says as River pulls her away.

"Later, bish!" says Penny. I just give them a little wave before I start digging my locker for my books.

"Boy, I wish we can mate with one of those hotties." she suddenly whispers as she stares dreamily over my shoulder.

I turn around to the sight of three male lycans walking down the hallway. They are so tall, about 6'5 or more.

You see, lycans are different than us regular werewolves. For one thing, they are known to be the direct descendants of the moon goddess, so they are treated like the nobility in the werewolf world. In fact, our king is a lycan.

Second, they are bigger, faster, fiercer, smarter, stronger and more powerful than any werewolves, even the alphas. They are like killing machines when provoked. You don't want to mess with them.

Third, in their human form, they are better looking and more attractive than us regular werewolves who are considered to be better looking than most humans...like way more. So, lycans are god-like smoking hot.

Fourth, they don't have to belong to a pack. They can travel anywhere alone and not be considered a rogue.

And fifth, they don't have mates chosen for them by the moon goddess like us regular werewolves. They get to choose their own mates, either another lycans, regular werewolves or even humans they're attracted to. They would form a bond, much like a werewolf's mate bond, or even stronger if they're both attracted to each other, to begin with. Once, I heard a story about a lycan who took an already mated she-wolf, leaving her mate broken since there's nothing anybody could do about it.

There are only three male and two female lycans in our school of over six hundred students. Only 10 percent out of those six hundred students are humans. All the teachers and the administration of this school are werewolves too.

The three lycans who are heading this way right now are Lazarus, Caspian, and Constantine. The female lycans who are not around right now are Serena and Milan. I haven't seen those two around for a few days now. They are, of course, drop-dead gorgeous.

I think Serena is mated to Lazarus, and Milan may or may not mated to Caspian. There are rumors that those three boys are closely related to our ruling king, but we don't know for sure. There's not much else that we know about the lycans in our school. Not even their last names. They keep to themselves and pay no attention to us mere werewolves and humans. That makes them so mysterious and much more attractive to the female population here.

So yeah, those three god-like looking Adonis are drop-dead gorgeous. Jaw dropping. Panty melting. And I so would be making a fool of myself if I don't stop drooling over them—like Penny—and all the other un-mated she-wolves around us right now.

I quickly turn back and start pulling books that I need from my locker. There's no way a lycan would be interested in an Omega like me. Lycans are attracted to strength, intelligence, and beauty. Besides, I might be meeting my mate today. Flutters of excitement start in my tummy at the thought. My wolf Ezra is getting excited. We've been waiting for this for years.

I grab Penny's hand and drag her along to get to our class before the bell rings. We share English lit class together.

"I can't wait to be out of this place soon. Thank goodness we only have a few months of school left." I inform Penny.

"Oh, I don't know...I don't mind school. There are lots of hot guys around, like those lycans." she says. " Or like those boys...too bad they're such jerks and man-whores," whispers Penny in my ear as we pass the popular group in our school.

Logan Carrington, our future Alpha is kissing or rather shoving his tongue down the throat of Mia Brown, the head cheerleader. They're together, but everybody knows they're seeing other people on the side. Zeke Walker, future Delta has his arms around Elle Johnson and Marie Jacobs, while talking to Hunter Stevens, the future Beta. I think Hunter isn't so bad. He doesn't seem like a player like the other two. He talked to me once or twice before and seems pretty nice.

"I wonder if he's digging for hidden treasure down her esophagus," I whisper back and Penny starts laughing.

Hunter turns to look at us, then his eyes shift to me, looking amused. I think his lips twitch a bit like he's trying not to laugh. Cuddly bunny and fuzzy slippers! He must have heard me.

I practically push Penny into our English lit class, while trying to hide my flaming face.

Yes, I do think that those boys are pretty hot. There's no way in hell would I admit it to anyone, though.

Logan and Zeke have this class with me and Penny. They enter the class ten minutes after the teacher started teaching. Not that she would say anything.

Logan slides into a seat in front of me and my wolf stirs. I stare at the back of his golden head for a bit. Logan is about 6'2", well-muscled; has high cheekbones and sharp features like a model; bright blue eyes and golden blond hair. When he smiles, wow. His straight white teeth and those adorable dimples are simply to die for. Well, maybe I have a bit of a crush on him. Just a little bit. I think a lot of the girls here do.

The rest of the classes went pretty well —boring and uneventful. Art is the only subject I look forward to. Did I mention that my mom is an artist? Well, she is, and I'm very proud of her.

Lavinia Fairchild is quite well known. Every werewolf household here has at least one or two of her prints or originals. My dream is to go to an art school and be as good as her.

We are sitting at our regular table during lunchtime when I suddenly smell that wonderful smell that I can't describe. Whatever it is, it smells awesome! Ezra, my wolf is fighting to be let out and take control. I guess I was born during lunch time. I stand up and start to follow my nose to identify where that smell comes from. I can't help it. I have to find it. I vaguely hear my friends calling my name, but I can't seem to focus on anything else but that smell.

My nose brings me to the popular group table. Oh no, I can't seem to bring my feet to stop. Ezra's taking control. Everybody stops talking. Logan Carrington? My mate is Logan Carrington? No no no no.

His beautiful blue eyes widen as he looks up at me. His eyes softened as they roam my face. I can see lust and hunger flitting across his face briefly as his eyes move up and down my body. But then he looks away quickly. His breathing ragged. My wolf howls with joy and my first instinct is to jump on him and stake my claim.

"Follow me," he says gruffly, and swiftly walks out the cafeteria through the back door.

I follow him across the lawn to an Oak tree. The tree provides us a bit of privacy from prying eyes.

"What's your name?" he finally asks. His beautiful eyes are not even looking at me. I can't seem to tear my eyes away from his perfect face. The sun is glinting in his golden hair. The shadows fall across the planes of his sharp features.

"Genesis... Genesis Fairchild," I finally answer.

"Fairchild? You're an Omega, aren't you?" he says. "I can't have an Omega as my mate. My pack needs a stronger luna, not someone weak like you. Besides, I love someone else. Mia makes a better Luna than you ever could." Each word is like a knife slicing through my chest. Ezra whimpers.

Oh no, suddenly I know what's going to happen. My heart starts to race, my breaths come out short and shallow. I don't know what's happening to me. All I know is that my heart is breaking.

"I, Logan Carrington, future Alpha of Shadow Geirolf pack, reject you, Genesis Fairchild, as my mate and future luna of my pack," he utters coldly, not looking at me once.

My wolf cries and howls in pain. She doesn't understand. Why is our mate hurting us so?

"Hey baby, what's going on?" says Mia, wrapping her arms around him. Where did she come from?

"Nothing to worry about, sweetheart," he answers.

She looks me over with disdain. She pointedly pulls Logan's head down and plants her lips on his for a claiming kiss. He wraps his arm around her waist, and then they turn and leave. I watch her whispers something in his ear and they both laugh.

I watch them laugh as I fall to the ground, clutching at my chest. Oh, goddess, it feels like he just plunged a knife deep into my chest and twisted it. Then he just keeps yanking the knife up and down, left and right over and over again until there's nothing left of my heart but a bloody, twisted ugly gash in my chest. Ezra curls up in pain then goes silent.

* * *

I'm lying on my bed now. Everything was a blur after I fell. I remember seeing my friends Penny, Reese, and River running to me, calling my name in panic. They were asking me what was wrong. River carried me to his car. Then I don't remember anything else. The three of them must've brought me home.

"Talk to me, honey. Tell me what happened," says mom gently, pushing my hair from my forehead.

"He rejected me, mom. My mate rejected me." My eyes are tearing up again. I still find it hard to believe that this is really happening to me. I was wishing that it was just a horrible nightmare.

There are a thousand different emotions chasing across mom's face. Disbelief, anger, pain, sadness....

All the pain comes back. I start twisting in my bed and mom wraps her arms around me. Even mom's comforting loving arms can't stop or ease the pain away.

"It hurts so bad. Make it stop...make it stop. Mom, please make it go away." I sob, clawing at my chest. "I'd do anything...just make it stop." Goddess, it hurts so much, I want to die.

"My baby. My poor baby girl," cries mom. Tears running down her face as she hugs me close, willing my pain to go away.

After what feels like hours, I calm down, or maybe I'm just too exhausted to even shed a tear. Only my chest is moving up and down. Sleep doesn't come easily. In the middle of the night, all alone in the darkness, tears leak out again, falling down my face silently. My wolf, Ezra, is completely silent now, but I can feel her crushing pain, as well as my own.

I had been looking forward to meeting my mate since I was four. Mom told me about it like it's the best thing to ever happen to a werewolf. I had been waiting for someone who would love me and protect me and be by my side no matter what.

All werewolves look forward to meeting their mates. It's very rare that a mate gets rejected, but it happened to me. What is wrong with me?

All werewolves know you only got one chance of having a mate. What now? Will I ever be loved and have a family? Will my wolf, Ezra, ever comes out and be the same again? A werewolf without his or her wolf is only an empty shell. Most would eventually die or go crazy after they lost their mates. Their wolves decide to disappear when the pain gets unbearable. Now I understand how very painful it is, and we're not even mated yet. Will I die or go crazy too? I hope Ezra is strong enough to stay.

How could the moon goddess do this to me? What did I do to deserve this? I didn't ask for an Alpha. She could've matched me to another lowly Omega and I'd still be happy. As long as I am loved, I'll be happy.

How did this day turn out so bad? Worst. Birthday. Ever.

If you enjoyed this sample, look for
Catching Genesis
on Amazon.

Luna Catherine

Yolanda Jolante

CHAPTER ONE

He had taken everything from me yet I'm still here. My own brother, Ronan.

Ronan lost himself a long time ago, and selfishly enough, he dragged me down along with him. I was of pure innocence, and he corrupted me. He made me bear witness to the most heinous of crimes, filling my mind with nightmares. I watched him in silence as he went down a black hole, returning to be what he secretly feared the most—a man with a dark soul.

He's claimed to not fear anything; a rebel who lives off instilling fear into others. He feeds off the control he has, the adrenaline rush he gets when a life ends by his hands. He can be irrational at times, a loudmouth, cocky, stubborn, dark, and twisted, yet still, he can't control one thing.

His love for me.

In his own twisted way, he loves me. He's done so much hurt and pain. He's been cruel and left me bare at such a young age, but still, he keeps me close. He feeds off my strength and breathes calmly in my silence. Now that he's grown, he can't find it in him to destroy me any further than he already has.

A murderer, a selfish and cruel man, and many more titles to everyone else but a frightened, confused, and an out-of-control little boy in a man's body, right in my view.

A storm is brewing, I can feel it. He knows it too because I told him before. He's tried so many times to ignore me, but today, he can't because, like always, I'm right.

A crash sound comes from the living room. He's breaking stuff again. He's earned everyone's attention, all movements still, in his outburst.

I watch him silently by the doorway while he loses his cool once again. He throws a glass to the nearest wall and makes one servant gasp in shock.

"Everyone, out!" he demands.

Not needing to be told twice, every present person scurries out of there, leaving us alone. Right after everyone has gone, he walks over to the drinks cabinet, pulling out a bottle of brandy.

I finally enter, walking over to stand by the large windows, not even sparing him another glance.

I hear him shuffling close, then the sound of liquid being poured before glass is slammed hard against the wooden table.

He loudly gulps down his drink. He's frustrated, I can feel it.

"Be careful, brother, before you kill yourself," I say.

He growls in answer, wanting to ignore me but he can't. I know he wants to have another, and if he does, he might lose his senses. That's never a good sign, especially today. A drunk Ronan is the worst Ronan.

"You've done wrong, brother. Now, you just might meet the outcome of your actions," I tell him calmly, like always.

"Shut up!" he growls in warning.

I do.

He paces up and down now.

"Damn troublemakers."

More like you, I want to say.

A cold, icy chill runs down my spine, and my body tenses in the process.

"The storm is coming. The storm is near."

I hear a growl before I'm spun around to face him, and his brown eyes darken. I don't even wince when he tightens his grip on my arm.

"Stop talking gibberish and say what you mean!" he seethes, his alcoholic breath fanning my face.

Like a lightbulb clicking in my mind, a certain wind washes over me. It's them. They are close. I don't know who they are, but they come with a mission.

"Be prepared . . . for just about anything," I tell him.

He growls in anger before he backhands me across the face, sending me flying and landing hard on the floor.

"If you have nothing better to say, then shut the hell up!" he shouts, leaving the room.

He has listened.

I close my eyes for a minute, blinking back tears and softly rubbing at my burning cheek.

"Oh no, miss!" Cara—one of the omegas—says, rushing over to help me up. "Please sit and let me treat you."

"There's no time. Please take care of the glass and then go into hiding."

Her eyes search my own until she gulps in realization of the situation. "Trouble is coming once again," she mumbles.

All I do is stare at her.

"You've always been the calm one out of everyone here, and the most truthful. Ha!" She sighs. "I will do as you say, Luna."

I close my eyes, holding back my tongue from telling her to stop referring to me as Luna.

Leaving her alone to attend to the scattered, broken glass, I decide to leave and go to my room, wanting to treat my cheek and to try to look presentable because I know Ronan wouldn't be pleased with me if I wasn't.

Coming back down the stairs in a long black jumpsuit with ballet pumps, I feel them really close, though I may not see them. It's a matter of time before they appear. I remain in the living room with half of my body visible through the window.

His footsteps echo as he appears, looking cleaner in dark jeans and a white shirt that hugs his muscles. I can feel his gaze on me.

"What the fuck are you wearing?" he shouts, and I almost jump out of my skin.

I turn to face him, opening my mouth to say something, when the cold chill comes at me like a bullet going through my chest.

"You have visitors, brother," I tell him, turning to face the window.

I hear his footsteps come closer.

"Shit," he curses before storming out of the door.

Ronan with his styled, cut, light-brown hair appears into view, standing on the front yard with about ten to fifteen men. A few minutes pass and no one shows up, making Ronan glance over his shoulder at me. His eyes narrow and I notice him try to fight off a smirk.

This is a promise that there'll be consequences if I'm lying, but I'm not. He's doubting me yet again.

All too soon, a group of tall men appear from the forest. Ronan's demeanour changes and his body tenses when he turns back front. Amongst the approaching men, I notice the one in the middle—the leader.

He is the most muscular out of the men; he's breathtakingly handsome with his midnight black hair, striking emerald-green eyes that meet mine, a strong jaw, and sculpted blank face. He shows no emotion to the onlookers, yet I can sense him. I'm stronger than him in this.

He is feeling everything, and he thinks I can't. His scent is of fresh pine and woods—earthy and pleasant to my nose.

I know without a doubt that he is my mate, the one I'm destined to be with, my soulmate. Yet what he represents, what he stands for, his views on mates, and all he's been till now forms a defensive shield against the bond.

He is just like my brother.

I sigh and slump in disappointment and defeat.

I watch the interaction between my brother and my mate. It's intense and doesn't seem like something good will be concluded. It's been a few minutes now, and I hold no hope for what may be.

Turning away from the window and meaning to walk away, I stop in my tracks when I sense it—a strong and intense gaze. I glance over my shoulder at the precise moment he nods my way. My heart flips at his intense eyes.

He has just caused the first real reaction from my already still heart.

When Ronan glances over his shoulder, I'm suddenly grabbed by arm and dragged out of the house, earning frightened eyes from pack members and hard ones from my mate's company. I'm shoved hard towards the ground, only for someone to grip my arm strongly to prevent me from going down any further.

Sparks erupt throughout my body, and I gasp at the contact. It's him, my mate.

I almost whisper it out but bite down on my tongue, not wanting to expose anything. Being pulled up, I sneak a glance to my mate. My breath hitches at the sight of his beautiful green eyes. I notice a small but deep and permanent scar on the side of his face; it still doesn't take away from his captivating looks. His scar is a sign of things he's gone through and conquered.

He catches me looking at his scar, and that makes his eyes harden with anger laced in them. I'm spun around to face my brother whose eyes are trained on me.

"So are we talking now?" My breath hitches when something sharp is pressed hard against my neck.

My eyes are only on my brother.

"What do you want, O'Connell?" my brother grunts, clearly annoyed by the situation we are currently in.

"You know what I want, Black. It's been long overdue now. Give me back my beta."

"Dead or alive?" Ronan arches his brow.

"Don't play games with me and give me what I want." My mate's deep voice sounds calm but deadly.

"Or what?" Ronan asks, clenching his hands into fists.

"Do you really want me to answer that? Alright, let me demonstrate." Without any warning, the sharp object is shoved into the side of my neck and pulled out. I'm immediately thrown across the yard, my body slamming hard against a nearby tree.

Growls erupt, bones crack, and bodies collide. I glance up from the ground to the horrific scene in front of me. Werewolves are everywhere; there's so much blood and fighting between my brother's wolf and my mate's right in the centre.

Pack members scream and run around, trying to get to safety.

Pain erupts from my neck and reaching up to where I was stabbed, a wetness coats the wound. Soon, I'll be bleeding out.

My attention diverts when I sense it, my brother's life is hanging in the balance. I sit upright, pressing against my wound and facing what now looks to be my mate's dark-gray gigantic wolf standing over Ronan's midnight-black one. My mate's eyes connect with mine just as he digs his teeth in my brother's wolf's neck.

My heart hammers hard against my chest. He won't hesitate to kill Ronan, but his eyes tell me that I've only got one chance to do something.

He's daring me to do something.

"Stop! Stop please!" I plead, struggling to rise on my feet.

I stagger close to them. A few of my mate's men remain, looking rather threatening.

"Alpha, I have a proposal. Let him go please." My brother's eyes narrow in threat, but I avoid his eyes, looking at my mate's.

I'll deal with my brother's wrath after. Right now, I need to manage the situation. Though it may be my first time being given the platform.

My mate doesn't let up. He puts pressure on my brother's neck, earning us both a growl and whine from my brother. Time is of the essence; I can almost hear him say.

"Your beta will be released, so long as you release our own." I take a ragged breath. "I will take upon any punishment and everything your beta endured in time of his captivity. I will accept with no argument or fight. The length of time he stayed here is the length of time I'll remain there."

I gasp when I feel myself really bleeding out now. I watch my mate's eyes take notice of this before he growls and takes a step back, loosening his grip.

"Please, release my brother. Brother for a brother." I gulp though I choke a bit.

My mate shifts into his human form, and I look away from his nudeness. From the corner of my eye, I see one of his men take a pair of grey sweats to him.

I'm getting dizzy now.

"What. Do. You. Think. You're. Doing?" my brother growls, his body shaking in anger. He is injured but I know he'll heal soon.

"I'm doing what's best, brother. You might not agree but it is. I-I will take my punishment once I return." I wish I didn't have to say this out loud, but it's for Ronan to clearly hear me and understand.

Ronan grunts before instructing one of his men to fetch the beta.

I sigh in relief for that—knowing a person will get to go home to his family. I stagger back due to the dizziness and almost fall, but my arm is gripped hard to the point of pain by my mate's men.

I mistakenly whimper due to the pain, but then, there's a growl. The grip on my arm is loosened and is being replaced by pleasurable tingles that I almost sigh out in relief.

The beta is soon brought out, beaten and bruised yet still standing. His fellow troops help him to one of the cars. I take a much-needed breath in preparation of me looking like him when I return. Well, if I don't die out due to all the bleeding.

Maybe I might just die here. That'll be fine with me.

"My beta," Ronan grunts.

All too soon, his beta is thrown at his feet, being helped up and taken in the house probably to the pack doctor.

I can't even watch anymore. My vision gets blurry, and my body weight takes over. I feel myself falling, only to land in someone's arms. The sparks give it away.

Before I can slip into darkness, I hear the parting words between my brother and mate.

"You know that I'll come back for her. She belongs here."

"No. She's mine now."

If you enjoyed this sample, look for
Luna Catherine
on Amazon.

ACKNOWLEDGEMENTS

I want to thank everyone on the publishing team. Thank you for your patience during the past year. I know I'm a pain in the ass. Thank you for guiding me, for improving my writing skills. But most importantly, thank you for publishing my first baby. This book is alive because of you.

To my friends, my mother, and grandparents who looked at me like I had three heads while I talked about my book. Thank you for kind words and patience. Brankich, you will always be my favorite English teacher and someone who understands my passion for writing.

And most importantly, I have to say thank you to my horse. You were always there when I was depressed, crying, and had a mental break down. And yet, you always found a way to make me happy. Even if you are a horse, an animal, you will always be my best friend and my closest companion. The reason why I live.

AUTHOR'S NOTE

Thank you so much for reading *The Female Lycan*! I can't express how grateful I am for reading something that was once just a thought inside my head.

I'd love to hear your thoughts on the book. Please leave a review on Amazon or Goodreads because I just love reading your comments and getting to know you!

Can't wait to hear from you!

Emily Dodd

ABOUT THE AUTHOR

Emily Dodd is an Australian author, has been writing since highschool on Wattpad, with over 15 million views

Printed in Great Britain
by Amazon